FLIRTING with the STRANGER

A REVERSE AGE GAP ROMANTIC COMEDY

GIA STEVENS

Flirting with the Stranger: A Reverse Age Gap Romantic Comedy by Gia Stevens

www.authorgiastevens.com

Published by: Gia Stevens

Print Edition ISBN: 978-1-958286-13-5

Editor: My Notes In The Margins

Publisher: Wild Clover Publishing, LLC

v061025

To Channing Tatum
It was such a chore watching you in Magic Mike…
With the dancing. The grinding. The thrusting.
I think you really owe me.

While this story is a romantic comedy there may be situations that are triggering to some. For a list of those triggers please visit my website and scroll to the bottom of the page.

FANCIED THE FUCK UP

Hollyn

With a steady hand, I pipe *Bitch* on the top layer of the light brown cake, smiling with every loop of the script letters. Once I'm finished, I step back with a hand on my hip and admire my handiwork. The script writing is some of the best I've ever done. I purse my lips together and exhale a sigh. With an icing spatula, I scoop up a dollop of frosting and smear it over the top. Too bad I have to cover it up. If you ask me, it would look better if it wasn't.

Nothing is worse than spending your entire afternoon decorating a wedding cake for the one person who's spent most of their life bragging about how much better their life is. Our parents have been friends since we were kids, so we grew up together. As kids, it was fun, until we became teenagers, and she'd constantly remind me and my twin sister, Parisa, of all the things she had that we didn't. But I always took the high road. So, the day she came into my bakery and the first thing she did was blatantly glance down at my empty left hand, I knew I was going to hate what came out of her mouth next. Sure enough, a little part of me died inside when she asked me to design her wedding cake. Five years ago, I was supposed to be the one walking down the aisle, but instead, I spent the night sitting on a hotel bathroom floor with a bottle of champagne. And when you're wallowing in your own self-pity, one bottle is never enough.

With a pair of rubber tipped tweezers, I delicately place the edible pearls in a swooping pattern around the center layer of the three-tier cake. Luckily, I don't have to attend the actual wedding.

Thank you, girls' weekend.

All I need to do is finish the pearl work and Della, the owner of The Sweet Spot, will finish the flowers before taking the cake to the reception.

The music blaring in my earbuds dims as an incoming call comes through my phone. Glancing down, Olivia's name flashes on the screen. I answer, putting her on speakerphone, but before I can even get a word out, Olivia's voice booms through the speaker.

"Girl, you better be at home, showered, bags packed, and fancied the fuck up."

"Well, not quite." I glance down at my black yoga pants with smears of buttercream frosting and a red flannel shirt with the sleeves rolled up to my elbows. "But good news is my bag is packed. Give me a couple of hours and I'll be ready."

Olivia's been friends with Parisa since they started working together at The Blue Stone Group. In turn, she's become one of my friends as well.

"A couple hours!?" Olivia screeches. "I'll give you an hour. If you're not home, I'm coming to the bakery and kidnapping your ass."

"Okay. Got it. See you then." I'm only half listening as I continue placing pearls on the cake.

"I'm serious. Sixty minutes!" Olivia's voice echoes through the kitchcn before I press end.

Because of the two extra hours I put in today, I got further than I was expecting. Now, Della will have less work tomorrow. I lift the cake and carry it to the commercial refrigerator and place it next to the other two finished tiers. As soon as I finish cleaning up the kitchen, I lock up and make my way home.

Once I walk through the door, I dump my purse on the couch and hustle upstairs to take the fastest shower imaginable. When I'm done, I throw on a sequin mini-dress and apply a light coat of make-up. Not five minutes later, a black stretch limo pulls up to the curb in front of my townhouse.

The instant I close the front door, the driver is already waiting next to the wide open car door. Olivia pokes her head out. "Hurry, bitch! We have drinks to drink and some celebrating to do."

"I'm coming! I'm coming! You guys started without me, didn't you?" My heels clatter on the cement walkway.

"Of course we did." Olivia's bright red lips pull into a wide grin as she holds up her glass.

The driver takes my bag, and I bend down to climb into the rear of the limo, careful to not show my ass to my neighbors. I flop down in the seat along the far side next to Liana, Charlie's soon to be sister-in-law, and Tatum, Olivia's sister. Olivia and Parisa sit across from me, while Charlie and a couple of her friends sit along the back. Charlie also worked at The Blue Stone group until things got serious with her co-worker, Bennett. Then they both left.

Parisa hands me a glass before popping open another bottle and pouring the bubbly liquid into the glass.

"Thanks. This is exactly what I need." I swallow a big gulp of the champagne. The bubbly taking off a little bit of the edge from earlier. But only a teeny tiny bit. "I don't know why I agreed to make Krystin's wedding cake. It's been a nightmare from day one. She's changed the cake flavors three times. Changed the type of frosting twice. Why do I put myself through this?"

"Because she pays well." Parisa shrugs.

And she does. Well, her parents pay well. She enjoys dipping into their pocketbook. "There has to come a time when I shouldn't sacrifice my happiness for money."

"The time will come." Parisa's voice is soft and soothing. "But on the plus side, you're done, and you don't have to go to the wedding."

"Thank God for that." I take another sip.

"With all that depressing shit out of the way. It's time to celebrate!" Olivia raises her flute. "It only took an engagement and a baby on the way to finally get together for a girls' weekend. Cheers bitches!" Everyone raises their glass except Parisa. She has a bottle of water as she's the one with the baby on the way, and we all toast.

Over the next two hours as we drive to the Cities, we talk about life, Charlie's wedding plans, and Parisa's pregnancy. Then somehow, the conversation turns to my love life, or lack thereof.

"You two are lucky you've found someone. Dating is hard." I tip back the glass, the last drop of champagne wetting my lips, and I glance between Charlie and Parisa.

"Your someone is out there. And he'll come around when you least expect it." Parisa rests a hand on my knee.

"After several years of not dating, I'm starting to lose hope. None of the guys I've gone out with this month have been the one. One guy was a blind date set up by this sweet old lady who comes into the bakery. She mentioned her grandson is around my age and single and she was *very* persistent that I meet him. I told her to have him come to the bakery, and he did. At first sight, he was attractive, well groomed. I had high hopes for the date. Everything was going great. Dinner was good. Conversation was decent. He even walked me to my door. And that was where the date imploded." I motion my hands like a bomb exploding. At the time, I wish there was an actual bomb.

"What happened?" Liana asks before taking a sip of her drink.

I bark out a laugh thinking about it. "He kissed me on the cheek and then whispered in my ear, 'What do you say we go inside and I turn your face into a daycare.'"

Parisa busts out laughing because she's heard this story before. And all I can do is nod vigorously, still in disbelief at his words, especially for a first date.

Once I regain my composure, I continue, "If a girl actually falls for those words, I feel sorry for her. Or maybe they get what they deserve."

"Are you sure you didn't go out with Trey? That seems like something he would say," Liana says, and another round of laughter fills the limo.

Charlie leans forward, eyes wide. "He did not say that to you!?!"

"Oh, he did." I nod. "Obviously, I very politely declined his offer and slammed the door in his face. The worst part was when I had to face his grandma when she came into the bakery. I had to bite my tongue and not tell her that her grandson wanted to give me a facial."

"I don't know if grandma would know what you were talking about." Olivia hides her giggle behind her glass.

"And I wouldn't be the one to tell her. Plus, I couldn't taint her view of her grandson. That would be all sorts of bad karma. Maybe my expectations are too high." I wrap one arm around myself as my other hand holds my champagne flute inches from my lips.

"You deserve the best. Don't let yourself think otherwise," Tatum says as she nudges me with her elbow, breaking me from my self-loathing.

"I would like to think so, but my other date was equally as bad, if not worse. A guy took me to Bella Italia. The place with the beautiful brick arch way."

Charlie points a finger at me. "Yes! Their chicken piccata is to die for. But it better be for forty-dollar parking."

I nod. "I totally agree. Anyway, the conversation was flowing, but his gaze kept darting around the restaurant like he was looking for someone."

"Oh, shit. Drug dealer?" Olivia leans forward, resting her elbows on her knees.

"I wish. That would have been less awkward. Ex-girlfriend."

Soft gasps fill the car as everyone's eyes go wide.

My head bobs like a bobble head, still in disbelief myself. "Turns out she's a waitress at the restaurant, and he wanted to see if she had been cheating on him with a co-worker like he suspected. I figured this out when he saw her talking to another server and he stormed over to them. I was done after that."

Some shake their heads as others giggle at my expense, and I can't blame them. I want to laugh at myself too.

"This only happens to you," Charlie says.

"I know. I can't make this stuff up." I bite back my

laughter. "There must be a magnetic current in me that only attracts assholes and creepers. Do I have a sign that hangs above my head that says, 'If you're a dick, come date me.'"

"Maybe they get that confused with 'if you have a dick'?" Charlie snickers.

"Perhaps you should find a guy for some fun versus trying to find the one?" Parisa lifts a perfectly shaped eyebrow.

"Easy for you to say. You've found your one."

My sister fell in love with her former co-worker. They hated each other, but after a snowstorm stranded them in a motel together, they put their differences aside and banged it out. Now, they're expecting their first child together.

"Either I've forgotten how to date in the past seven years, or the pool of guys is getting smaller and perhaps, even dumber."

"I think Parisa is on to something." Olivia tips her glass of sparkling champagne toward her. "Let loose and have a good time tonight. Scope out the guys and if you find someone who catches your attention, go for it. Also, I got you a little present." She reaches next to her, grabs a small gift bag, and sets it in my lap.

"You didn't have to get me anything. This night isn't for me." Slowly, I dig through the tissue paper.

"This night's for all of us. Plus, I know you wouldn't have brought this for yourself and safety and all that." Olivia's bright, red lips are visible through her glass of champagne.

My fingers wrap around a box, and I yank. Pieces of tissue paper come with it and flutter to the floor. I hold the box out in front of me. "Condoms. You got me condoms." I stare at the box and shake my head. "And a twelve pack.

How many times are you expecting me to have sex tonight?" I ask with a giggle.

"Three didn't seem like you were trying hard enough and thirty-six seemed like overkill. Twelve was perfect. But look, they're ribbed for her pleasure." Olivia points to the description on the box. The entire limo falls into a fit of laughter.

I stuff the box of condoms back into the gift bag. Of course, my plan was never to hook up with anyone tonight and I didn't come prepared. A part of me is thankful for Olivia's thoughtfulness but the other part is nervous if it will happen. One-night stands aren't my thing. Every person I've had sex with, I've also been in a relationship with. Is this what people do? Who makes plans to have a one-night stand with a total stranger? Olivia apparently, and she's using my vagina to do it. Perhaps they're right. I'm thirty-four years old and it's time to try something new. "If that's going to happen, we'll need way more of these." I hold up my empty glass.

CHAPTER TWO

FLEET OF STRIPPERS

Hollyn

Olivia twirls around to face the group and throws her hands in the air. "Welcome to Heaven and Hell."

We all glance around the large loft style room in one of the most popular nightclubs in the city. Sheer white curtains drape from the ceiling and pool on the floor. Soft white lights shine up from below, giving the space an open and airy atmosphere, as if you were in heaven. A large leather sectional sits in one corner and two leather armchairs sit kitty-corner. In front of the sectional is a coffee table with candles resting on top. Places like this are not my usual style, but I will take full advantage while I'm here.

I grip the railing and peer over the edge. Below us is

hell. Large video screens cover all the walls as fire dances all around. Like flickering flames, people dance in slow, hypnotic movements as red spotlights shimmer over them. It's not even 10 p.m., and the place is wall to wall people. Based on the line outside that snakes down the block, it's going to be wall to wall people all night.

Olivia stands next to me, looping her arm through mine. I turn toward her. "How did you score this place?"

"My dad knows a guy who knows a guy and called in some favors. He said this room is booked out for months, but made it work for me. We deserve the best of the best. Also, I have the black card so the night's on me." She brushes her long golden locks off her shoulder as her signature red lips stretch into a dazzling smile. All she would have to do is flirt with someone and she could get what she wants.

"I've heard people need to get here early if they want a chance to get in." I glance over the railing again.

"That's exactly why we needed to come here. What do you say we get this party started?" Olivia glances toward the private bar, drops my arm, and beelines it in that direction. The bartender pours seven glasses and a sparkling juice. "Bitches, get your asses up here. We're toasting!"

The loud bass booms through the speakers and reverberates through the entire room and through my chest. I scan the crowd below as people dance and have fun. That's one thing my life has been severely lacking in the past seven years. Fun.

"Hollyn! Get over here!" When I turn, Olivia's holding up a champagne flute for me.

Releasing my grip, I push off the railing and stroll over to where everyone is seated. I grab the delicate stemware from her grasp and hold it up with the rest in a circle above us.

"Congratulations to Charlie and Parisa and all the wonderful things yet to come. And to the rest of us sad and single ladies." A collective laugh spreads around our circle. "Here's to our night of fun and debauchery." We all clink our glasses together.

Several hours and even more drinks later, I'm standing next to the railing again, swaying my hips to the music thumping below. A pang of jealousy floats through me as I watch couples pair off and dance together. For years, I've been content with my life. I put all my time and energy into the bakery and the thought of dating never appealed to me, especially after I got burned. But with Charlie engaged and Parisa starting a family, it makes me wonder if I'm missing out.

Movement next to me catches my attention and I turn to find Parisa standing at my side. "There's quite the selection of guys here tonight."

I take a sip of my drink. "Oh yeah, I'm sure I'll find a high-quality man at a dance club on a Friday night." I point to a group of people gathered below us. "Like that guy, who may or may not have just vomited behind that pillar."

"He doesn't count." She waves him off. "But also, no one said he had to be high quality. Just someone to take the edge off." She tosses me a flirty wink. "I know the ex left an enormous dick shaped hole in your heart, or a small dick might be more accurate. But I think it's time to stop letting him ruin your life and live it for you again. Think about it." She rests her hand on mine and gives it a gentle squeeze before going back to the couch with the other girls.

I nibble on my bottom lip. Maybe she's right. We're two hours away from home, so if I do hook up with some stranger, it's not like I'll run into him in Harbor Highlands. I volley the idea back and forth in my head, mostly to see if a reason why I shouldn't hook up with a random stranger appears. Still unsure with what I should do, I rejoin the group.

"Olivia, why do you keep checking your phone?" Charlie asks.

"No reason." Olivia pulls her phone away from her face and sets it on the table in front of her.

"Oh, I know that look! That look says you're up to something." Charlie points her glass in Olivia's direction.

"There may or may not be a surprise coming." A devilish smirk forms on Olivia's lips.

"Wait, you didn't get a stripper, did you?" Charlie narrows her eyes at Olivia. "You did! I knew it! You've always wanted to throw a stripper party."

"It's only fitting for an engagement party." Olivia shrugs her shoulders, but she can't hide her sly smile.

"Typically, those are for the bachelorette party," I say.

"Well, I guess we get to do this twice then," Olivia sing-songs.

"I bet the guys didn't get strippers." Parisa takes a seat on the armrest of the couch next to Olivia.

"Of course they did. They're with Trey. I'm sure they got an entire fleet of strippers." Olivia spreads her arms wide.

"A stripper train." Tatum pretends to pull a train horn cord. "Toot toot."

Charlie's fingers type away on her phone screen. A few

seconds later, she peers over the edge of her phone screen. "Bennett says they didn't get strippers."

"This is supposed to be a classy girls' night. No talking to the guys." Olivia flails her arms in the air. We all giggle at her overly dramatic display.

"I don't think classy and strippers really go together," I say.

"He's not a stripper. He's an exotic dancer. There's a big difference," Olivia deadpans.

"How? Like one slaps his dick on your face and the other doesn't?" Liana asks.

Olivia points her glass toward her. "Yes. Exactly." I double over from laughter along with everyone else.

"If I wanted balls in my face, I would have stayed home and had Bennett do that for free," Charlie says.

"I bet that's a Saturday night for you." Olivia raises her glass to Charlie and everyone giggles.

"Ugh. That's a visual I don't need." Liana fake gags.

"Speaking of the stripper. Where is he? He's almost an hour late. I'm going to call and get my deposit back." Olivia picks up her phone again.

"Wait." I rise to my feet, and all the blood rushes from my head. With a slight wobble in my legs, I grip the back of the chair until I'm stable. Perhaps I should slow down on the champagne. "Let me go see if he's here. Maybe he doesn't know where to go."

I turn around and walk toward the stairs. My hand glides along railing as I descend the steps that lead to the main floor. The music pumps through the speakers as scantily clad twenty-somethings mill around. I glance down, watching my step, and before I reach the bottom, a pair of black shoes meet my black peep toe pumps. My gaze slowly drifts up, and standing in front of me is a young, gorgeous man with dark hair and wearing a smile that makes my nipples pebble and my thighs clench. I give him a once over, tight jeans, black shirt that stretches over his broad shoulders and hugs his muscles, something I wish I could do right now. I shake off the thought. This must be our guy.

Glancing up, I meet his dark eyes. "Finally, you're here."

STRIPPING TO BOY BANDS

Van

The entire day was shit and the final nail in the coffin… I got fired. I was half tempted to ask my foreman, or former foreman, where in the employee handbook it states an employee can't take part in any extracurricular activities with another employee while off the clock. Granted, those activities involved his office and his daughter bouncing up and down on my cock while screaming my name. Even so, I was off the clock. But his tomato red face and protruding vein in his neck told me otherwise. Plus, my pants were still wrapped around my ankles, and I don't think I would have gotten very far kangaroo hopping out.

Instead of scouring the internet for a new job, I'm at the club, Heaven and Hell, on a Friday night because a friend needed a wingman. Why not spend what little money I have on ten-dollar drinks that are the size of a shot glass? Sounds like what any responsible adult would do. Tomorrow I'll start the new job search. Masonry jobs are a dime a dozen. I doubt I'll have any issues finding a new one.

I've only been to this club twice. It's a little too fancy for my liking and waiting twenty minutes for an overpriced drink is not my idea of a good time, but I'm taking one for the team. I'm crammed behind a group of girls as they giggle and flirt with the bartender, with hopes to score a free drink. My irritation increases as I get jabbed in the back with an elbow.

Finally, when I see an opportunity, I wedge myself between two people and rest my elbow on the bar. Over the next five minutes, I repeatedly attempt to flag down the bartender, but get ignored for a girl in less clothing than the last. Eventually, the bartender passes me the expensive ass whiskey sour I ordered. The glass is so small I'll have it empty in two swallows. Shit. I should have gotten two. By the time I squeeze out of the crowd, my drink is already empty. Fuck. There is no way I'm going back into the lion's den for another drink. Then I remember there's another bar on the second floor. I bet I could score a drink up there and no one would be none the wiser.

I maneuver my way through the rest of the crowd until I find the stairs that lead up to the second floor. Before I can place a foot on the first step, a thick arm hits my chest, halting me in my tracks.

A big, burly man with almost black eyes bore directly into my soul as if he wants to shove his fists down my throat and rip out my heart Mortal Combat style. "Private party. Do you have a wristband?"

Of course I don't have a wristband, but he doesn't need to know that. "They never gave me one."

"Can't get up there without a wristband." His tree trunk of an arm still blocks the stairway.

"Listen, man. I only want a drink. It's a fucking zoo at the bar." I hike my thumb in the direction of the now even larger crowd that's gathered. "I promise, I'll go up and be back so fast you won't even know I'm gone." Maybe I can bribe him? I reach into my pocket and pull out the first bill I grip. When I glance down, all I see is a five. Shit. I'm sure it would take ten more of these to get him to consider moving.

"Okay."

My head sling shots up. His expression unreadable. "Okay? Cool. Thanks, man." A wide grin covers my face. I wasn't expecting it to be that easy. This might be a good night after all. I take a step forward, but his arm is still blocking my way. I duck down to try and crawl under, but it's too tight of a squeeze. Standing to my full height, I peer down. "Your arm's still in the way."

He snarls his lip. "Get the fuck out of here. No wristband. No entry."

The smile falls from my face. Can't one thing go my way for once? Now might be a good time to follow through with the bribe. I shove my hand back into my pocket to find the five again when a fight breaks out to my left. The big, burly guy mutters under his breath before pushing me aside to take care of the situation.

My gaze darts to the open stairway, then back to where the big, burly bouncer is manhandling one guy while fending off another. If I'm going to end up getting man handled like that, I might as well get a drink first. Without a second look, I climb the stairs. I only make it a few steps before I'm stopped again. Except this time instead of a burly guy, I'm greeted by an auburn-haired bombshell in a tan sequined mini dress. One look at her and instantly I forget all about the whiskey sour. Hell, I forget my own name.

"Finally, you're here."

"Oh. Um." *Play it cool, Van. Don't let the hot girl get you tongue tied.* "Of course, where else would I be?" I flash her a dimpled smile.

"No, seriously. You're an hour late. The least you could've done was call. We have a group of girls who are ready to see you take your clothes off. Let's go." Her dainty fingers wrap around my wrist. The warm contact sends a current of electricity coursing through my body as she tugs me up the stairs.

"Wait." I plant my feet. "What are you talking about? Take my clothes off? I think I deserve dinner before I get naked." I flash her a seductive smile.

"Dinner? Are you kidding? We weren't told we had to feed you." She drops my hand and rests it on her hip. "Look, we have a thousand dollars for you plus tips, if you're good, to take your clothes off and shake your ass while we all ooh and ahh over your ripped abs. You have ripped abs, right?" She lifts the hem of my shirt, exposing my hard six pack. "Oh yes, that'll do." Her gaze lingers on my exposed stomach for a few extra seconds before she reluctantly drops the fabric. "So, are you coming or am I calling your boss to tell him you won't do your job?"

Fuck. She thinks I'm a stripper for her party. But it pays a thousand dollars plus tips. Since I'm jobless, I could use the cash. I wager the battle in my head for a split second and, fuck it. First time for everything. "Lead the way."

She spins around and climbs the stairs, the shimmering sequins on the ass of her dress hypnotizing as her hips sway back and forth. As the giggles and laughter grow louder, I second guess myself. I've never done this before. I mean, I've gotten naked before, just never with more than one girl watching.

"Our entertainment has arrived!" the bombshell announces to her friends. All their heads turn my way and I give them a small wave and sheepish smile, still not entirely sure how this is going to play out. A blonde comes up and introduces herself as Olivia. She directs me to an area next to the bar where I can get ready and let the bartender know what music I want played. I strut to the curtained area as if I know what I'm doing, when in reality, a bead of sweat pricks my temple. After I'm on the other side of the curtained room, I peek my head through and get the attention of the bartender and order another whiskey sour. She passes the drink to me, and I slam it. I'm going to need a lot of extra liquid courage for this.

I take one shoe off and kick it to the side. Wait, do I take my shoes off? It's not like I have pants that easily rip off. Unless you're Arnold Schwarzenegger; I bet he could rip my pants off. Then again, I wouldn't want him ripping anything off me. I side shuffle to collect my shoe and slide it back on. Reaching for my phone in my back pocket, I pull it out and search for stripper playlists. There has to be something out there. After I get somewhat of a list together, I pass it along to the bartender. She glances at the list, and then up to me and shakes her head with a smile. All I can do is shrug my shoulders because fuck if I know what I'm doing. I need this to be convincing enough that they give me the cash and I can bolt out of here.

The bartender hits a button and smoked glass descends from the ceiling. The noise from the downstairs club grows quieter and quieter until the glass locks into place on the floor. Silence fills the room. *Holy shit. That's fancy as fuck.*

The first note of "Pony" by Ginuwine thumps through the speakers. An eruption of hoots and hollers come from the girls. I guess I'm doing this. I peel back the curtain and make my grand entrance as a group sits in a semi-circle on the couch while the others occupy the armchairs. Mentally, I come up with a game plan. First, I'll hit up the girls on the couch and then the ones in the chairs. I suppose I should do something extra special for whoever the party is for. But I really want to go after the auburn-haired bombshell I met earlier. I've heard that if someone is a good dancer, then they're good in bed. Well, I'm good in bed, scratch that, phenomenal in bed, so I must be a good dancer.

I saunter to the couch first and swivel my hips while lifting the hem of my shirt so they get a glimpse of my abs. Can't give everything away right from the start. Gotta keep them wanting more. One girl's eyes go wide as another has a grin that splits her face. Another shoves a few dollars into the waistband of my jeans. When I get to the last girl, I do a double take. Holy shit. The bombshell has a twin. Luckily, she's wearing a black dress, so at least I'll be able to tell them apart. I swing my hips and turn around to shake my ass. I've always been told I have a nice ass. All the squats from lifting bricks have paid off. A round of whistles followed by clapping surrounds the couch. I move over to the two girls sitting in the chairs, one of them is the bombshell. I hike one leg up on the arm of the chair and swivel my hips, my crotch mere inches from the tip of her nose. Her hands fly up to cover her face.

Bending down, I grip her wrists and peel her hands away and gaze into her eyes. "Just enjoy the show."

"I'm not used to being this up close and personal to a stranger's…" She waves a hand around the front of my pants.

"Don't worry. It won't bite unless you want it to." I toss her a flirty wink.

A small chuckle escapes her, and her lips turn up into a smile. Finally, she drops her hands to her side. Olivia strolls over to us, grabs her hand, and deposits a stack of bills into her palm. Olivia glances at the money, then at my crotch, then at the bombshell, and nods firmly. The bombshell hesitantly wraps her fingers around the stack of singles.

"You don't get to leave that chair until you shove all those in his waistband." A wide grin spreads over Olivia's face before she's turning on her heel and retreating to her friends.

Not wanting to waste another second, my hands go to the button of my pants, and I flick it open. Slowly, I pull the zipper down. Her eyes fixate as each tooth passes through the zipper. Her teeth sink into her bottom lip. How do you say you're turned on without saying you're turned on? Look like the girl in front of me. There's something exhilarating about having the power to turn someone on. Maybe later she'll be thinking of me while she touches herself because I know I'll be thinking about her.

With the top of my boxer briefs exposed, her soft fingers brush against my heated skin as she shoves a dollar into the waistband. I find the rhythm of the music and sway my hips back and forth. Like a pendulum, her gaze follows my movements. Lust pools in her irises as I swivel my hips inches from her face. This time, she shoves handfuls of bills into my waistband until she's out of money. Feigning disappointment, I drop my leg to the floor and move on to the next girl. repeat the process, giving her a similar show to what I gave the bombshell.

When I finish, I glance around. Shit. Now what am I supposed to do? Thinking quick, I find an empty chair and place it in front of the couch. Using it as a prop, I channel my inner Channing Tatum and grind my hips on the chair, giving each and every one of these girls the fantasy of wishing they were this chair. Maybe I've missed my true calling.

The song changes and I realize this one-man show is getting lonely. I stroll to the bombshell still sitting in the chair and hold my hand out for her. She glances at my open palm before glancing up at me, eyebrows pinched together.

Bending down, I place a hand on each of the armrests, caging her in. My breath, warm against the shell of her ear. "Take it. It's your turn for some special attention." Even in the dark, I can see the pink color of her cheeks.

"Girl, get it!"

"Rip his shirt off!"

"Let's get to the good stuff!"

Voices yell around us, but I'm not sure who's saying what. Reluctantly, she rests her palm on mine. Her soft skin a contrast against my rough hand as her fingers wrap around mine. I'm half tempted to forget this party and take her behind the curtain. I shake the thought from my head. Instead, I hoist her out of the armchair and guide her to the chair in the middle of the room.

Once she's seated, I bend down again and whisper in her ear, "Is it okay if I touch you? Just on your hands and arms." Her gaze darts from me to her friends as if she wants them to give her an answer. Hoping to reassure her I add, "Because you can most definitely touch me."

Her eyes meet mine and she nods before choking out, "Yes."

That's all I need. I straddle her legs and swivel my hips. I grab her hand and run it under my shirt. Her warm fingertips drag across my skin. When she reaches the middle of my chest, I remove my hand, but she keeps hers there. Her fingertips roam down my chest, caressing every dip and valley of my abs as they dance with my movements. There's something hot and sensual with the way her fingers graze over my skin. I don't know what it is, but I don't want her to stop. When she reaches my waistband, she drops her hand to her lap. A pang of disappointment hits me from the loss of her touch. I love having her hands on me.

Then another idea pops into my head. Grabbing her hands, I take a step back, giving her enough room to stand in front of me. This time, I grab both of her hands and place them at the hem of my shirt. I bend down until I'm at the shell of her ear and whisper, "Take my shirt off."

Slowly, I lean back and study her face. Her forehead wrinkles, but her fingers continue to caress the hem of my shirt. She nibbles on her bottom lip, and I'm so tempted to take over and nibble it myself. I nod my head, encouraging her to continue. Her fingers grip the fabric and drag it up, exposing my heated skin to the cool air. Once she's removed my shirt as far as she can reach, I take over and pull it the rest of the way off. With one side of my shirt in one hand, I wrap it around her waist and grip the other end with my other hand and tug, causing her to press up against my chest. Electricity courses through me as I sway my hips back and forth against her body to the music.

Just as I find my grove, the song changes. The first few notes of "It's Gonna Be Me" by NSYNC blares through the speakers and I freeze. In fact, everyone in the room freezes. My gaze darts to the bartender. This song certainly wasn't on the playlist I gave her. All she does is give me a one shoulder shrug.

Never one to turn down a challenge, I turn my attention back to the girl in my arms and move my body to the beat.

The bombshell barks out a laugh. "You are not stripping to NSYNC."

"Oh, but I am. And I'm going to look good doing it, too." I flash her a sexy smirk.

At least the song has a beat I can work with. And offers plenty of opportunities to thrust my hips. Starting at my shoulders and down to my stomach, I roll my body like a slow-moving wave. At the end I thrust my hips and all the girls clap and cheer. Their encouragement spurs me on more. I bend at the knees, and dress be damned. I pick her up and wrap her legs around my waist. She gasps and rests her hands on my shoulders for support. Swiveling around, I peer over her shoulder and find what I need. Within a few steps I'm standing in front of the chair. I release her legs, and she slowly slides down my body. My dick rubs against her the entire way down. There's no way she can't tell how much she turns me on.

Once her feet are firmly planted on the floor, she flashes me a saucy smile. "I didn't know boy bands turned you on?"

Now it's my turn to laugh. "It was all JC." She chuckles. I love her laugh. It's soft and sweet and I want to spend the rest of the night making her laugh, amongst other things. With an arm wrapped around her waist, I tug her toward me so she's snug against my chest. "Actually, that's only for you. What do you say we get a drink after this?"

Her gaze droops to the floor. "I don't think that's a good idea."

"I think it's an excellent idea. Probably the best I've ever had." All I want is to spend more time with her and I'll do whatever it takes to make that happen.

"Maybe you should give everyone else a dance." Her

voice is so soft I almost don't hear her, but her fingertips lightly brush my bare chest.

"But what if I don't want to give anyone else a dance? You're the only one I want to dance with."

A few of the other girls woot and holler while another one screams out, "Rip his clothes off!"

"It sounds like your friends want you to rip my clothes off. I'd hate to disappoint them." I trail a finger down her flush cheek and she shivers from the contact. It's not just me who feels the chemistry radiating between us in waves. She wouldn't be this hesitant if she didn't feel it either. I can see it in her eyes. The way she brushes against me. The way her cheeks turn crimson from my touch.

"We paid you to dance for everyone, not just me." Her eyes shift back and forth, searching mine, waiting for my response.

As much as I don't want to, I drop my arm that's keeping her captive against me. I'll be patient for her. Good thing the night's still young. Her chest heaves as she drags a finger down my chest. She takes one step backward, then another. Until finally she twists around and makes her way to the bar. I watch her every step until the song changes, and I then remember why I'm here. Sadly, it's not to convince her to spend more time with me even though that's the only thing on my mind.

CHAPTER FOUR

STRIPPER FANTASY

Hollyn

When I reach the bar, I order a lemon drop martini. The champagne is no longer cutting it. First of all, I've never had a guy dance for me like that and second, it's so fucking hot. The bartender places my drink in front of me. Immediately, I grab it and swallow a big gulp, needing something to settle my erratic heartbeat. Something about him dancing in front of me, my hands on his body, people watching, sent my body ablaze. Honestly, I want to finish ripping his clothes off. If we were alone, chances are I would have. My pebbled nipples brush against the cool silk of my dress, sending a shiver down my spine. Where did these thoughts come from? Even when I was with the ex-fiancé, I never had an animalistic desire to tear someone's clothes off. I lift the glass up to my lips for another drink.

"I didn't know what to expect when I ordered a stripper, but I think he is well worth the money." Olivia comes to stand next to me at the bar, pulling me from my stripper fantasy. She flags down the bartender and orders herself a Cosmopolitan.

All I can do is sip my lemon drop martini as my gaze wanders to where he's thrusting his hips, slow and seductive, in front of Charlie's friend.

"I think you're drooling." Olivia bumps her shoulder with mine.

"I am not." Nonchalantly, I swipe at the corners of my mouth.

"Anyone can see the chemistry smoldering between you two. Plus, he hasn't taken his eyes off you the entire night. You should see what he's doing later." She wiggles her eyebrows at me.

"The stripper?"

"Yes! See if those dance moves translate into moves between the sheets. Because, damn, his hip thrusts could do some serious damage to a girl's vagina. Bring him back to our room tonight. I'll have a key if anything happens."

"Where will you stay?"

"I'll figure it out." Olivia shrugs a shoulder.

"I won't lie. The guy is fucking gorgeous. But..." I scrunch my nose, "he looks so... young."

"And I bet he has stamina like a wild stallion. You need to saddle up and take him for a ride." Olivia motions as if she's throwing a lasso while bucking her hips.

"I don't know. I don't know him." As much as I'm attracted to him, I'm still not convinced I can go through with a random hook up.

"That's the point of a one-night stand. No getting to know you. No awkward first dates. You dive right into the good stuff. Be spontaneous for one night. Don't think. Just do. Him." Olivia smirks behind her glass.

"The first time I saw him take his clothes off, all my friends did too." I cringe. "Not too many people can say that."

"And I one hundred percent approve. After seeing what he's packing, you need to see what else he has to offer. Stop trying to talk yourself out of it. A night of fun and debauchery, remember?" Olivia holds her drink up to me and we cheers.

I swallow a big gulp of my martini. I'd be lying if I said I wasn't curious about what a night between the sheets would be like with him. The erotic way he swings his hips. Slow and seductive. I can only imagine what it would be like with him hovering above me, grinding his hips like that.

When I get back to the couch and take a seat, I'm surprised when a piece of black fabric covers my face. When his woodsy spice scent hits me, I know exactly who it belongs to. With one last sniff, I peel it off and I'm greeted with a devilish grin from Olivia as she nods her head to the left. When I twist around, a shirtless stripper is stalking towards me. Olivia scurries off the couch, leaving me all alone with Mr. Tall, Dark, and Oh So Delicious.

"We meet again." A smile teases his lips.

"Or you're stalking me." I mimic his same teasing smile before taking a sip of my drink.

"What can I say? I'm drawn to you like a stripper to a waving dollar bill."

A laugh bubbles out of me. I slap my hand over my mouth in hopes of not spewing my drink all over his stomach. Chalk this up to the first guy who's turned me on and made me laugh within the first hour of meeting him.

"How about one last dance before the night's over?" He holds out his open palm.

I eye it suspiciously, unsure of what to do. If I take his hand, a part of me thinks this night might end in more than just a dance, and if I don't, I might regret it. For a brief moment, I wage the war inside of me. This time the devil wins. I place my hand on his and he tugs me off the couch. With our hands between us, he intertwines our fingers. When I glance up and meet his eyes, a mix of lust and playfulness dance in his dark irises. I make the mistake and glance down to his mouth as his lips tip up into a smile. My chest heaves as my heart rate speeds up from this single action.

"I think I'm affecting you the same way you're affecting me." He pulls me to him so our bodies are flush.

"No. This is my natural reaction when a shirtless guy pulls me to his chest." I smirk.

"What's your name?"

The question is innocent, but do I want to give him my real name? My heart beats erratically as my gaze shifts back and forth over his face. "Holl—and. Holland."

"Holland." The name rolls off his tongue, deep and growly. I could listen to him say it over and over again. Too bad it's not my name. "Van. My name is Van."

"Hi, Van."

"Now that we got that out of the way, what do you say I give you some more one-on-one time?" Before I can respond, Van's tugging me toward the vacant chair in front of the couch. Van whirls us around. Once the chair brushes against the back of my knees, he's pushing me down until my butt hits the seat with a thump.

He strolls to the bar, leaving me all alone, and leans over the wood bar top to whisper to the bartender. His muscles flexing and tightening as he rests his hands on the rail. She gives him a slight head nod. A few seconds later, "Ride" by Chase Rice pours through the speakers. When he turns back around, a seductive grin fills his face and my thighs, instinctively, clench together. He prowls toward me like a lion hunting its prey and I've never wanted to get caught as badly as I do right now. Everyone is watching from a distance, but I hardly notice. My focus is solely on the man stalking toward me. My chest heaves in sync with each of his footfalls. When he comes to a stop in front of me, his crotch is at eye level. The outline of a very impressive bulge stares back at me. He places a calloused finger under my chin and forces me to meet his gaze.

"Eyes up here." A smile teases his lips.

He bends down and rests his hands on the back of the chair, caging me in. My eyes never once leave his. He leans in, his lips a mere inch away from mine. The smell of spice and man invade my nose. I'm convinced he's going to kiss me. My lips part a fraction and my eyes flutter closed as I brace for impact. Seconds pass, but it never comes. Instead, the prickly stubble on his cheek brushes against mine. His breath tickles the shell of my ear. "While I love this dress on you, I wish you had on something else."

"Why's that?" My voice is a whisper.

Van pulls back slightly, so I can see his face, my gaze fixated on his lips. "So, I could spread your legs and show you what I really want to do to you."

My nipples pebble into stiff peaks from his words. I nibble on my bottom lip, imagining what that would be like. Never in my life have I ever had a guy speak to me like this. And holy shit, it's hot as hell. Dress be damned, I'm tempted to climb this man like a tree and let him have his way with me, right here in front of everyone. But before I can do that, he rises to his full height.

Instead of spreading mine, he's hiking a leg over my

lap and straddling me. He grabs my hands and brings them to his ass. My palms are flat against the stretched denim. Once he's satisfied with their position, he brings his hands back to the front, each one on either side of me, resting on the back of the chair. He pumps his hips, only making slight contact with each upward thrust. What I really want to do is raise my hips in time with his for more contact. Instead, I savor the moment, imagining what it would be like with him thrusting into me. Naked. The muscles in his backside move and flex with every swivel. The worn denim of his jeans is rough against my fingertips as I give his backside a gentle squeeze. His hands move to grip the side of my head and he tilts it up. Lust and desire swirl in his eyes. My heart rate spikes and my breathing quickens knowing he sees the same in mine.

The music stops, but Van doesn't move. He continues to stare into my eyes, then his gaze drifts down to my mouth. Once again, I think he's about to kiss me and if he did, I wouldn't stop him. My lips part, almost as an invitation for him to press his lips to mine. He tilts his head and moves a fraction of an inch closer. My eyes flutter closed. He's about to kiss me.

Suddenly, loud clapping and cheering comes from all around us. My lids lift just as Van pulls away. He moves off me so he's no longer straddling me, but his gaze never leaves mine. Slowly, he takes a step back, and then another, before he's turning around and retreating to the room behind the curtain.

SUCH A CASANOVA

Van

I was seconds away from pressing my mouth to her soft, plump lips. To claim her. Let her know I wanted more from her. Instead, the clapping from her friends burst our lust filled bubble, and I retreated. What the hell am I doing? Since my life was thrown into a tailspin four years ago, I've lived life in the moment, but chalk this up to be the craziest thing I've ever done.

I yank the singles from my underwear and place them on a chair sitting in the corner. I fasten the button of my jeans and grab the bills, flipping through the stack before shoving them into my pants pocket. As I pull my shirt over my head, a voice from behind me causes me to spin around.

"That was a good show. Everyone had a good time."

Holland pulls the curtain to the side, creating a hole large enough to poke her head in.

"Thanks. All part of the job." I assume that's something a stripper might say.

"Can I come in?"

"Yeah." I wave her in as I pull the hem of my shirt the rest of the way down. Her gaze lingers on my stomach before she realizes she's staring and looks away. Even in the dim light, the blush covering her cheeks is visible.

"So anyway, I wanted to give you the rest of the money." She hands over a white envelope of cash. "You can count it if you want, but it's all there."

"No, I trust you." I tuck the envelope into my pants pocket with the other bills. "So, what are you doing after this?"

"Everyone is pretty tired, so I think we're going back to our hotel."

"If you want to stick around for a while, I'll be here. We can do some actual dancing." The last thing I want is for this night to be over. I've gotten the appetizer. Now I want the main course. The sparkle in her eyes give her away. Girls like her need to be challenged. Don't ask, but demand. So, I switch tactics. "Come dance with me." This time it's not a question, but a statement.

"Oh, I don't know. I don't want to leave my friends." She turns her head to glance at everyone else.

With my fingers, I grip her chin and direct her attention back to me. "Your friends will be fine. Come dance. Don't be so uptight. Let loose."

"I am loose." There's a little defiance in her tone. I can't help but quirk an eyebrow. "Not like that." She huffs and rests her hands on her hips.

"Then prove it. Come dance with me."

Several seconds pass before she exhales a huff in

defeat. "Fine." She holds up her pointer finger in the air. "One dance."

"That's all I need." I smirk.

We exit the small room and I stroll over to the stairs. Before descending, I turn around, and she's talking to her friends. I'm assuming she's telling them she's going to the dance floor with me. My suspicions are confirmed when five heads, all wearing the same wide smile, swing toward me. I give them a small wave and a smile of my own. Finally, she saunters my way. The lights glimmer off her dress, causing it to sparkle, and I imagine slowly peeling it off her body. One strap. Two straps. And then it floats to the floor, leaving her in nothing but a thong. Quickly, I shake that thought from my head. One thing at a time.

Once at the bottom of the stairs, I spot the burly bouncer and flash him a cocky grin. He glares at me as if he wants to eat me for breakfast. Luckily, I'm with Holland so his breakfast will have to wait. I turn around and hold out my hand. She glances down at my open palm before placing her hand in mine. Her gaze wanders up to mine as a smile covers her face.

"Such a gentleman."

I lean down so only she can hear. "Believe me, you wouldn't be calling me a gentleman if you knew what I want to do to you right now." Her cheeks flush crimson. "But first, let's see what kinda moves you've got."

With her hand in mine, I guide her to the dance floor, squeezing in between bodies until we find enough space for the both of us. I spin around so I'm facing her, my hands go to her hips as hers wrap around my neck. Both of us sway our hips to the music. Her fingers play with the hair at the back of my head. The innocent touch sends all my blood rushing south. I don't know how she does it. The simplest touch from her drives me wild. One of my hands slides to her lower back, resting above the curve of her ass. I tug her so her body is flush with mine. My hips grind against her. She tilts her head up, a seductive smile gracing her lips.

Bending down, my warm breath whispers across the shell of her ear. "That's what you do to me."

She throws her head back in laughter. "Oh, I'm sure any girl rubbing her body against you would cause that."

"Well you're not just any girl. And right now, it's all you." I drag my fingertips up her spine of her open back dress. Even though it's hot in here with all the people, a shiver takes over her body.

"You're such a Casanova. Do those words work on all the girls?" She tilts her head, a teasing smirk on her lips.

"You tell me?"

"Cocky much?"

"Call it confidence."

"Or conceited."

"I could show you my skills and then you can tell me, confident or conceited."

"I'm sure that's exactly what you want."

"Hell yeah." I cup the sides of her head and tilt her head, forcing her to meet my eyes. "I've wanted to do this all night. In five seconds, I'm going to kiss you and if you don't want me to, say the word. Five." I scan her face for any signs she doesn't want this. "Four." I inch closer to her. "Three." Her lips part a fraction. "Two." My gaze flicks from her mouth to her eyes.

Before I can get to one, she's tugging me closer, and her lips crash to mine. The sweet taste of her lemon drop martini still on her lips. I run my tongue along the seam of her lips and she opens for me. Our tongues caress one another's as if they are doing their own slow dance. I trail my hands from her cheeks to her waist. Her body flush against mine is what dreams are made of. I've been with my fair share of women, but I've never felt an attraction like this. Like if I let her go, I'll lose her, and right now I never want to let her go.

Reluctantly, I break the kiss but keep my lips millimeters from hers. "What do you say we get out of here? Go someplace a little more quiet."

With hooded eyes, she pauses while she contemplates my question. "I have a hotel room a couple of blocks away. We could walk there."

"I'll follow you wherever you want to go." I flash her a dimpled grin.

She gives me a beaming smile in return and then shakes her head. "There you go with the lines again. Let me tell my friends where I'm going. I'll be right back."

We pull away from each other and I walk her back to the stairs that lead to the private room. Getting fired from my job is turning out to be the best thing that's happened to me. Scored over a thousand dollars cash, plus I'll be spending my night with a gorgeous woman.

A few minutes later, Holland's descending the stairs. I greet her with my hand held out. "Ready?"

A smile tips the corner of her lips as she eyes my open palm before she rests her hand in mine. "You really like this hand holding."

"Any way I can touch you." We stroll toward the exit, hand in hand. I hold the door open for her as she steps through and I follow, the warm spring air hits us.

"So, what brings you downtown?"

"Celebrating a friend's engagement and my sister's pregnancy."

"And you needed a stripper for that?" I raise an eyebrow.

"That was Olivia's idea. It was all part of our night of fun and debauchery."

"I'm glad I could help with the debauchery part of the evening. We could get started right now." I bend down and whisper into her ear. "I could push you against the wall down that dark alley. All the sounds from the city would echo around us, drowning out your cries of pleasure as my tongue laps at your needy pussy." Her steps falter from my words. I'm sure she's already dripping wet for me.

"Oh, well. If we weren't at the hotel, I might have taken you up on your offer." She points to a building a half a block from us.

"We can walk around the block again."

She releases a throaty laugh. "Too late. We're here."

NIGHT OF FIRSTS

Van

When we enter the hotel lobby, she directs us to the right, past the check-in desk, and down a hallway until we reach a bank of elevators. She presses the button and we both watch as the red numbers above the doors count down. The seconds feel like minutes as we wait. The anticipation to be alone with her nearly kills me. Finally, the doors open with a ding.

With my hand on her lower back, I guide her to go first. As I turn around and stand near the back wall of the elevator, she presses the button for the suite level. Holland moves to stand in front of me. "What is it about elevators? The close quarters?"

"Or perhaps it's the cameras," I lean in and whisper. "Because I know you like when people watch."

Her breath hitches as goosebumps sprout up her arms. She knows I'm not wrong. My suspicions are confirmed when she plants her palm against my chest and shoves me until I hit the back wall with a thump.

"Maybe we should give them a show." She rises on her toes and presses her lips to mine. I grip her hips, my fingertips digging into her soft flesh through her dress, and haul her to me. The elevator comes to a stop. I pull away from Holland and peek over her shoulder. Quickly, she steps to the side of me as a group of six people enter the elevator.

Once the doors close, I wrap my arm around her shoulder and slowly drag my hand down the open back of her dress. My fingertips caress her heated skin as I inch my way downward until I reach the curve of her ass. She shivers at the contact, and I give her a wink before my fingers dance down to the hem of her dress. Luckily, her heels give her a few extra inches and I don't have to bend down as much. When I reach the edge, I slide my hand underneath, naturally hiking the back of her dress up, exposing her backside. But we're so crammed in here that no one pays attention.

As the elevator continues to climb, my hand travels down. Holland's chest rises and falls with each passing second, as if she knows what I'm about to do and is expecting it to happen. While everyone else in the elevator talks amongst themselves, I bend my knees slightly and run a finger down her crack until I reach the apex of her thighs. Knowing what I want without having to say anything, she spreads her legs slightly to give me better access. The pad of my middle finger runs along the silk of her panties. Her teeth sink into her bottom lip as her eyes flutter closed. I draw small circles on her pussy over the fabric, which has now become damp with her arousal.

Leaning down, I whisper so only she can hear, "Does knowing anyone could catch us right now turn you on?" Her lips fall open and she exhales a small gasp.

The elevator comes to a halt and the doors open. I remove my hand, drop the back of her dress, and smooth it down, mostly so I could run my hand over her ass again. Everyone else files out of the elevator followed by Holland and myself. I catch up to stand next to her, my hand resting on her lower back. Any opportunity to touch her, I'll take it. Though we're silent the entire walk, the sexual chemistry radiates off us in waves. I'm drowning in her and right now I don't want saving. Once we reach her door, she pulls out her key card. A split second later, the light flashes green, and she pushes the door open. I reach over her and hold the door while she walks into the narrow foyer.

As soon as the door clicks shut, I tug her wrist and spin her around, crashing my lips to hers in a bruising kiss. Not being able to kiss her this entire time has been torture. She wraps her arms around my neck as I deepen the kiss. I turn us around and slam her back against the nearest wall. Using it for leverage, I wrap a hand around her knee, hiking her leg over my hip, all while never breaking our kiss. Finally, I get to touch her like I've wanted to all night. Slowly, I drag my hand up her silky-smooth thigh until my fingertips reach her panties. With the pad of my finger, I rub slow, lazy circles over the soaking wet fabric covering her pussy. A moan escapes her throat and I swallow down every sound. I repeat the motion but this time her head falls back, breaking our kiss.

"Oh, God. I'm going to combust any moment." She releases another whimper when I brush over her clit. Her breathing shallows as she pushes out the next words. "Wait. Hold on." I instantly freeze. "Just so you know, I don't normally do this. Find a random guy at the bar and take him home for sex."

"You don't need to explain anything to me."

"I needed to get that out."

"Do you feel better now?"

"I do."

"I'm glad I'm the lucky guy, then." I place an open mouth kiss on her collarbone, then move up to her neck. She tilts her head to give me better access, and I take it.

She bucks her hips against my hand, and I take that as my cue to keep going. Her breathing is heavy as she mutters, "Don't stop."

"I have no intentions of stopping until I get at least seven orgasms from you."

"Overachiever." She squirms in my arms. A throaty moan escapes as I brush over her clit.

"Determined," I mumble against the side of her neck.

"You better get to it. We don't have all night."

"Yes, ma'am." I push her panties to the side and slide two fingers between her folds, her sweet honey covering my fingers.

"Oh, fuck," she cries out in pleasure. "Also, don't call me ma'am."

I laugh. My warm breath skates across her damp, sensitive skin. I press against her tight opening before plunging a finger in.

"I take that back. Call me whatever you want. Just. Don't. Stop." Her words come out in breathy pants. She wraps her arms around my shoulders. Her fingers comb through my hair before her nails dig into my scalp, clutching my dark strands.

I pull out and add a second finger, stretching her even more when I push back in. Her hips grind against my hand each time I pull out and plunge back in. With my free hand, I pull the strap of her dress off her shoulder and place kisses across her chest. When I reach the swell of her tits, I suck the soft flesh, leaving tiny bite marks in my wake. I pull down the top of her dress, her pebbled nipples exposed to the cool air. While I continue to pump in and out of her, I suck one hardened peak into my mouth. Pumping faster, I swirl my tongue around her nipple. Her moans get louder until she finally detonates, screaming my name. Her nails dig into my scalp. She rides out her orgasm as her pussy clenches around my fingers.

I release her nipple with a pop. "I believe that's number one. Hold on." With her arms still wrapped around my shoulders, I lift her other leg until I'm carrying her weight, her body pressed up against mine. I turn around and enter the rest of the enormous suite. "Where do you want your next orgasm? On the couch? The table may be sturdy enough. Against the window? Then the city below can see how fucking sexy you are as you come for me." Her breath hitches at the last one, telling me that's her answer.

When I'm standing in front of the floor to ceiling window, I drop my arms holding Holland up and she slowly slides down the front of my body. Once her feet are firmly planted on the floor, I take a step back.

"Take off the dress."

She raises her right arm and with her left hand she tugs on the zipper until it stops at the end. One strap at a time, she pulls them over her shoulders until the fabric flutters and pools at her feet. She steps out of the dress and lifts her leg to pull off her heels.

"The shoes stay on."

A smile flirts on her lips. She drops her leg and stands to her full height wearing nothing but a tan silk thong and heels. My heart stops. Time ceases to exist. I'm surprised I don't pass out when all my blood rushes south.

Once I pick my jaw up off the floor, I say, "Turn around and walk to the window. Put both your palms flat against the glass."

She does exactly what I say. I stalk up behind her, my reflection like a double exposure against the lights of the city below.

I place my hands on her waist, lean over, and whisper in her ear. "Are you ready for your next orgasm?"

She turns her head and eagerly nods. My hands skate up and over her rib cage and wrap around her front until I cup both of her tits. I roll each hardened nipple between my finger and thumb. A small whimper escapes her throat.

"Van. If you don't make good on your promise. I'm going to do it myself."

I bark out a laugh. "A woman who's self-sufficient, I like that. But don't worry, cupcake, I got you."

Bending down, I grip the thin straps of her panties and glide them over her hips and down her tone legs. Now, she's in front of me in nothing but her black high heels. My hands grip her hips, my fingertips dimple her soft flesh and pull back, forcing her to bend at the waist. Still on my knees, I slide my hands down to the globes of her ass and squeeze the tender flesh. A low, breathy moan sounds above me.

I slide one hand down the crack of her ass, between her legs, until I find her soaking wet pussy. With her spread open, I circle her clit. Her arousal coats my finger. When I find her entrance, I tease the opening for a few seconds before pushing in. Her tight walls grip my finger. Fuck, if this is how she feels with only a finger, I can only imagine what it'll be like with my dick filling her.

I continue to pump in and out, faster and harder with every thrust. Then I add a second, stretching her more. Her moans and whimpers grow louder as she pushes back against my hand. Wanting more. Needing more. And who am I to deny her?

I pull out and she whimpers from the loss. "I need to taste you."

Before she can say anything, I'm spreading her wide from behind. I trail my tongue down the crack of her ass until I find her needy pussy. Her honey hits my taste buds and I release an animalistic groan. Like a starved man, I lap at the sweetness.

"Oh God! Ahh! That feels incredible. Don't stop."

Her legs quiver and she continues to grind against me, needing all the connection she can get. I flick my tongue over her clit and she exhales another throaty moan.

"Keep going. Oh Van. I'm about to come."

With my hand wrapped around her, I continue rubbing her clit while I lap at her pussy at the same time. Her moans and whimpers fill the room as her orgasm takes over and coats my tongue. Her entire body trembles, but I don't stop.

With the flat of my tongue, I lick bottom to top. Then I tongue fuck her while alternating between hard and soft pressure on her clit with the pad of my finger. Her legs quiver as she's exploding again, screaming out my name. This time, I slow my movements until she comes down from her high. The room goes silent except for her breathy pants. I rise to my feet, wiping my mouth on the back of my hand, and stand behind her, my lips at the shell of her ear.

"Everyone down on the streets witnessed number two and three."

Her hands fall from the window, and she turns to face me. Her body flushed and her chest still heaving "And I want four and five to be with your cock."

All the girls I've been with have never had this type of

confidence with sex. Usually, they have me take the lead, which I'm okay with, but I'm finding this confidence from a woman sexy as fuck.

"When you put it that way, I can't deny you what you want."

I prowl toward her. One step. Two steps. My movements forcing her to retreat until her back hits the cool glass. I wrap my hands around the sides of her head, my fingers combing through her silky hair, and slam my lips to hers. My tongue peeks out and presses against the seam of hers, seeking entrance. After a little coaxing, she opens, and our tongues caress each other's. I know she can taste herself on my tongue, but she doesn't stop. The kiss is slow and sensual at first but grows more ravenous with each passing second. I need inside this girl. I pull away, her lips plump and swollen from the kiss. Her eyes slowly flutter open and meet mine.

"Do you have a condom? I don't think I can wait another second without being inside you."

She takes a moment to digest my words. "Yes. On the nightstand. In the bedroom."

"I'll go get it." I turn around and glance around the large room, unsure where the bedroom is. She notices my confusion and points me to a door on the left. I barrel toward the closed door and throw it open. Flipping on the switch, light floods the room. Quickly, I glance around until I spot the box of condoms sitting on the nightstand. When I rush over to it, I yank a foil pack out and an entire strip comes with it. Not caring, I return to Holland in a flash, the foil packets fluttering behind me. She's still standing where I left her, arms wrapped around herself, nibbling on a fingernail. She catches sight of me and drops her hand, a twinkle in her eye. Then she notices the trail of condoms behind me and a laugh bubbles from her throat.

I stop in front of her. My chest rises and falls with my labored breath. I hold up the accordion style strip of condoms, unable to hide my boyish grin. She plucks the condoms from my hand, tears off a foil packet, and holds it between two fingers.

"Now, I think it's only fitting that this night ends the same way it began. And there's one of us wearing too many clothes." She finds her phone and taps on the screen. "No Diggity" by Blackstreet fills the room. She tosses her phone on the couch and sways her hips to the music. It has to be one of the hottest things I've ever seen.

I take a couple of steps back, giving myself some room. My fingers grip the hem of my shirt and slowly drag it up over my abs, flexing with each movement. When I pull the shirt over my head, her heated gaze is watching my every move. I toss my black shirt at her, just like I did at the club. She catches it and clutches the fabric to her chest. The shirt drapes between the valley of her full tits. Next, I slowly pop the button of my jeans and peel the tops away, exposing the band of my black boxer briefs. She nibbles on her bottom lip in anticipation of what's next. I want to be the one nibbling on that lip right now. I hike my thumbs in the top of both my jeans and boxers and slowly tug down until both fall to my feet. My cock springs free, bobs up and down, and juts out toward her. Like me, it knows exactly what it wants. Her. A small gasp escapes her lips as she stares at my thick dick.

"If you keep staring at it like that, you'll give it a complex." I step out of my jeans, not wanting to waste another minute not being inside her.

"Sorry. It's just. Wow." She sucks her lower lip into her mouth.

In a few quick steps, I'm standing in front of her. I rip

the condom from her fingers and look into her eyes. "Are you ready?"

Without missing a beat, she says, "More than you'll ever know."

I push her against the window again, except this time I hike one of her legs over my hip. Using the window for leverage, I lift her other leg until she's fully wrapped around me. The head of my dick slides down the seam of her pussy. I rock my hips back and forth, collecting her wetness on my shaft. Thoughts of pushing into her, condom be damned, flit through my mind. The last bit of blood rushes south as I imagine her stretching around me with no barriers between us. But I can't risk it. The tip of my cock teases her clit and she whimpers. She rocks against me, seeking any sort of friction she can find.

Not wanting to wait another second, I rip into the foil packet with my teeth and discard the wrapper on the ground. I reach below us and roll the condom on. Once it's in place, I rub the tip through her slick pussy, gathering her wetness. On my last stroke down, I find her entrance and push her down onto my cock.

"Fuck. I think your pussy was made for me. It fits so perfect." A deep moan rumbles from my chest as her pussy clenches around my dick, her heat enveloping me. I've never felt anything this good.

Her hands fly to my shoulders and her nails dig into my muscles. Her mouth falls open as she adjusts to my size. "Oh shit. You're so big."

She throws her head back, and I take the moment to suck on her soft flesh at the base of her neck. I pull my hips back and thrust back in. Repeating the motion over and over again as I nip and suck on her heated skin. She uses my shoulders for leverage to bounce on my dick, meeting my thrusts. The sound of our skin slapping mixed with our moans of pleasure fill the room. Between us, her tits bounce, causing her pebbled nipples to brush against my chest. She throws her head back again, pushing out her chest, the featherlight sensation I'm sure driving her wild, too. I continue to pound into her, my orgasm on the brink of exploding, but I need her to come first.

"Fuck. I'm not going to last much longer. You're so tight. I need you to come for me."

"I'm almost there."

She pulls herself closer to me so we're chest to chest. She rotates her hips as I continue to thrust into her, her clit rubbing against the base of my cock. Her pants and moans mix with my grunts and gets louder with each thrust. A few seconds later, her pussy contracts around me, squeezing me like a vise grip. I can't hold out any longer. White hot heat floods my body as my seed spurts out, filling the condom as I roar out my orgasm. I slow my thrusts until she's milked every last drop out of me. I pull out of her but never let her go. Using the window, I press her back to the glass for the leverage to keep her upright. Both of our chests heave from exertion. She wraps her arms around my neck, and I nuzzle into hers.

"That was a first." My gaze meets hers.

"First time having sex?" Uncertainty laces her tone.

I bark out a laugh. Her eyebrows knit together, still unsure where I'm going with this. "No, not sex. First time… against a window."

But what I really want to say is it's the first time where I've felt so consumed by someone else. The first time it's felt that intense.

She releases a laugh of her own, soft and sweet. "Oh. Yeah. Same." There's a brief pause as she contemplates what she wants to say next. "Earlier, you called me cupcake. Why's that?"

Surprised from her question, I nuzzle my nose into her neck. "You smell like vanilla. It reminds me of the cupcakes my mom would bake for me."

"You're thinking of your mom right now."

"Uh… no. Well, it's now been replaced with memories of you."

"Always the charmer."

"But also, let's not forget, I still owe you three more orgasms. And I'm a man of my word. Perhaps, if you're a good girl, I'll even toss in two extra." I flash her a dimpled smile. But mostly, I don't want this night to end.

FAKE STRIPPER

Hollyn

Hangovers are no joke. My head feels like over mixed batter as if someone put my brain in a stand mixer and turned it to ten. The culprit of this displeasure goes by the name of lemon drop martini. I crack an eyelid and I'm greeted with a mop of brown hair. I freeze. Oh shit. Everything from the night before comes rushing back to me. The stripper. The elevator. The window. So much nakedness. And so many orgasms. I roll over and slink out of bed. When I stand, an ache between my legs reminds me of everything that happened the night before.

Then the cool air hits my naked body, once again reminding me of what went down last night. And Van did a lot of going down. Shit. Where are my clothes? On the other side of the room, I spot my shoes haphazardly laying on the floor, but no dress. Tiptoeing around the foot of the bed, I find my weekend bag and pull out a bra. I throw the straps over my shoulders and clasp the back. I go back in and grab a pair of yoga pants and a t-shirt.

Once I'm dressed, my gaze darts from one side of the room to the other. On the nightstand, I spot a ripped foil packet and shrug. At least we used protection. Do I wake him and tell him it was fun, but it's time for him to leave? Will he want another round? I quirk an eyebrow at the thought. But then the tenderness between my legs tells me I can't handle any more of Van for a few hours or, hell, a few days.

Last night… I don't know what came over me. He made me feel beautiful and confident, and like I could have anything I wanted. And God, I wanted him. Even without all the alcohol flowing through my veins, I know my feelings wouldn't be different. But now what do I do? This is uncharted territory. I need reinforcements. With one last glance behind me, I scurry out of the bedroom and exit the suite.

A minute later, I'm pounding on Parisa's door. I wrap my arms around myself as I wait. I'm not the girl who partakes in random one-night stands. It was exhilarating, but now what?

The door flies open. "Oh, good to know you're still alive." Parisa throws her arms around me in a hug before she moves out of the way, and I advance through the open door.

I glance around the room. "Is Seth around?"

"He's still in the bedroom." Parisa hikes her thumb toward a closed door.

"I wasn't interrupting anything, was I?" I ask.

"No, you're fine. You look nervous. What's up?"

"What did I do last night?" I pace back and forth. "I

don't do one-night stands, especially with guys I've just met."

Parisa pulls out a chair at the small nook in her suite next to me. "Here, take a seat. I'll let everyone know you're here."

I sit down, but a few seconds later I'm standing again, trying to rid myself of this anxiety. A few minutes later, there's a knock on the door. Parisa answers and Olivia, Charlie, and Tatum stroll in.

"Where's Liana?" I ask.

"She and Mark are taking full advantage of a weekend without kids. And I know that because my room shares a wall with them. Next time, I'm remembering ear plugs," Tatum says.

"Speaking of taking full advantage… you look like you had a good night last night." Olivia plops down on the sofa in the small living room.

"I think I can say the same to you. Your hair's a little disheveled this morning." I flick a loose strand of hair that didn't make it into the messy bun plopped on the top of her head.

"Where did you sleep last night? I'm assuming you let Hollyn have the room," Tatum asks.

"I made Trey share his room with me." Olivia's gaze wanders down as she picks at a piece of invisible lint from her shirt.

"Wait? Trey? Like our friend Trey?" Charlie asks.

Olivia nonchalantly shrugs. "Yeah. We've become close friends."

"Like friends who show each other their privates?" Parisa wiggles her eyebrows.

"We kept our privates to ourselves, thank you very much. But there was some cuddling. I guess you could call it cuddling." Olivia leans in and whispers, "He liked being the little spoon." The entire room bursts into laughter. "You guys can't tell anyone." Olivia glances at everyone in the room.

Tatum and Charlie motion like they're zipping their lips while Parisa and I nod. Of course, we are all doing this while attempting to bite back our laughter. "Enough about me. Hollyn, how was your night with the stripper?"

I fall back against the couch and throw my forearm over my eyes. "It was the best sex of my entire life. I think I'm ruined for any other guy. But also, did sex change in the last seven years? I don't remember it being so intense. So hot." I fan myself.

"That good, huh?" Charlie asks.

I hold up seven fingers and mimic Monica from *Friends* as I mouth seven.

"Girl, what the hell are you doing here? Go get eight, nine, and ten." Olivia smacks my arm.

My hands drop to the couch. "I've never done this before. I don't know what protocol is."

"Well, first you don't leave him alone in the room," Olivia exclaims.

"Oh, that." Parisa points to Olivia. "It sucks waking up to a cold bed when you're expecting a warm body next to you. Seth did that to me twice. It's a confidence killer, for sure."

"What did I do?" Seth strolls in from the other room.

"Left me in a cold bed without a word." Parisa beams up at Seth.

"I believe I made that up to you many times." Seth bends down and places a kiss on Parisa's forehead. "Good morning, ladies. Hollyn, how was your night with the fake stripper?"

"Fake stripper?" I pinch my eyebrows together.

All the color drains from Seth's face as his wide-eyed

gaze darts around the room, looking at everyone but me. As I follow his movements, all my friends avoid me as well. Parisa crosses her legs away from me and drops her gaze to the floor. Olivia pretends to dig in the couch cushion. Charlie stares at her phone screen, while Tatum looks over her shoulder.

"What's going on? Why did Seth say *fake* stripper?"

Charlie's shoulders deflate and she sets her phone down. "Seth, Bennett is in my room. You should go see him." Without asking any questions, Seth bolts towards the door without another word.

"Will someone tell me what's happening?" My heart rate spikes as my gaze pauses on each and every person in the room, waiting for an answer.

Olivia moves to sit next to me. "After you left the club, a guy showed up who was the real stripper we hired. Apparently, he got stuck in traffic and couldn't get to the club on time. He wanted to call, but his phone was dead."

My head snaps back so fast to face her I'm surprised I don't get whiplash. "Wait, so the guy I slept with last night wasn't a stripper?"

"Yay! You didn't sleep with a stripper!" Olivia enthusiastically throws her arms in the air, shaking her hands like a cheerleader with pom poms.

"Were you guys going to tell me I took a complete stranger back to my room!?" I screech.

"I mean, either one was a stranger." Parisa shrugs her shoulders.

"Were you guys going to tell me?" I shriek.

"What were we supposed to do? Pound on your door while he was pounding you and say what? 'He's not really a stripper. Carry on,'" Olivia deadpans.

"Yes! That! You should have done that." The decibel

level of my voice is so high I'm sure only dogs across the city could hear me.

"Let me ask you this. Did you have a fun night?" Olivia crosses her arms over her chest and narrows her eyes at me, waiting for an answer.

I glance everywhere but at her. I can't deny that it was one of the best nights I've had in… forever. But it was all under false pretenses.

"I will take your silence as you did." A smug smile graces Olivia's face.

I exhale a huff. "But he lied. He lied about who he was, and he stole money from us." I jump to my feet and stomp toward the door. "He can't get away with this."

"Where are you going?" Charlie asks.

"I'm going to confront the stripper. Or fake stripper. Or whoever the hell he is." I throw open the door. It slams behind me as I stomp down the hallway. My hands shake as adrenaline courses through my body. Who pretends to be a stripper? And I'm the idiot who slept with him. This is why I don't do one-night stands with strangers.

Once I reach my room, I lift the key card up to the door and the green light flashes. I press the handle down, throw open the door, and charge into the room. Quickly, I glance around to find the dark-haired stranger. "Van!" I shout. "If that's even your name," I mumble under my breath. Stomping through the suite, I get to the bedroom, the door partially ajar. Pushing it open, I storm in and yell, "How dare you!" My stomach clenches into a giant knot when my gaze fixates on the empty bed. Then I glance down to the floor. No jeans and no black shirt. I whirl around and my heart jumps to my throat. A sliver of light shines through the crack of the bathroom door. I bolt in that direction and push the door fully open. I blink once. Twice. Empty. He left.

ONE MONTH LATER
THE SWEET SPOT

Van

I pull up to the curb in front of The Sweet Spot. The same neon cupcake sign hangs in the front window. Five years have passed since I've been here. And if I think about it, it's five years too soon. I turn off the ignition and sit in silence. I never imagined I would be here, especially under these circumstances. But here I am.

When I got the phone call from Keith Goldberg, my mom's friend and lawyer, my gut told me something was wrong. That's when he said Mom was in the hospital. She'd suffered a brain aneurysm. I dropped everything and drove two hours north to Harbor Highlands. I made it to the hospital just in time to spend a few hours with her before she passed.

Now a few days later, I'm parked outside the bakery

she opened when I was two years old. Well, technically, it's my bakery now. I throw open the door of my fifteen-year-old sedan and step out onto the blacktop. As the sun dips into the horizon, I pull my shades off my eyes and hang them from the collar of my shirt. Slamming my car door, crumbles of rust drop to the ground, and I stroll to the entrance. I shove the key into the lock and twist. The bell above the door chimes as I enter. Vanilla and sugar assault my nostrils. Smells like home. Or what was my home, at least.

I glance around to find a light switch when a clatter from the back catches my attention. My head snaps toward a dim light that shines from the end of the hallway. With careful footsteps, I slink down the narrow hall. When I come to an open doorway, I stop dead in my tracks. Before me stands a woman with auburn hair tied up in a bandana, a red flannel shirt, and a bowl tucked into the crook of her arm. She whisks the contents inside, all while swaying her hips back and forth quietly singing "What's Love Got To Do With It" by Tina Turner. A slight smile tugs at my lips in amusement. Clearly, she isn't breaking in to steal everything. But instead breaking in to bake a cake? Interrupting the show, I rap my knuckles on the wall. She doesn't turn around, so I knock a little louder. This time, she jumps and whirls around, and instantly her eyes go wide as recognition sets in.

"Oh. Shit," she gasps. The bowl of melted chocolate tumbles from her grip and splatters on the floor. She yanks her earbuds from her ears. "Fake stripper?"

"Holland?"

"Who?" Her eyebrows scrunch together.

I tilt my head. "Holland. You told me your name's Holland."

"Oh." Her eyes go wide. "Yeah. No. Hollyn. My name is Hollyn."

I point to my chest. "I'm Van. Not fake stripper."

"Fake stripper. Van. In my bakery."

All the color drains from her face. Her hand stretches out to steady herself against a table as her legs wobble. A second later, her eyes flutter closed, and her body goes limp. Acting fast, I'm at her side, catching her before she hits the floor. With Holland—or Hollyn—in my arms, I carefully lower us to the ground. As I sit next to her, I hold her to my chest. I've never had anyone faint in front of me before. I stare down at her face. The same sloping nose and full lips I remember from our night together. I brush a loose strand of hair from her forehead. Slowly, her eyes flutter open, and I'm greeted with gold speckled hazel eyes.

"There you are." I smile down at her.

"What happened?" Her brows furrow in confusion.

"You took one glance at my handsome good looks and fainted." Her eyes flit back and forth as she searches mine to see if I'm telling the truth. "Maybe not the first part, but you did faint."

"I'm sorry." She moves to sit up, but falters.

"Slow. Take it easy. Let me get you some water." I help her to a sitting position and glance around the kitchen, unsure of where anything is.

"There's some bottled water in the black fridge." She moves to stand, but I stop her.

"I'll grab it." I locate the fridge on the far side of the kitchen. Once I reach it, I open the door and fetch a bottle. With hurried steps, I'm back in front of her. I crouch down and sit on the floor next to her. I twist open the cap and hold the bottle out to her. She takes a sip and then turns to me.

"Thanks. I'm sorry. I'm sure I look like a mess." She

glances down at her wrinkled flannel shirt and yoga pants. Then her hand flies to her mop of hair in a messy bun held up with a bandana. "Wait, why are you here?"

"It appears when my mom passed away, I inherited her bakery." I wave a hand in front of us before dropping my arm in my lap.

"Your mom is Della?" Her head flinches back slightly.

"Yes."

She peers off into the distance as if she's deep in thought. "You're Della's son Vance?"

"That's me. My mom was the only one who called me Vance. Everyone else calls me Van."

She presses her fingers to her thumb as if she's counting. "So that makes you twenty something. At least twenty-one since you were at the club…"

"Twenty-four."

"Oh. Shit." Her eyes go wide again.

"How old are you?"

"Not twenty-four."

I bark out a laugh. "Let's move on to a more neutral topic. You know my mom, so you're not a stranger robbing the place. It's my turn to ask, why are you here?"

"I work here with your mom. Worked. Sorry about her passing." Her features soften and she rests a hand on my forearm.

"Thanks. But why are you here right now? Baking?"

"Oh." Hollyn pulls her hand away and rests them in her lap. "Before your mom… passed, we were in the middle of a couple of orders. The customers had already paid, and we already had all the ingredients, so I wanted to make sure I got those fulfilled."

"So, you break in and bake?" I give her a slight smile.

"I have a key. So technically, I didn't break in. When Mr. Goldman called me to tell me about what happened to

Della, he also told me she gave him firm directions to have me finish these orders and he would take care of everything else. She couldn't bear the thought of her customers having to settle for some leftover store-bought baked goods, her words not mine." She takes a sip of her water.

A small laugh escapes me. "That sounds exactly like something she would say. She takes a lot of pride in her work."

"And she loved her customers. They came to this bakery because they loved the passion your mom puts into her baking. And I didn't want that to be forgotten." Tears prick her eyes, then a lone droplet rolls down her cheek.

Normally, emotions are not my thing, unless it's caused by an orgasm, but this is different. I wrap my arms around her and hug her tight to my chest. I get a whiff of her familiar sweet vanilla scent. Thoughts of our night together over a month ago flit through my mind. Fuck. Now is not the time to think of her naked body against mine. She drops her head to my chest and soft sobs escape her throat, pulling me from my daydream. "I didn't know my mom meant that much to you."

Hollyn sniffles and mumbles into my shirt. "She's been there since I finished culinary school. She took me under her wing and taught me everything I know. I can't fathom the idea that she's not here anymore. Not only for me, but the entire community. Everyone loves this bakery."

Her arm wraps around my waist and she holds me tight. Slowly, I rub small circles up and down her back. I've held her in my arms before but this time she feels so small. "My mom always told me, 'Don't cry because it's over, smile because it happened.' I know if she was here right now, she'd tell us not to cry because she's gone, but smile because we knew her."

She exhales a small laugh. "That sounds exactly like something she would say."

I rest my chin on the top of her head, my grip on Hollyn never wavering. "She always looked toward the future and not back at the past. I know she wouldn't want us to be sad."

"Yeah." She pulls out of my grasp and my arms tumble to my sides. With both hands, she swipes the moisture from her cheeks. "Sorry, I think I got your shirt wet." She brushes at the wet spot as if she's trying to erase it.

I glance down at the darkened cotton from her tears. "Don't worry about it." I rise to my feet and hold out my hand for her. A jolt of electricity courses through me when she places her much smaller hand in mine. I tug her to her feet and reluctantly drop her hand. This isn't the time or place to act on my thoughts, instead I step away, needing some space. "All this feels so… surreal."

"Tell me about it." She releases a nervous laugh as she crosses her arms over her chest. "What's the plan with the bakery?"

"I'm not sure. Put it up for sale?" Her face falls at my words. "I know nothing about running a bakery. Plus, I don't live here. I don't know how that would work."

"I get it. I contacted our other two part-time employees and told them what happened, and they won't be needed for the time being." There's a brief pause. "All I ask is that you let me finish these last two orders. I'd hate to disappoint the customers." She holds still, waiting for my response.

I nod. "I can do that. Thanks for reaching out to the others."

"It was the least I could do. Since I won't have any

extra hands, maybe you can help me?" Her hands fall to her sides and she inches closer to me.

I laugh. "I don't have the slightest idea how to bake."

"You can do the easy stuff… like stirring." She beams up at me.

"First day here and you're already putting me to work." I quirk an eyebrow. It's been a month since the last time I saw her, and she left me alone in a hotel bed and yet I can't fight the magnetic pull drawing us together. All I want to do is be near her. Never in my wildest dreams did I expect to see her again. Maybe dreams do come true.

"Let me clean up and we can meet back here tomorrow morning? Are you staying at a hotel?" She pulls out a washcloth, runs it under hot water, and cleans up the chocolate.

"I'll help you." Her lips tip up into a small smile at my offer. I pull out another washcloth from the same place she got hers. "Actually, I'm staying at my mom's apartment."

Her washcloth falls to the floor and she stares at me. "Is that… hard? Being around all her things."

"A little, but mostly it's comforting. With all her things around me, it's like a part of her is with me. I do sleep on the couch though. Sleeping in her bed would be weird."

She softly laughs. "I can see that."

We spend the next twenty minutes cleaning the kitchen. Mostly, it's Hollyn bossing me around, but nonetheless, we work seamlessly together. And I enjoy being with her. Something about her drives me wild. And the longer we're together, bumping against each other, innocent grazes as we move about the kitchen, the more I want to clasp her cheeks and kiss the hell out of her. I've spent the last thirty days reminiscing about our night together. But it would be a dick move if I tried to kiss her right now, even though I want to. Bad.

COUGAR LIFE

Hollyn

As soon as I left the bakery, I called the girls for an emergency meeting. I needed drinks and to vent. Because everything that's happened in the last two hours is like a lucid dream. Like at any moment, I'm going to wake up in my bed, blankets wrapped around me, and all of this will be a figment of my imagination. I pinch my forearm. *Ouch.* Isn't this when people wake up? I pinch myself again, a little harder this time. Shit. This isn't a dream. Now, I'll have two bruises as my souvenir.

I tip back the martini glass, the vodka burning down my throat, but that's the last thing on my mind. "I can't believe the fake stripper, I mean Van, is Della's son. She mentioned her son, Vance, but I never put two and two together." I swallow another big gulp, emptying my glass.

"Sure, Della had pictures of her son in her office, but twelve-year-old Van looks *nothing* like twenty-four-year-old Van. Thank God for that, but how could I have ever known? And in what universe would I end up shoving dollar bills down his boxers and then sleeping with him, only for him to show up a month later as my new boss."

I glance around our table and spot Olivia's full drink. Without asking, I grab her martini and swallow down the contents. I think I need this more than her right now.

"Girl, slow down. We have all night." Olivia plucks her glass from my hands. "You gotta breathe."

I rest my elbows on the table and narrow my eyes at her. "Did *your* one-night stand show up out of nowhere as your new boss?"

"Good point." She pauses. "Hold on, I'll get you another drink." Olivia stands and makes her way to the bar at Porter's.

"Do you know what he's going to do with the bakery?" Charlie asks.

"I don't know. I was too preoccupied picking my jaw up off the floor to think about it. In fact, I'm still trying to wrap my head around everything."

Olivia sets a fresh martini in front of me, and I take a gulp. There isn't enough alcohol to get me through all this. "I'm at a loss for what to do. I love my job. For the past six years, I've been working for Della with hopes of me eventually buying the business when she retires. Now everything has gone up in smoke." I trace the base of the glass with my finger.

"You think he'll sell it?" Parisa asks.

"I'm not sure. He mentioned doing that, but he phrased it more like a question than a statement. He doesn't have any reason to keep it. In the seven years I've been there, I've never seen him come in."

"Maybe you can buy it from him?" Tatum asks.

"No bank will approve me for a loan. Not yet anyway. My credit is still shit. While I have some money in savings, it's not enough." I stare at the olive submerged in the bottom of my drink.

"Perhaps you can convince him not to sell? Show him that the community loves the bakery and would be lost without it." Charlie takes a sip of her martini.

My head snaps up. "You might be onto something. He agreed to let me finish a couple of orders and he said he'll help."

"Does he have any baking experience?" Tatum asks.

I release a humorless laugh. "That's a big fat no. So, it should be fun."

"Okay, all that aside. How was seeing him again? Did you get the urge to rip his clothes off? I won't lie. I wouldn't mind seeing more of his dance moves." Olivia leans in, elbows resting on the table.

Heat creeps up my neck. I attempt to hide my smile behind the rim of my martini glass, but by the way everyone is gawking at me, I'm failing miserably. Van wasn't a hit it and forget it kinda guy. He's entered my dreams, uninvited, on multiple occasions.

"I'm going to go out on a limb and say she's getting her dollar bills ready for another show," Parisa says.

"No. No. It wasn't anything like that. Yes, he's gorgeous. Anyone with eyes can see that. But circumstances have changed. He's technically my boss now. And not to mention ten years younger than me."

"You're our first cougar!" Olivia shouts.

"Quiet." I press my pointer finger to my lips, shushing her. "I don't think the people down the street heard you."

"Girl, own it. You had an amazing night with this young, hot stud and guess who comes back into your life.

At the very least, it could be fun. That's all I'm saying." Olivia shrugs.

"My night with Van was the best I've had in—ever. But that's all it can be. My top priority is the bakery, keeping my job, and convincing him not to sell. I can't worry about anything else." I glance down at my half empty drink.

"You've made the batter, now you need to put it in the oven and let it bake. Then you can eat cake off each other's naked bodies," Olivia says.

"That. You should do that." Charlie points her drink in Olivia's direction, nodding her head.

"Orgasm coercing would do the trick. Is that a thing? It should be a thing," Parisa says.

"I'm not going to sleep with him so he keeps the bakery." I glance between the four girls.

"Sleep with him for you. If he keeps the bakery, that's a bonus." Olivia flashes me a salacious smile.

"You guys are ridiculous. I need to show him why the community loves The Sweet Spot, not spend our time between the sheets." But the thought of him hovering above me, his lips on mine in a searing hot kiss exactly like our night at the hotel, has me clenching my thighs together.

"Well, try it your way first and if it doesn't work, get naked." Olivia shimmies her shoulders.

All the girls clink their glasses together. The angel on my shoulder is whispering to use my words while the devil is shouting to rip off his clothes. Right now, one is more tempting than the other. I'll find out tomorrow when I see him which one wins.

CHAPTER TEN

LICK SOMETHING ELSE

Van

"Keith, keep an ear out if you hear of anyone who's looking to buy a business or a bakery."

"I can get in touch with a realtor if you'd like." His tone is stoic through my earbud.

I drum my thumbs on the steering wheel. "Nothing's set in stone yet. Just keep an ear out."

"Will do, Van."

The phone call disconnects as I pull into the empty back parking lot of The Sweet Spot. All night, I tossed and turned, all my thoughts on Hollyn. Never in my wildest dreams did I think I would see her again, and trust me, I've had some intense dreams about her. Now, she's here. In the flesh. It's my mission to get a repeat of our one night together. My phone buzzes in my pocket, drawing my attention from my daydreams. I pull out my phone and stare at the screen. Annoyance spreads through my body as I read the message from an old hook up.

A knock on my driver's side window startles me. When I glance up, Hollyn's bright smile and hazel eyes greet me. She nods her head toward the door and heads that way. I pluck out my earbud and toss it into the center console. As I step out of the car, I tuck my phone back into my pocket. Following her footsteps, I enter the back door and turn right into an open doorway. Now that I'm slightly less distracted, I familiarize myself with the kitchen.

In the center sits two tables, a shorter wood table on one side and a higher steel table that butts up to the wood one. A sink and dishwashing station across from the tables. One wall is lined with ovens, while another has several commercial refrigerators and a couple bakers racks full of various stand mixers and blenders.

She fidgets with a towel that sits on the wood top. I move to stand next to her, and she glances up at me. "Are you ready for today?"

"As ready as I'll ever be. Where did you park?"

"Out front. I walked down the block to get these." She twists around, grabs a to-go cup of coffee, and holds it out to me. "I wasn't sure if you like coffee. Maybe if I stuck around after our one morning together, I would have known. Anyway, if you want some." A pink blush covers her cheeks as she rambles with nervous energy.

We've seen each other naked, given each other multiple orgasms. There shouldn't be any awkwardness.

"Coffee is definitely needed. Thank you." I grab the cup from her grasp. Our fingers brush against each other's, sending a jolt of electricity coursing through my body. There's a brief pause before she pulls away. Every touch from her makes me want more, and the wantonness behind her irises confirms she wants it too. "So, what are we making today?"

She turns to face the smooth worktable in front of us. "We have four dozen unicorn cupcakes for a little girl's birthday party."

My eyes go wide at the idea of that many cupcakes, especially unicorn ones. "Is it too late to back out?"

"Yes." She smiles up at me. "I promise you, it won't be as daunting as it sounds. It'll be fun." Her eyes sparkle at the last sentence, telling me how much she loves her job.

I huff out a humorous laugh. "Says the woman who does this for a living."

"I bet you'll end up enjoying it by the end. I'll even let you lick the spoon." She gives me a wink.

Fuck. Now, I'm reminiscing about what she tasted like when I had her spread wide against the window at the hotel. "I'd rather lick something else."

She whirls around, a smile tugging on her lips. "Excuse me?"

I turn to look behind me because there is no way I said that out loud.

When I turn back around, she's standing with her hand on her hip, narrowed eyes, but her smile never falters. "Did you just say what I think you said?"

"No." But I nod my head yes.

A blush covers her cheeks, then her gaze returns to mine. "First the spoon, and if you do a really good job with the cupcakes, maybe you can have that something else."

Holy shit. Is she flirting back with me? I think she's flirting back. Fuck. I want her to be flirting with me because flirting leads to kissing, which leads to groping, then getting naked, and I really want the last one. Badly.

My feet carry me over to where she's standing next to

the worktable. I'm ready for whatever she wants. Cupcakes or no cupcakes. She pulls out a tablet from her bag and with the swipe of a finger, it comes to life. With a few more taps, a picture of unicorn cupcakes fills the screen.

"This is what we're making. They'll be a vanilla cake with the multicolored buttercream frosting with fondant ears and a horn." She reaches behind her and grabs something off the back table. "Then they will go into these sleeping unicorn cupcake holders. Aren't they adorable?"

"Very adorable." I keep my gaze locked on hers. She turns her head in my direction, catching me staring at her. Her lips tug into a small smile as pink dusts her cheeks. She's never been more beautiful. It's my new life mission to make her blush.

"We better get started." She takes a step away from me as if space will break the attraction that seems to tether us together. She points to the opposite side of the kitchen. "Grab two of those stand mixers."

Luckily, I spent many years watching my mom bake in the kitchen at home and know what a stand mixer is. I set off to the far side of the kitchen and pluck two mixers off the shelf. When I set them down on the table, she has measuring spoons and bowls set out in front of her.

She rests her palm on the table and turns toward me. "So, I'm dying to know. Why did you pretend to be a stripper?"

I throw my head back in laughter. When I come to, I rest my palms on the cool wood surface while I contemplate what to say. "A gorgeous girl approached me and asked me to take my clothes off." I give her a wink. "The money was a bonus. I would have done it either way."

"Honestly, I don't know if you're lying or telling the

truth." She releases a small laugh. It's such a sweet sound, one I could listen to all day and night.

"To be honest, it was for the money. I lost my job the same day, and I would have been a fool not to take it." I pray she doesn't ask why I lost my job. That's a conversation I would rather not have at this moment, and I don't know if I could lie to her. Before she can ask, I keep talking. "I'm surprised you all didn't catch me."

"We were at least ten bottles of champagne deep, so we would have been excited for anyone to take their clothes off." Her sweet laugh fills the room.

"My turn to ask a question. How did you find out I wasn't a stripper?"

"Apparently, after we left the club, the real stripper arrived. He got stuck in traffic, so that's why he was late and his phone was dead so he couldn't call. The next morning, I went back to the room, but you were gone."

"You came back to the room? Hoping for another round?" I wiggle my eyebrows.

"No." Pink covers her cheeks. She turns away from me and then twists back to face me. "Well, technically yes, but that was before I found out you weren't a real stripper. Since you're not a stripper, how did you know how to move like one?"

"Raw talent." I shrug a shoulder.

She throws a towel at me, hitting me in the chest. "Now I know you're lying."

I pick up the towel and lean in toward her. "You've experienced my moves between the sheets. Who says it can't come naturally?"

"Fine, I'll admit, you have moves. But how did you know how to use them?"

"I'm that good." I flash an enormous grin.

"No. I don't believe you. No one wakes up and knows how to dance like a stripper."

"Fine." I cover my mouth with my hand and fake a cough. "*Magic Mike.*"

Her eyebrows reach her hairline. "Wait. The movie? You watched a movie with a bunch of guys who take their clothes off and dance?"

"Well, it wasn't by choice."

She laughs. "Someone held you at gunpoint and duct taped your eyelids open? Please explain."

"I was watching The Transporter, a very masculine movie by the way, and when it was over, Magic Mike came on next. The remote was on the other side of the room and I was very comfortable on the couch." I shrug my shoulders as if this is what people do every day.

"So, you willingly watched a bunch of half-naked guys dance around?"

"I believe it paid off because I didn't hear any complaints that night. But also, not the worst movie I've seen. It was like Channing Tatum was speaking to my soul." I rest my palm on my chest. "He wanted to do more with his life than just be a stripper."

"And you want to do more with your life than... what?"

"Be a stripper."

She snorts out a laugh. "You're such an ass."

"Honestly, I'm not sure. I started doing masonry because it was decent money and they hired me. But now, I'm the proud owner of a bakery. And I know nothing about pastries except how to eat them." I give her a tight smile.

"Good thing I'm going to teach you. The key is in the measurements. Too much or too little of an ingredient can throw off the entire batter. It must be like mixing concrete. You need to have the perfect consistency in order to have the best finished product."

"Mortar. But when you put it that way, I suppose."

"See, you're already halfway there. Let me show you." She grabs my hand and leads me to a back room.

Her hand is warm and silky as her fingers wrap around mine. "A dark room. Hollyn, are you bringing me back here to make out? I normally don't kiss on a first date, but I could make an exception for you."

She glances back at me. "Good thing this isn't a date."

"Either way, I'm definitely going to kiss you."

She whirls around until she's facing me. I bend down, close my eyes, and pucker my lips. Suddenly, a piece of fabric is tossed onto my head. I yank it off. A pink apron with yellow flowers hangs in my hands, and Hollyn is nowhere in sight. Turning around, she's tying her own apron around her back.

"How come I get the pink one while you get the blue?" I tie my apron around my waist.

"Blue is more my color." She pulls out a couple of mixing bowls and measuring cups and measures ingredients.

"That's cool. I'm comfortable enough with my masculinity to wear pink. I look good in anything. But even better in nothing." I toss a wink in her direction. Moving to stand next to her in front of the worktable, I bend down and whisper in her ear. "The pink in your cheeks most definitely looks good on you."

"Well, aren't you the charmer? Here, stir this." She shoves a bowl and a spoon at my chest.

"Have I ever told you I like it when you get all demanding?"

She smirks. "No."

"Well, I do. More so when we're naked."

She stands up straight and squares her shoulders. "You may have charmed my panties off once, but you'll need to try a lot harder than that if you want to do it again."

"Is that a challenge, cupcake?" Bending down, I whisper against the shell of her ear, "Because I like a challenge."

The corners of her lips tip up into a smile. "Keep stirring."

We spend the next hour working side by side. She's telling me what to do and I'm enjoying every second of it. Mostly because I love listening to her sweet voice. Once we've mixed all the batter and poured it into cupcake liners, we put them in the oven.

"We have about thirty minutes until the cupcakes are done. And then we have about another thirty minutes to let them cool." She sets the timer and places it down on the table.

"I can think of a few things we can do to kill the time." I grip her waist and pull her toward me.

"Is that so? Would it happen to involve long, smooth strokes?"

I tip my head toward the ceiling and groan. "Fuck. Are you reading my mind?"

When I glance back down, she's biting her lower lip. Bright hazel eyes stare back at me and she nods her head. She reaches around me, and I get a whiff of her sweet vanilla scent. My dick twitches, remembering the last time I was with her.

"Good. Because the frosting won't make itself." She shoves a spatula in my hand.

I bark out a laugh and grip the spatula. "Oh, I see what

you did there. I'm a patient man. For you, I'll wait even longer."

"That's good, because once these are done, we have another two dozen to make." She gives me a wink.

Two hours later, we are wrapping the last batch of cupcakes to be frosted tomorrow. Even though I didn't have a clue as to what I was doing, we work perfectly together. Having Hollyn there to guide me step by step made everything so much easier. Not to mention, I loved stealing glances her way, taking every opportunity to touch her, even if it was a slight graze. After thinking my time with her would only be for a night, I want to savor every second I get with her right now.

"I'm so tired." When I turn around, she's tossing a towel onto the table, resting a hip against the edge. "But you did really great. I think you're getting the hang of everything."

I grab a towel and dry my hands from washing the dishes, then move to stand in front of her. "Thanks. You make it worth trying."

"Your mom would have loved to make those cupcakes. She always had a knack for creating fun and whimsical decorations." A somber expression covers her face.

I place my finger under her chin and force her to meet my eyes. The small contact sends a jolt of electricity through my finger, traveling all the way to my toes. "She would have been proud of what you came up with."

My gaze travels from her eyes to her mouth, where a small smile graces her lips. I linger there, wanting to press my lips to her pillowy soft ones. To taste her sugary sweet lips once again. Instead of talking myself out of it, I make the move. I bend down and press my lips to hers. She's exactly as I remember, but I keep the kiss short and pull away. Her expression is unreadable. Shit. She didn't like the kiss.

"Sorry. That was a mistake," I blurt out.

She casts her gaze downward, digesting my words. "What do you say we call it a day and get out of here?"

I flash her my signature dazzling smile, wanting to remove the awkward tension floating between us and replace it with the fun and flirty Van. "Where are we going? Your place or mine?"

Hollyn playfully slaps my chest, but before she can pull away, I capture her hand in mine, holding it against my body. Her hazel eyes glance up to meet my brown ones. Without fail, the sexual tension once again crackles between us like a freshly lit fire, waiting to engulf us all.

"You go to yours. I'll go to mine." And she pulls the pin on the figurative fire extinguisher.

"Fine then. At the very least, let me walk you out."

"Such a gentleman." She flashes me a sultry smile.

"If you knew the thoughts I'll be having about you later tonight, you might change your mind."

"I can't with you." She laughs and shakes her head. "I'm parked on the street, so I'll leave out the front."

"I'll lock up the back and meet you there." She saunters down the hallway toward the front of the bakery and I can't help but watch her hips sway back and forth. It would be better if she were coming toward me instead of away.

A minute later, I'm meeting her at the front, while she stares out the large window.

"What are you looking at?"

"Huh? Oh. Nothing. Ready?" She grips her hands together. "Actually."

My ears perk up. Maybe she wants to take me up on my offer to take her back to my place.

"Maybe we should swap numbers? You know, in case anything comes up… with the bakery and we need to get in touch with one another."

And all my thoughts deflate like a popped balloon. "Yeah. That's a good idea. That way, if I have any bakery ideas in the middle of the night, I can text you, or call, or FaceTime."

She playfully laughs. "Give me your phone." She holds out her hand. I dig out my phone, unlock it, and pass it over. Her fingers type away on the screen. A ding sounds from her bag. "There, now you have my number and I have yours."

"Perfect." I hold the door open and she steps past me. She waits on the sidewalk as I shut the door and turn the key in the lock when a deep, unfamiliar voice catches my attention.

"Hollyn. It's good to see you again."

I swivel around, and she gives the guy a small wave. "Hi, Lucas. How are you doing? How's Lucy?"

He stands in front of Hollyn, too close for my liking. "I'm good. Lucy's good. She's excited for her party. I was at Posh and Peony confirming all the balloons and decorations for the party. You don't want to know how much rainbow balloon garland costs."

She reaches up and tucks a loose strand of hair behind her ear as she giggles. I glance to Lucas, and a sly smile covers his face. The way he's ogling her irritates me. He takes a step closer.

"We're excited to see everything. Van and I were finishing the cupcakes, which I'm sure will go perfect with the rainbow balloon garland."

"Hi. I'm Van." I step up next to Hollyn and hold out my hand to Lucas.

He glances down at my hand before meeting my eyes. "Lucas. Very nice to meet you."

I squeeze his hand harder than normal, but he doesn't seem to notice. When I release my grip, his hand drops to his side and he directs his attention back to Hollyn.

"So, I'll see you at noon tomorrow?" Lucas asks.

"Yes. See you then."

"Both of us," I interrupt.

Lucas glances at me, then at Hollyn. "Great."

He brushes his hand along her arm, and I'm tempted to shove him into traffic. I clench my jaw so hard I'm surprised I don't crack a molar.

His gaze wanders up her body before focusing on her lips. "Have a good night." With that, he's strolling down the sidewalk.

Once he's out of earshot, I turn to her. "What's with that guy? I'm pretty sure he was undressing you with his eyes."

"He was not. Lucas is a nice guy. I've done a couple of birthday parties for him."

"He was one hundred percent flirting with you." I narrow my eyes at her.

"No, he wasn't." She crosses her arms over her chest.

I take a step closer to her so I'm inside her bubble and brush my hand down her arm, mimicking the same look Lucas gave her. Her breath hitches once my eyes meet hers. We stare at each other for a moment. Her hazel eyes hypnotizing. Slowly, I lean in, wanting her warm lips on mine. Suddenly, a car horn bursts our little lust bubble, and she pulls away.

"Uh. I-I should get going. I need a shower and out of these frosting covered clothes." She picks at chunks of blue and pink dried frosting.

"Yeah. Me too. So, I'll see you tomorrow. Meet you in the morning?"

"Yeah. Good night, Van."

"Night Hollyn." I cross my arms over my chest as she turns on her heel and saunters to her car. My night will be filled with sweet dreams with Hollyn taking the leading role.

LICK YOUR FROSTING

Van

Why did I agree to do this? I don't know what I'm doing. I've never done this before. My palms rest on the worktable in the kitchen of The Sweet Spot. And most of all, they're kids. Glancing to my right, I spot a partially open box of cupcakes. I pluck one out and shove it into my mouth.

"Hey! What are you doing?" Hollyn slaps my hand away before I can reach for another cupcake. "These aren't for you."

"I weat when om stwessed," I mumble around a mouth full of cake and frosting.

"Chew. Swallow. Then talk." She places a hand on her hip and glares at me.

I finish chewing, then swallow. "I eat when I'm stressed."

"What could you possibly be stressed about?"

I throw my hands in the air. "I don't know what I'm doing. I can't say I've been to many kids' birthday parties. The last time was probably when I was a kid myself."

Her hands grab my wrists and places them to my sides, then she locks eyes with me. "We're not there to play with the kids. We are only there to stuff them full of sugar and be on our way. I've gone over this with you." Her voice is soft as she talks me off the ledge.

I inhale a deep breath. "Okay. We get there. Set up. Hang out in the background. Then clean up."

"That's all we have to do." I reach for another cupcake, but she slaps my hand away. "What are you stressed about now?"

"Nothing. These are fucking delicious."

"Oh my god. You're ridiculous. Get to work. These boxes won't move themselves." She shoves a stack of unfolded boxes at my chest.

I wrap an arm around her waist and tug her so the boxes are sandwiched between us. "Did I tell you how much I like it when you boss me around?"

"I'm starting to hear that more and more."

A hearty laugh escapes me. Something about being around her makes me feel alive again. Like I want to do more with my life than just coast by. She makes me want more.

We work side by side making boxes, filling those boxes with cupcakes, and moving them into the back of the delivery van along with tables and display stands. Once everything is packed, I climb into the driver's seat and she hops in next to me. I program the address into the GPS and shift into drive. We drive in comfortable silence for several minutes. Then my mind drifts to Lucas and his interaction with Hollyn yesterday and I have questions, so now seems like the perfect opportunity to fish for answers.

"So, what's the scoop on this party? Obviously, it's a unicorn party based on the number of horns I had to twist into shape and place on top of the frosting. What about the guy? Who's he?"

"Lucas." She taps her finger on her chin, thinking. "He's been coming to the bakery for the last several years. I know we've done a few birthday parties for his daughter."

"His wife ever come in?" I glance over at Hollyn.

"No wife. They got divorced several years ago. Rumor has it she was cheating on him with the pool boy."

"Someone else who likes them younger." A small smile stretches across my lips, but my gaze never leaves the road. From the corner of my eye, I see her shake her head.

"You've reached your destination." The robotic voice from the GPS sounds.

I slow down and flip on the turn signal. An open wrought iron gate frames the paved driveway. As we creep up the red maple tree lined blacktop, a massive slate blue Victorian house with a wraparound porch comes into view. No wonder this guy spared no expense for the birthday party. I'm sure he wipes his ass with hundred-dollar bills.

I stop the van in front of the house on the circular driveway. As soon as I turn off the ignition, Lucas steps out the front door. Was he watching out a window, waiting for us to arrive? Probably couldn't wait to flirt with Hollyn again. His dress shirt is pristinely pressed, and his slacks are perfectly tailored. A glint of silver in his hair shines in the early afternoon light. This is a kids' birthday party, not a funeral. When we step out, he directs us where to set up, his gaze never leaving Hollyn, and that fuels the fire already raging inside me.

After we're all set up, party goers start arriving in

droves. Kids of all ages run around with bubble wands, screams of laughter sound as they jump around in the bounce house, and there's a petting zoo. What kid needs a freaking petting zoo? Normal kids get arcade games and pizza with an adult dressed up in a creepy-as-fuck mouse costume, not this.

All afternoon kids, parents, and *Lucas* come up to the table to take a cupcake or two. Hollyn's so graceful as she makes sure to bend down as each kid approaches so she's eye level with them and tells them all about the magical unicorn cupcakes. All the kids absolutely adore her, and I can see why. Hell, I adore her.

As the party winds down, Lucas prowls to the table for the tenth time today. Still wearing his overpriced suit and sticking out like a sore thumb. Of course, the first thing he does is flash her his pearly whites as she stands in front of the table organizing cupcakes. Then he turns to me, his smile not as bright. I give him a tight smile and a head nod, but what I really want to do is punch the smugness off his face.

"Everyone loved your cupcakes. They were a tremendous hit with the kids and the parents." Lucas stops next to Hollyn.

"Thank you so much. The compliment means so much to us," She points a finger between us, "and the bakery."

"What's the trick for the extra burst of flavor in the frosting? Or is that because you made them?" His eyes crinkle in the corners.

She laughs and brushes her hand down his bicep. He glances down at her hand, his smile growing wider. *Don't cause a scene, Van.* I repeat that over and over in my head because if I don't, I might hurl my body across this table and tackle his old ass to the ground. We're both about the same height, similar body build, though I think I'm more agile than him.

"You're too sweet Lucas. Actually, the secret is an extra pinch of salt. It enhances the sweetness, so the flavors burst on your tongue." Her tongue peeks out to wet her bottom lip. His gaze lingers there, watching her every movement.

"Well, anyway. I wanted to come over here and thank you for the cupcakes. My daughter loved the unicorn decorations." He pauses. "But also, if you aren't too busy, would you want to get a cup of coffee sometime?"

Her cheeks flush pink as she fumbles for her words. "Oh. Um."

Unable to hold back any longer, I ask, "Do you always try to hook up with women at your kid's birthday parties?" The bite to my tone is clear.

She whirls around and shoots daggers my way. If literal steam could come out a person's ears, hers would be bursting. All I can do is shrug. I call it like I see it.

Lucas laughs nervously before directing his attention back to Hollyn. "I'm sorry if I made you uncomfortable. That was never my intention. It was nice to talk to another female, especially one who isn't seven and only using me to buy her toys."

"No. It's alright. Since the party is over, we better get cleaned up and out of your way."

"It was really nice talking to you."

"You too, Lucas."

Once Lucas is out of earshot, she turns to me, brows furrowed, nostrils flaring. "What the hell's wrong with you?"

My eyes go wide. "Me? I'm not the one trying to find my next lay at my kid's birthday party. And he's like twice your age. Maybe he should find someone closer to his own age bracket."

She flings her arms in the air and exhales an exasperated sigh. "Sure, he's a little older, but he's not twice my age. He's probably closer to my age than you. Anyway, we were only talking. Two adults having a conversation. As if you would know anything about that."

"If it walks like a duck and quacks like a duck—"

"That makes you an asshole." She turns and stomps away.

"No. It makes it a duck!" I yell to her back. "Fuck." I turn back toward the table and kick the leg. "Shit." I rake my hands through my hair. When I come to, a pair of innocent brown eyes stare up at me from the opposite side of the table. "Dammit. Don't repeat that. Any of that." I scan the table and pluck a left-over cupcake from the rack and hold it out to the little boy. "Have a cupcake." He snatches it from my fingers and runs off, shoving the frosting in his face.

I finish boxing up the left-over cupcakes, take down the displays, and fold up the table. When I'm done, I haul everything to the driveway, where I find Hollyn throwing boxes around in the back of the van to make room for the tables and racks.

I drop the table to the ground. "I'm sorry. I didn't mean to upset you."

"It's fine, Van. Just get the stuff so we can get out of here."

She doesn't spare a glance my way, so I turn around and collect everything to load into the van. The entire ride back to the bakery is silent. She sits with her arms crossed, staring out the passenger door window while I white knuckle the steering wheel. Jealousy and anger bubbling over. I hated how he looked at her, how he touched her. And she let him. I have no claim to her, but fuck, I want one.

When we arrive back at The Sweet Spot, I'm still in a foul mood. We get out and unload the van. Each of us grab an armful of items and haul everything into the bakery. Watching another man flirting with her in front of me was maddening. And she didn't realize she was flirting back. The brushing of his arm, laughing at whatever he said. If that doesn't give a man mixed signals, I don't know what does. But what if she was purposely flirting back?

Finally, I break the silence. "You didn't find it inappropriate that he was flirting with you?"

She halts in her tracks. "We're doing this again? He wasn't flirting. He was being friendly."

"Friendly?" I scoff. "He was borderline stalking you. Constantly seeking you out. Touching you at every possible moment."

"You know what? Maybe he was flirting." Her tone is sharp. "Why can't a guy flirt with me? Is something wrong with me that I'm unflirtable?" She throws her hands in the air.

My teeth grind as I get into her face. "It's because he was doing it right in front of me."

"I'm not yours to claim, so I don't see what the problem is! Plus, you already told me you don't want me. So, what? No one else can have me either?" She drops a foot back, separating herself from me.

My face falls and I blow out a breath. "I never said I didn't want you."

"After the kiss, you said it was a mistake." She wraps her arms around herself.

I turn and rest my palms on the worktable. "I kissed you during a vulnerable moment. That was the mistake. If I had it my way, I would kiss you and never stop kissing you."

"He just wanted to tell me how much he enjoyed my cupcakes, especially the frosting."

At the sound of her voice, I turn to face her. My nostrils flare thinking of Lucas near her, telling her how much he likes her baked goods. And she's right, she's not mine. Not yet anyway.

"What's that look for?"

The thought of her with someone else drives me mad. And fuck if I know why, but I don't like it. So, for the time being, I'll kiss the hell out of her until she forgets any other man exists. I step into her personal space again, she cranes her neck up to meet my eyes. "Because I want to be the only one to lick your frosting." The words are a whisper off my lips.

The air between us crackles with electricity. Her eyes shift back and forth, searching mine. Her voice is low when she says, "Why do I have a feeling frosting no longer means... frosting."

"Because it doesn't." I inch my lips closer to hers.

"Then what does it mean?"

"Exactly that. I'm going to lick your frosting."

CUPCAKE VIXEN

Hollyn

Without a second thought, his lips crash to mine. Demanding and frantic. My hands cup his cheeks and I hold tight. I need him to keep me afloat, so I don't drown in a sea of heat and passion. Because it would be so easy to get lost in him. Lost in this.

He whirls us around and pushes until my lower back hits the stainless steel table edge. A small whimper escapes me.

"Fuck. I'm sorry," he mumbles against my lips.

"It's okay. I fully expect you to make it up to me."

"I can manage that." He kisses me again.

Van grips my waist and lifts until my butt contacts the top of the cool metal. He twedges himself between my spread legs while never breaking our kiss. His hard cock presses against the apex of my thighs and I fight the urge to rub against him like a cat in heat. Instead, I tug him closer and let him do the rubbing.

Not waiting a second longer, Van rips at the buttons of my chef's coat until the sides fall open, exposing my white, almost see through camisole and light pink bra. Van's gaze wanders down my chest, admiring every inch of me before coming back up to meet my eyes.

"Shit. This is what you've been wearing under this the entire time?"

"It gets hot, so I need to wear as little as possible underneath." My breathing quickens from his heated stare.

"I'm going to get hard every time I see you in your chef's coat because I'll know this is what you're wearing underneath." His hands wrap around my waist under my coat. The light brush of his fingertips sends goosebumps sprouting across my body.

"Maybe one day I'll surprise you and have nothing on underneath." I bring a hand up and cup his cheek. My thumb brushes over the light stubble and I imagine what it would feel like between my thighs. Instinctively, I rock my hips against him, wanting to feel it right now.

He closes his eyes and groans, then presses his forehead to mine. "You would do that. You cupcake vixen. Perhaps I should punish you for that."

"What are you going to do?" I challenge.

"Bring you to the cusp of orgasm, but not let you come."

I gasp. "You wouldn't."

"Keep teasing and you'll find out."

I reach down between us and cup his rock-hard cock, giving it a playful squeeze before running my hand up and down his shaft. His eyes pinch shut as if he's in pain but then his lips part, forming an O. I continue with the motion of gripping, squeezing, and stroking until his hooded eyes meet mine.

"This will definitely get you a punishment."

He grips my wrist to halt my movements and then lifts my hand to set it on the tabletop, the warmth of my palm contrasting against the cool steel. Then he repeats the motion with my other hand.

"Lean back," he demands, and I do as he says. With a flick of his wrist, he undoes the snap of my pants and pulls the zipper down. "Now lift yourself up."

Using all my strength, I lift my butt off the table. Luckily, Van is quick and slides my pants over my hips and drags them down my legs. My heated skin falls to the metal and sends a shiver coursing through my body. Van rises to his feet. His calloused fingertips drag up the side of thighs until his hands are at the top of my ass. With a firm grip, he squeezes the soft flesh before lifting and pulling me forward until I'm resting on the edge.

"There. Right where I want you."

He runs the pad of his finger down the front of my now damp panties. I rock my hips to get more friction, but it's useless. He pulls his hand away.

"Now, now. We were going to do this your way, but you didn't listen, so now we're doing it my way."

I nibble on my lower lip in anticipation of what he's going to do next. He moves his hand back between my legs, rubbing my aching pussy again, but this time using two fingers. Only a thin piece of fabric keeps him from plunging inside of me. He continues to rub up and down while he lowers his head and places a kiss on the swell of my breast. Then he does the same on the other side. I bring a hand up and thread my fingers through the hair on the back of his head. Arching my back, I press my chest toward him. I want to feel more of him. All of him.

Everywhere. He continues sucking, nipping, and kissing my breasts all while still rubbing me on the outside of my now soaked panties. I'm ravenous for his touch. Like at any moment, I'm going to combust. Because I haven't been touched like this since the last time his hands, his lips, his expert tongue were on me. And his tongue is what dreams are made of.

Using one hand, he tugs down the neckline of my camisole, taking the cup of my bra with it, and exposing my pebbled nipple to the cool air. His tongue swirls around the peak before sucking it into his mouth. He bites down, causing me to throw my head back and moan. I grind against his hand, my grip on his hair growing tighter. The buildup has me on the edge of climaxing, when suddenly Van pulls away. A whimper escapes me from the loss.

He stares at me with mischievous eyes. "I told you I'd bring you to the edge and not let you fall."

"I hate you. If you won't finish what you started, I will." I move my hand to the front of my panties, but Van stops me. A deep growl rumbles from his throat.

"Not so fast. I didn't say I wouldn't finish."

I quirk an eyebrow, challenging him.

"I think it's time I taste some of your frosting."

Van bends down and hikes one of my legs over his shoulder. He runs his nose along my wet panties. With one hand, he moves them to the side and holds them there while he uses his other hand to spread me open. His tongue darts out and licks up my slit. My breath hitches and a tremble courses through my body. He repeats the motion using the flat of this tongue this time and I moan out his name, which turns into a chant. Like if I keep saying his name, he'll continue lapping at my pussy. Because I need more. Need him.

"Keep going. Don't stop." My words come out in breathy pants.

The tip of his tongue flicks my clit before he dives back in, licking me from bottom to top again. His saliva mixing with my arousal. He finds my opening and tongue fucks me. My hips buck, wanting more of him. More of everything.

"Oh Van. I need you. More. More."

My pleas don't go unanswered as his grip on my panties grows tighter until the sound of fabric ripping fills the room. Now with his extra free hand, he shoves a finger into my needy opening. Thrusting in and out while he flicks my clit with his tongue. Every action sending me one step closer to orgasmic bliss. He enters me again with a second finger, stretching me more. My moans and pants echo around the kitchen as Van continues pleasuring me.

I thread my fingers through his hair. My fingers grip the strands, holding him in place. The stubble on his cheeks rubs against my thigh, it's rough but God it feels good. The slow buildup grows stronger with each passing second. He wraps his lips around my clit and sucks, and that's my undoing. My entire body vibrates as my orgasm floods through me. My screams of pleasure fill the kitchen. Van's thrusts become harder and faster as he sucks on my clit. My toes curl as another orgasmic tsunami washes over my entire body and Van continues to lap up every last bit of my arousal.

Finally, my orgasm subsides and Van stands. He wipes his face with the back of his hand. "Fuck. You really do taste as sweet as frosting."

"Any time you have a sweet tooth, you are more than welcome to do that again." My chest heaves as I collect my breath.

"Trust me, I'll take you up on that offer. But right now, I'm not done with you."

Van steps between my legs again. He cups my cheeks and presses his lips to mine. I can taste myself on him and I'm not the slightest bit bothered by it. His fingers thread through my hair at the back of my head while his other hand travels between us. Without missing a beat, he's undoing the button on his pants and shoving them down. He grips his cock, the head sliding through my wetness starting at my clit and moving down. Then he repeats the process, using my arousal as lube. When he's at my opening, he pushes in, stretching me. I break our kiss and throw my head back, savoring every delicious inch of him entering me.

"Fucking hell. Your pussy clenching around me… amazing." Van pulls all the way out and slides back in. Once he's fully seated, he stops. "Shit. I don't have a condom."

I lower my head until our foreheads touch. "I'm on the pill."

Without another word, he presses his lips to mine in a bruising kiss while he pulls out and thrusts back in. His hips piston in and out. My fingers grip his hair and hold on as he pounds into me. With each thrust, he drives deeper and deeper. He pulls away from our kiss and drops his head to my shoulder. He brings a hand between us and circles my clit. The double stimulation drives me over the edge once again. His mouth comes back to mine and swallows my moans. His hips continue to jack hammer in and out of me. The slapping of our bodies, mixed with our moans and grunts, fills the kitchen. After a few more thrusts, his hips jerk as his hot seed spills inside of me. Eventually, his movements slow until he comes to a stop.

"That was… fuck. Amazing." His breathing labored as he snuggles into the crook of my neck.

"It was." He places a soft kiss on my collarbone and then another at the hollow of my throat. I tilt my head to give him better access. "If you keep that up, we'll need a round two."

His warm breath skates across my heated skin as he laughs. "I have no issues giving you what you want." He pulls out of me, and I can't help the small whimper that escapes from the loss of him.

"Looks like we have a new mess to clean up."

CHAPTER THIRTEEN

PENIS CUPCAKES

Van

"Dammit." I toss the hockey puck, also known as a cupcake, onto the worktable. "What the hell did I do wrong this time?"

A few days after the birthday party and hot bakery sex with Hollyn, I decided to attempt this baking thing alone. Mostly, I want to do it to impress her. Show her I can actually do this.

All morning I've been trying to bake cupcakes and with each and every batch something goes wrong. The first batch, I filled the liners too full and when they rose, they spilled together and formed a dick and balls. It's pretty badass if I wanted to make a dick and balls. I save it for Hollyn, anyway. And now the new batch, they are so hard I could use them as a deadly weapon.

I rest my palms on the table and stare at the mess in front of me. Something's gone wrong, but what? Exhaling a sigh, I reach for the large garbage can and with a sweeping motion I dump all the bad cupcakes inside. A cupcake will not defeat me.

Once again, I set up all my ingredients and read over the recipe one more time. I've read this card so many times, I'm surprised I don't have it memorized yet. Carefully, I measure out the dry ingredients and dump them into a bowl. I do the same with all the wet ingredients and pour them into a separate bowl. Then I mix the two. Gently, I scoop the batter into the cupcake liners and place them in the pre-heated oven. I set the timer and stare through the oven window, willing the cupcakes to turn out this time.

When the timer dings, I open the oven door. They look like cupcakes. With oven mitt covered hands, I lift the pan up to my nose and take a whiff. They smell like cupcakes. I set the pan down on the table and stare at the lightly browned cakes. I puff my chest out. I might have successfully made my first batch. Growing impatient, I pluck one from the tin. Steam rises from the still hot cupcake as I toss it back and forth in my hands, trying not to burn myself. Once it's cool enough, I peel the wrapper down and take a big bite. As soon as the fluffy cake hits my taste buds, I chew once, twice, and wet bits of cake tumble out of my mouth as I spit it out. Why the fuck is it so salty? When I glance at the table, the teaspoon is sitting next to the sugar, and the tablespoon is next to the salt. Fuck. There's the issue. I can't do this. I need Hollyn.

Pulling my phone from my pocket, I scroll until I find Hollyn's number and hit call. After a few rings, it goes to voicemail. I hang up and send her a text.

VAN

Where are you? I need you. I may have
made a penis cupcake.

Just kidding. I did. It's for you.

But seriously, I need your help. Everything
I've made has turned to shit.

I set my phone down on the table and stare at it like I did the cupcakes, willing her to answer. When several minutes pass with no reply, I clean up my mess. I'm not attempting another batch. The cupcakes may have won this battle, but I will win the war. My phone buzzes with an incoming message.

HOLLYN

Are you at the bakery?

VAN

I am, but I'm done. A man can only take so
much failure. What are you doing?

HOLLYN

Oh no. You'll have to tell me about it. I'm
lying in bed.

VAN

It's noon and you're still in bed?

HOLLYN

I think a kid at the birthday party got me
sick. I've been miserable all morning. I'll
spare you the details, but I can't keep
anything down.

VAN

I'm coming over. Text me your address.

HOLLYN

You don't need to do that. I'm just going to
sleep some more.

VAN

I insist. Let me take care of you.

For several seconds, there's no reply. I worry I've come on too strong. She's an independent woman. I doubt she wants anyone taking care of her. Finally, my phone buzzes, putting me out of my misery.

HOLLYN

542 Balsam Way Apt B. Door code is 2253

VAN

On my way.

Thirty minutes later, I'm pulling into the short driveway of Hollyn's townhome. I turn off the ignition and grab a bag from the passenger seat. When I get to the front door, I pull out my phone and punch the code she gave me into the keypad. I press the last number, and it hits me. CAKE. A smile tugs at my lips. Of course, the baker would have cake as her door code. I twist the knob and step inside. The door opens to a small entryway. A set of stairs is directly in front of me that leads to the second floor. To the left of the stairs is the open living room. Snuggled on the sofa, blanket wrapped around her, sits Hollyn.

"Hi." Her voice is soft.

"Hi." I toe off my shoes and make my way toward her. I set the bag on the coffee table before taking a seat next to her on the sofa.

"Sorry, I look so terrible." She smooths down her hair.

I grip her chin and force her to meet my gaze. "You look beautiful."

"Even with snot dripping out of my nose and my voice sounding deep and husky?"

"Especially with the snot. And you'll have to talk dirty to me later with that husky voice of yours."

"I can't with you." She lets out a laugh that turns into a cough. When she's collected herself, she points to the table. "What's in the bag?"

I reach for the brown bag and pull out the items. "I got you some water with electrolytes so you stay hydrated. Also, I stopped by my favorite café and got you some chicken noodle soup." I pop off the lid. She leans in and inhales the comforting chicken broth.

"That smells so good."

"Want some?" She vigorously nods her head. I pull out a plastic spoon and pass it over to her. "Crackers?"

"Oyster crackers and soup. Where have you been all my life?" She beams up at me.

"No worries. I'm here now." I flash her a small smile.

She leans back and dips her spoon into the broth, blows on it, and slurps it into her mouth. "This is so good. Where did you get it?"

"The Waterfront Café. When I was a kid and got sick, my mom would always get me soup from there. She was an amazing baker but couldn't cook for the life of her."

"I never would have guessed." She sips more broth, her eyes close as she savors the comforting taste. "Do you miss her?" There's a brief pause, then she shakes her head. "Sorry, that was a dumb question."

"No. It's fine." I lean back against the sofa. My gaze wanders up toward the ceiling. "I'll always miss her. One thing she always told me was not to dwell on the past and constantly look toward the future. So I know she wouldn't want me to be sad. That's how she was, so I try to live my life the same way."

"I can see that. She always looked for the good in everything. I remember one time when a delivery came to the bakery for Valentine's Day and we were supposed to get two cases of strawberries to make chocolate dipped strawberries, but we got raspberries instead. Without missing a beat, she immediately switched gears and made lemon raspberry cupcakes. She inspired me every day."

"I see a lot of her in you. You both have a similar drive. Similar passion."

Her eyes meet mine. "I know she didn't want a service, but I would like to do something small at the bakery. Maybe make her favorite cupcakes and hand them out to customers. One last cupcake on Della."

"I think she would like that. We can do something, but after today, you'll have to bake the cupcakes."

"That bad, huh?"

I nod my head. "It was a disaster."

"I'm proud of you for trying." She laces her fingers with mine. "How about we make them together. I think Della would be surprised I got her son into the kitchen."

"She's in heaven tossing sprinkles into the air." I laugh.

"She totally is." There's a pause. "I cherish every moment I got to work with her. She's an amazing woman. And she raised a pretty amazing son." She bumps her shoulder with mine.

I stare into her dazzling eyes. Even when she's not one hundred percent, they still sparkle. "If you didn't have the plague, I would kiss you right now."

She barks out a laugh that turns into a coughing fit. I wrap my arm around her shoulder and rub small circles along her back until she finishes.

"By the way, I like the code for your door." She turns toward me, eyebrows knit together. "Cake. It's very fitting."

Her eyes crinkle in the corners. "It was the first thing that came to mind, so I went with it."

With my arm wrapped around her shoulder, I tug her

close. She snuggles into my chest as she rests a hand there. I use my other hand and pull the blanket so it covers both of us. I pick up the remote and go to the home screen of the streaming app. "What are we watching? Something with guns, blood, and blowing shit up?"

"Or there is a *Magic Mike 2* we could watch. Maybe you could pick up some new moves?"

My chest rumbles with laughter. "You would like that, wouldn't you?"

"I wouldn't complain." She steals the remote from my hand. "How about something with Gerard Butler?"

"Okay. I can get behind that. He's in some pretty good action movies."

"Don't get too excited. This one also has Katherine Heigl, and it's called *The Ugly Truth*." She beams up at me.

"Sounds like a romantic comedy. But since you're cute, I'll watch it." She releases a tiny squeal of delight and presses play. "But next time, it's Gerard Butler in *Law Abiding Citizen*."

"I mean, I won't say no to anything with Gerard Butler. He's hot."

I roll my eyes as Katy Perry plays through the TV. "So, if Gerard and I were standing in a room together, who'd you pick?"

She nibbles on her bottom lip for a moment as she contemplates her choice. "Both. I want a Van and Gerard sandwich."

"Oh! Is that how you like it? My dirty girl."

Oh shit. Did I call her my girl? I want her to be my girl. But I don't know where her head is at. Maybe she didn't hear me? I glance down and she's staring up at me. Nope. She heard me. Awkward. I flash her a smile and she reciprocates with a small one of her own.

"The movie's starting." She snuggles into me as we turn our attention to the movie.

Several hours later, I stir awake. Still in the sitting position, I crack my eyelids and raise my bowed head. I lift my hand and rub the stiff muscles at the back of my neck. When I peer around the room, the tv screen is black. In fact, the entire room is dark and I'm missing the cute red-head who was cuddled up to me. The flush of a toilet draws my attention. When I listen more carefully, I hear the sounds of dry heaving. I jump to my feet and follow the sound through the living room and into the open kitchen, when I notice light shining through a partially closed door. At first, I debate if I should knock or let myself in, so I decide to do both. I tap my knuckles to the wood door before slowly pushing it open. She's on the floor, kneeling in front of the toilet. She doesn't acknowledge me until I crouch down beside her.

"Sorry you have to see me like this." Her voice echoes as she speaks into the porcelain bowl.

"Don't worry about that. What can I do?" I rub lazy circles over her back.

"Make me feel better."

"If I could, I would swap places with you in a heartbeat. So, instead, how about I make sure you're okay?"

She releases a muffled groan before replying, "Okay."

I stand. Next to the sink is a rack with towels so I pluck a washcloth from the stack and run it under warm water. I pass it to Hollyn, who's now resting her head on her arms that are draped across the toilet. She wipes her face and mouth before passing back the washcloth.

"Let's get you up and off the floor. I'll help you to your room." I lift her from the tile and wrap an arm around her waist. "Where's your room?"

"Wouldn't you like to know?" Her lips pull into a weak smile. Even when sick, she still has a sense of humor.

"Yes. Yes, I would. But right now, my motives are for a different reason. We'll make up for that when you haven't been hugging the toilet." I guide her out of the bathroom, but she stops me.

"Wait."

She turns around, opens the medicine cabinet above the sink, and pulls out a bottle of mouthwash. She twists off the cap, takes a swig, and swishes the green liquid around for a few seconds before spitting it out into the sink. She places the bottle back into the cabinet.

"I don't want barf breath."

I chuckle. "That's fair."

We exit the bathroom and head up the stairs to her bedroom. She pulls back the covers and crawls under. I tug the blanket over her and sit on the side of the bed. I brush a loose strand of hair out of her face and tuck it behind her ear.

"You get some rest."

"You're not staying with me?" Her sad, hazel doe eyes stare back at me.

"As much as I would love to. You need some rest." I lean down and press a kiss to her forehead. "I'll talk to you tomorrow."

When I glance down, she nods slightly. I rise to my feet and make my way toward the door. I glance back at the bed and she's rolling to her side, snuggling the blanket to her chest. Dammit. I don't want to leave. I turn around, crawl onto the bed behind her, and throw my arm over her, hugging her to me.

"Just a few minutes," I whisper into her hair.

WATCHING YOU SLEEP

Hollyn

The next morning, I stir awake and attempt to roll over but can't. When I peer down, I realize why, a heavy arm drapes over my waist. I can't fight the smile that takes over. He stayed. With careful movements so I don't wake Van, I roll over to face him. He's sleeping on top of the blanket and still wearing his clothes from last night. Something about that sends an eruption of butterflies through my chest.

I study his face, his long, dark eye lashes fan down his cheeks, his messy dark hair contrasts against the white pillowcase, a light stubble of hair covers his jaw. This man has me more and more in awe of him every day. Not only for everything he's gone through but also for how hard he's trying with the bakery. Slowly his eyelids flutter open, and I'm met with deep, chocolate brown eyes.

"Good morning." My words are soft.

"Were you watching me sleep?" His voice is gruff.

"Maybe." I tip up one side of my mouth. "I'm surprised you stayed."

"I was too comfortable to leave. Plus, I could get used to waking up like this." He lifts his hand and brushes a strand of hair off my face. His warm fingertips graze across my skin, sending goosebumps down my arms. "How are you feeling?"

"Much better. Must have been a twenty-four-hour bug or something."

"I'm glad to hear that. It looked a little touch and go there for a moment. I was wondering if you'd make it."

"Oh, stop."

"You hugged that toilet as if it were your best friend."

"You're so mean." I playfully shove at his hard chest, but he doesn't budge an inch. Instead, he grabs my wrist and tugs me to him. The blanket folds over, creating a barrier between us as he pulls me on top of him. I'm unable to control my giggling.

"You know you like me."

"Maybe. Sometimes. You're kind of growing on me." I shrug one shoulder.

His eyes widen in disbelief. Then his fingers tickle my sides. I squeal out an uncontrollable giggle as I squirm on top of him.

"You're not playing fair!" I screech in between breaths.

Van gives in and stops. I place my cheek on his chest while I collect my breath. Once my heart rate evens out, I prop my chin on his chest.

"What's on the agenda today?"

"Oh! I have to show you my penis. At the bakery."

I blink once. Twice. Wait, what? "You have to show me your penis at the bakery? This isn't something we could do here?"

"No. That came out wrong. I can explain."

My eyebrows raise. "Please do."

"Yesterday, before I came over, I was attempting to do some baking on my own. Which went terribly wrong, except for the penis cupcake."

I motion my hand for him to continue because that can't be the entire story.

"Apparently, if you over fill a cupcake tin, the batter spreads into all the holes when it bakes and makes a penis. I made you a penis."

I giggle. "Aww. I don't know if I should be more flattered that you attempted to bake, or that you made me a phallus shaped cake."

He runs his hands up and down my back. "I'm a man of many talents. I'm thinking I should make an entire line of penis cupcakes. Big ones. Little ones. Maybe not little ones. No one wants those. Maybe I can use some sprinkles to simulate—"

I slap my hand over his mouth and all I hear is a few muffled words. "Please don't finish that sentence. But I am impressed that you tried to bake without me." I remove my hand. "What do you say we go see what you've been working on? Meet up at the bakery in an hour?"

"Okay. I can't wait to show you my penis." He tosses me a wink and I roll off him.

"Go home and take a shower, Casanova. I'll see you soon."

Van hops off the bed, flashes me a boyish grin before he's out my bedroom door and running down the stairs. A few moments later, I hear the door open and close with a soft click. I twirl around and flop down, my back flat on the mattress like a schoolgirl with a crush. What am I doing? I don't remember the last time I felt like this. Is this what fun feels like? Whatever it is, I can't keep the smile from forming on my lips.

Sure enough, he baked me a cock and balls. I'm actually impressed. It's perfectly formed and proportionate. I glance up to Van. A proud, beaming smile covers his face.

"How about we make some more cupcake batter and then we can move on to the frosting?"

"You're the boss."

I pull up the recipe for a basic cupcake batter and direct Van to take the reins, and I'll be his assistant. He reads through the recipe and then pulls out all his ingredients while telling me what bowls and which measuring utensils he'll need. I happily collect everything he needs and place them on the worktable. With his lips pursed together in concentration, he mixes all the dry ingredients together, then moves on to the wet. He pours the dry into the wet and mixes them together. In the meantime, I prep the cupcake tins for the finished batter. I show him how much to fill each cup to avoid any more penis cupcakes. After we fill all the cups, he grabs the tin and places it inside the pre-heated oven.

Van closes the door and turns toward me, his chest puffed out and a knowing grin on his face. "This batch is money."

"The batter looked perfect."

Van's shoulder bumps with mine and he peers down at me, his eyes bright and glossy. "I don't think I could have done it without you."

My belly does cartwheels from his words along with the

way he stares at me. Heat creeps up my neck. Needing to steer this conversation elsewhere before I mount him like a bull at the rodeo, I add, "You did all the work. I was only here for moral support. What do you say we attempt frosting?"

"I don't know. I feel like I just got the handle on the batter and now we add another step… this might be too much for one day."

I invade his personal space and drag my finger down the center of his chest. My voice soft and seductive as I say, "How about this? If you make it, I'll let you lick the frosting off my body." Maybe I'll be mounting him after all.

He captures my hand with his. Desire pools behind his hooded eyes. "You need to be more specific. Which frosting?"

I glance up. "Both."

A groan rumbles from his chest. "Let's do this."

I step away, needing a little space between us before I rip his clothes off and run my tongue over his body as if he was my own personal cupcake and tasting *his* frosting. Reaching for the tablet, I pull up a simple buttercream frosting recipe. Not for me, since I've had this recipe memorized since culinary school, but for Van, so he can follow along.

We work seamlessly together as Van unwraps the unsalted butter and tosses the sticks into the bowl latched to the stand mixer as I measure out the salt and dump it in. I lift the lever to raise the bowl and Van turns on the mixer. The paddle swirls, mixing the ingredients. Once the two ingredients are whipped together, I slow down the paddle and both of us slowly sift the confectioner's sugar into the bowl. Our hands bump together occasionally, neither of us can hide our smiles when they do. I stop the mixer, scrape down the sides, and Van starts it up again to repeat the process. When everything is mixed, each of us grabs a tablespoon. I measure out the vanilla and Van measures out the cream. At the same time, we pour our liquid into the mixing bowl.

"Now we mix it until it's nice and fluffy." I glance up at Van standing next to me, my shoulder almost touching his bicep. He wraps an arm around my back, resting his palm on the table, caging me in. With his nose, he nuzzles the back of my neck.

"Smells like you." His breath is warm against the shell of my ear.

I tilt my head so my lips are an inch away from his. My eyes scan his, then drift to his lips. If I move a sliver, my mouth would be on his. My heart hammers in my chest at the same speed of the mixer. Each passing second feels more like minutes. I don't know how he does it, but he's electrified my life, like there might actually be a guy out there for me and that guy is him.

The oven timer dings, pulling me from his hypnotic trance. "The cupcakes are done." My voice is low and soft.

"I'll grab them." Van waits a moment, his eyes still searching mine before pushing off the table and stepping away.

I use the free moment to collect my thoughts. The bakery. Focus on the bakery. I switch off the mixer and lower the bowl so I can remove the paddle. Then I remove the bowl from the mixer and set it on the table.

Van places the cupcakes next to the bowl and rubs the palms of his hands together. "Let's ice some cupcakes."

"Frost. We frost cupcakes."

"Aren't they the same thing?"

"No. Icing is thinner and more flowy and mostly consists of sugar. It's mostly used for donuts, cinnamon rolls, and some cakes. You didn't learn this from your mom?"

"I was more interested in eating everything she baked, and less about *how* they were made. So, we frost the cupcakes?"

"Correct." Van reaches for a cupcake in the tin, but I stop him, pulling his hand away. "But first they need to cool, otherwise the frosting will melt. You can frost your penis cupcake, though."

Van's eyes light up with delight like a child meeting Santa for the first time. He darts to the opposite side of the kitchen to grab the plate with his cupcake resting on top. When he returns, he places it in front of himself. His excitement is contagious as he bounces back and forth on the balls of his feet. I pull out a pastry bag and a large star tip.

"Hand me the spatula over there." I point to a spatula resting on the counter near the sink. Van reaches over and plucks it off the counter and passes it to me. "So, the trick is to put the pastry bag in a glass so you can fill it. It makes it one hundred times easier."

I wrap the plastic around a glass, scrape the bowl, and plop a heaping scoop of frosting into the bag. I pass the spatula to Van so he can do the next scoop. When the bag is full, I pull up the side and twist the bag closed. I give it a gentle squeeze until the frosting peeks out of the tip and then pass it to Van. He eyes the pastry bag, then his cupcake, and then me, a blank expression on his face.

I can't fight the smile that takes over. He looks absolutely adorable when he's confused with his big puppy dog eyes. "Here, let me show you."

I grab the pastry bag from him with one hand and direct his larger hand to wrap around my smaller one. He moves to stand behind me and wraps his other hand around mine. I guide the piping bag over part of his cupcake and squeeze, causing the frosting to flow out. I move our hands over the cupcake in a circular motion, creating a cone of frosting.

"Here. You give it a try."

"How about you show me one more?" He pulls his hands off the pastry bag.

"Okay…"

My eyebrows pinch together, unsure of what he's up to. I pipe the frosting onto the next part of his cupcake when something cool swipes across my neck. Then Van's warm mouth is covering the same spot, licking and sucking.

"Tastes sweet like you, but I still prefer how you taste more."

Oh. I can get on board with this. I tilt my head to give him better access. Another dab of frosting glides across my neck. Van's mouth covers the spot again. My lips fall open and I can't control the moan that escapes. A shiver rolls through my body and my nipples harden to stiff peaks beneath my shirt. Van continues to nip and suck on my heated skin.

The pastry bag tumbles from my hand and hits the table with a clatter. I whirl around in Van's arms, grip his cheeks, and haul his lips to mine. He wraps his arms around my waist and tugs me to him. He rocks his hips and his hard cock presses into my stomach. I reach down between us and grip his length in his jeans, alternating between rubbing and squeezing.

A deep rumble sounds from his chest. "Fuck. Cupcake. Keep going."

His breath becomes more labored with each stroke. I reach down with my other hand and flip open the button of his jeans. Now, with more room, I shove a hand inside. There's only a thin layer of cotton between him and my hand. I grip his cock through the fabric, fluctuating my pressure on each upward stroke. I glance up at his face. He pinches his eyes closed at the same time his lips part. His chest heaves under his shirt while he anticipates what I'm about to do next.

"It's my turn to taste you."

From my words, his eyes open to half-mast and a smile plays on his lips. I grab the frosting bowl and crouch down. I set the bowl on the bottom shelf and turn toward Van. When I glance up, he's hunched over with his hands resting on the table, eyelids half open. My tongue peeks out and wets my lips. Reaching up, I grasp the sides of his jeans along with his underwear and tug down. When I pull the fabric over his bulge, his cock springs free, bobbing up and down until his jeans are at his ankles. Holy hell. I knew he was big from the way he stretched me but being up close and personal to his weapon of mass destruction is an all-new experience. I wrap my hand around his thick girth, my fingers far from touching. I pump once. Twice. Then I bring my mouth to the tip, licking the head. The salty pre-cum hits my taste buds.

Van releases a deep groan. "You're going to look so fucking hot with my cock in your mouth. Your pretty lips wrapped around my dick, tunneling in and out." Moisture pools between my legs from his dirty words.

I reach behind me and dip a finger into the frosting. I smear the buttercream on the tip of his cock. With the flat of my tongue, I lick it off, and then suck the head into my mouth. I release it with a loud pop.

"Mmm. Cock and frosting. Now this is something I could get used to." I smear another dollop of frosting on his shaft. Again, I lick it off. I repeat the same thing on the other side. A guttural groan sounds above me.

"I want to see you take my cock. Suck it into your mouth. Fuck. Hollyn."

I love the way Van makes demands, knowing it's me that drives him crazy. I grip the base with one hand and stretch my lips around the head and slide down. The flat of my tongue runs along the underside. I pull up and slide back down. I continue the motion except I twist my hand on the way up. Van's hand reaches down and threads through my hair. He guides my head as I bob up and down on his dick. He bucks his hips slightly, causing his cock to hit the back of my throat. I swallow and he groans.

"Fuck. Yes. You're so beautiful with your plump lips wrapped around me. Swallowing me down. Taking every inch of my cock like a good girl." His words spur me on more. I speed up and increase the pressure of my hand and my lips. "Keep going. I'm going to come."

His muscular thighs tremble beneath my hand as his movements become jerky. A moment later, his hot seed spurts out, hitting the back of my throat, and I swallow him down. His movements slow until I've sucked every drop from his cock. When he's done, I release him with a pop. With my finger and thumb, I rub away any moisture from the corners of my mouth.

I rise to my feet, still between Van and the table, a sultry smile on my lips.

Van presses his mouth to mine, not caring my lips were just on him. He pulls away and rests his forehead against mine. "If I knew baking was this much fun, I would have started sooner."

"Only because it's baking with me."

His voice is soft and sweet. "You're the only one I want to bake with."

His words and the way he says them spark something inside me. Hope, perhaps?

The muffled vibrating from my phone sounds from the other side of the kitchen, pulling us from our moment.

"I should get that."

Wordlessly, Van pushes away from the table. I move away, when I peer over my shoulder Van is pulling his pants up and clasping the button. I turn back around and find my open bag with my phone sitting on top. A missed call and several text messages pop up after I tap the screen. I scan the messages from Olivia before glancing back up to Van.

"My friends are meeting at Porter's later. Are you interested in coming with? Meeting my friends?"

Van stalks toward me until he's standing in front of me. "Meeting the friends. That's a big deal. Are we ready for that kind of commitment?"

I let out a humorous giggle. "It's only drinks. Do you want to come?"

"If you want me there, I'll be there."

"Great. I'll let them know." I type out a reply to Olivia to let her know to expect us. When I'm done, I toss my phone back into my bag and turn toward Van. His expression is half excitement and half lust. I tilt my head to the side. "What's that look for?"

Van wraps an arm around my waist and tugs me to him. "We still have some frosting left, and I haven't had my fill of you yet."

YOU'RE ONE OF US

Van

I'm sweating bullets and I shouldn't be. She invited me out to the bar to meet her friends for drinks, but fuck. Why does this feel like more than just meeting her friends for drinks? Probably because I'm falling hard for this girl. Whenever I'm near her, it's like all my problems disappear. She genuinely makes me happy, and I haven't been happy for a long time.

After some more fun with frosting and another round of Hollyn screaming my name, we went our separate ways. Mostly because she wanted to get cleaned up. If I could, I'd wear her scent on me all day, so then everyone knows she belongs to me.

I glance down at my watch, 6:45 pm. She told me to meet her here at seven. Will I appear desperate if I show up early? I pace in front of the door of Porter's Ale House, unsure of what to do. People on the sidewalk pass me, scrunching their eyebrows and glaring. You haven't seen a grown man be nervous about a date? Shit, is this a date? It can't be a date. Unless it's a couple's date. Maybe I should pick up flowers.

I glance down at my watch again, 6:47 p.m. Shit. She's not like any of the other girls. Who cares if I'm early? There's nothing wrong with being excited to see her. I reach for the handle and tug, the metal cool against my clammy palm. My eyes take a moment to adjust to the dim lighting inside compared to the bright sun outside. With a quick glance around the bar, I immediately spot Hollyn sitting at a table with a couple of other people. Here goes nothing. As I stroll over to the table, I notice a guy take the seat next to her and wrap his arm around the back of her stool. Instantly, I come to a halt and my body tenses. All I see is red. Heat floods my entire body when she laughs at something he says. Then she turns toward me and her face lights up. Jumping out of her seat, she saunters over to me. She's wearing a pale-yellow sundress that hugs her chest but flows at the waist. But my favorite thing is her breathtaking smile.

"You made it." Excitement lights up her face as she stops in front of me.

"I did." I give her a beaming smile of my own.

"Good. Everyone is dying to meet you. Well, again, I guess. But this time you get to keep your clothes on." She jabs me in the ribs with her elbow.

Shit. "That's right. Half your friends saw me practically naked. And the other half are their significant others. Maybe we shouldn't do this."

She takes my hand in hers, intertwining our fingers. "Nonsense. It's only Bennett and Seth who are the significant others. It'll be fine. Plus, I'll be here to protect you." She winks.

She tugs me along as I follow close behind. Once we reach the group, she steals a chair from a neighboring table and places it next to hers, so I'm seated at the head of the table.

"If everyone remembers, this is Van. Van, this is everyone." Hollyn sweeps an arm over the table as everyone introduces themselves and the guys shake my hand. Maybe this won't be so bad.

"So Hollyn, how does it feel knowing you saw your boyfriend half naked the same time all your friends did?" Trey lets out an "oomph" as Hollyn back hands him in the stomach.

"Ignore him. He has no filter," Bennett says. "What can we get you to drink?"

I wipe my palms on my jeans. "A beer would be great."

Several rounds of drinks later and everyone knows the stripper story and how I now own a bakery. But also, how I'm a horrible baker. Hollyn made sure to tell everyone those stories, but she also mentioned how much I've improved. And how I now know the difference between frosting and icing.

Suddenly, Bennett stands up and rests a hand on the back of my stool. "You know, I think it's time the boys have a chat with Van. Man to man." Seth and Trey also rise to their feet.

My gaze darts between the three guys and then Hollyn, unsure of what's happening right now. My heart pounds as if it's going to crack through my rib cage.

"You guys, is this really necessary?" Hollyn whines.

"Yes, it's very necessary. He's an outsider. We need to make sure he's a good fit for not only you, but also our family." Trey rounds the table to stand next to Bennett.

"If you guys are assholes, I swear to God, I'll kick all your asses." Hollyn narrows her eyes and points her finger at Bennett, Trey, and Seth. She turns to me and clasps my hand in hers, giving it a gentle squeeze. "It's best to get this over with now. It's like ripping off a band aid."

All I can do is nod because I don't know what's happening right now. Bennett clasps me on the shoulder and directs me toward the back of the bar. My mouth goes dry and I swallow hard.

"Is this where you take me out back and beat the shit out of me as part of an initiation?"

Trey turns to me, his expression stoic. "And if it was?"

"I would rather not take part."

"Well, you don't have a choice." Trey's sinister tone sends a brick dropping into the pit of my stomach.

Seth pushes Trey out of the way. "Don't listen to him. We suspect they dropped him on his head as a child. There's no solid evidence, just speculation."

The glowing red exit sign at the end of a hallway draws nearer. Luckily, we take a sharp turn and Bennett directs me to sit on a stool on one side of the table, and the three of them sit on the other side like a jail house interrogation. All that's missing is the two-way mirror.

Bennett clears his throat before locking eyes with mine. "What are your intentions with Hollyn?"

"I-um—" Out of nowhere, a flashlight shines directly into my face. I lift my hand to shield my eyes from the blinding light.

"Trey, what's with the flashlight?" Bennett asks.

"It seems appropriate for the questioning."

"Why is it so bright?" I whine while still attempting to block the light.

"It's a tactile flashlight. 3000 lumens. It's used for self-defense. I got it at the surplus store downtown. The best part, if someone tries to kidnap you, shine the flashlight in their eyes." Trey moves his hand to assault Seth with the light.

Seth slaps his hand down. "Turn off the flashlight. Plus, no one's going to kidnap you. And if they did, I bet your ass they would return you within five minutes. Probably try to sue us for emotional distress."

"Fine. You guys are a bunch of fun suckers," Trey grumbles and clicks off the flashlight.

"Now where was I?" Bennett rests his elbows on the table and leans in. "Oh yeah. What are your intentions with Hollyn?"

I run my hands along the top of my jeans. "Um. Well, I like her. A lot."

"Did you touch my future wife at the party?" Bennett narrows his eyes at me.

Seth rests his forearms on the table and leans in, mimicking Bennett. "Or my pregnant girlfriend?"

My eyes go wide. "No. To both." My gaze flits between the two of them. "The moment I saw Hollyn, I was instantly drawn to her. I wanted to spend my entire night with her, but she insisted I give the other girls some attention. I promise you I didn't touch them."

"Obviously, all the girls are very close and protective of Hollyn, and so are we. If anything were to happen to her or you hurt her, you know you'll be hearing from us." Seth's gaze bores into mine.

"Don't let the bow tie fool you. He knows how to throw down. I've witnessed it." Trey nods toward Seth.

"I have absolutely no intentions of hurting Hollyn.

Hell, I don't even know where we stand. All I can say is I like the girl. She's all I think about. When I'm not with her, I'm thinking about her. When I'm with her, I'm thinking of her. She consumes me. Frankly, it's kinda terrifying."

Bennett leans back in his chair with a wide grin on his face. "That's what those girls do. They suck you in and never let you go. In the best kind of way, of course."

Seth nods, confirming what Bennett is saying is true.

"Alright, now onto the rapid-fire question portion of the evening. Don't think, just answer." Trey reaches for his flashlight again.

Seth stops him. "Enough with the flashlight." Trey pouts.

"What's your full name?" Bennett asks.

"Vance Michael Bailey. But everyone calls me Van."

"How old are you?" Trey asks.

"Twenty-four."

"Oh, we've got a young buck." Trey rubs his hands together, a sly smile covering his face.

"When's your date of birth?" Seth asks.

"February twentieth."

Trey flits his gaze between Seth and Bennett, before turning to me. "What's your social security number?"

"Um. I don't want to answer that."

Trey tilts his head and shakes his finger at me with a smirk on his face. "Good. You're sharp." Before Bennett or Seth can say anything, Trey asks another question. "Who's your favorite Disney princess?"

"Sleeping Beauty."

"Hell yeah. Good answer." Trey raises his hand for a high five. I hesitantly lift my palm to meet his, not entirely sure if it's a joke or if he's serious.

Seth turns to Trey. "Sleeping Beauty? I guess it makes sense. The only girls you can kiss are unconscious."

"I resent that." Trey shoves Seth.

Bennett shakes his head before asking, "What was your job before the bakery?"

"I did masonry."

Trey leans in to peer at Bennett. "Oh, that could be helpful for the new patio you want to put in."

I nod my head. "Yeah. I could help with that."

Bennett rubs his chin as if he's thinking.

"Do you watch sports?" Seth asks.

"All the major ones. Football, baseball, hockey."

"Group meeting," Bennett says.

Trey stands and Bennett and Seth turn their backs to me. The three guys huddle together like a football team deciding on the game winning play. All I can hear is whispered murmurs as they discuss whatever it is. Trey glances up at me with a wide smile on his face, then ducks back down to the group. I've never been interrogated like this before. My heart thumps like a bass drum at a rock concert. I continue to wipe my hands on my jeans, unsure of why I'm so nervous.

The guys separate and all stare at me with impassive faces. My gaze drifts between all three of them, but their eyes give nothing away. Bennett is the first one to crack. His eyes crinkle in the corners as a grin covers his face.

"Welcome to the group. You're one of us now." Bennett holds out his hand for me to shake. I exhale a sigh of relief before I meet him in the middle of the table with my hand. We all stand, and the rest of the guys offer handshakes and one handed back pats.

"I won't lie. That was a bit intense and a little terrifying." I laugh.

"Oh, that was nothing. If you cross those girls, you're in for a world of hurt," Bennett says.

"Noted."

Bennett and Seth make their way back to the table with the girls. Trey wraps his arm around my shoulder and stops me until the other two are out of ear shot.

"If you ever decide the love thing isn't for you, come find me." Trey digs into his back pocket and pulls out a business card. I flip it over and read the lettering.

"We meet on Thursdays. And bring snacks." With that, he wanders back to the table. I stare at the card and shake my head. Then I tuck it into my back pocket.

When I arrive back at the table, everyone's already seated, and I take the chair next to Hollyn. Everyone is quiet for a moment, then Bennett raises his beer. "Hollyn, we're keeping him."

The entire table erupts in cheers as everyone raises their glass. Hollyn wraps her arms around my waist and gives me a tight hug. I can't help the face splitting grin that takes over. Heat radiates through my chest. My mom was the only real family I had, especially after the breakup with my ex. And since she passed, I've had no one. But now these guys have welcomed me into their family as one of their own and I couldn't be happier.

THE NON-DATE DATE

Van

The night before with Hollyn's friends was one of the best nights I've had in a long time. When I came back to Harbor Highlands, I wasn't expecting to stay as long as I have. I was expecting a week max. Now, I'm contemplating whether I want to leave. It shows how falling for the right person can change your entire life. As I lie in bed, I get an idea. I pull up my phone and send a text.

VAN

Get ready. I'm picking you up in an hour.

HOLLYN

Sleeping.

VAN

Sleeping people don't text.

HOLLYN

I beg to differ. Sleep texting is totally a
thing. I'm doing it right now.

VAN

You have an hour before I'm coming to get
you. Ready or not.

HOLLYN

If you come over now, I can guarantee one
of us will be coming.

VAN

Oh, sleeping people have jokes now.

HOLLYN

I'm a multi-talented sleeper.

VAN

60 mins. Then I'm coming over.

HOLLYN

Is that a threat or a promise? 😉

Exactly an hour later, I'm pulling into the driveway
of her townhouse. I turn the ignition off, jump out of
my car, and jog up to the door. When I try the
doorknob, it's still locked, so I use the code and let
myself in. The living room and kitchen are both still
dark, so she must be in her bedroom. I climb the
stairs two at a time until I come to a stop in her
bedroom doorway. A blanket, formed in a Hollyn
shape, lies on the bed. Slowly, I creep into the room,
careful not to give myself away. Once I reach the end
of the bed, I grab hold of the blanket and rip it
off her.

She lets out a giggle and rolls on to her back. I take in
the sight before me. She's wearing a light blue tank top
that's practically see through with a pair of matching

panties. One leg is bent at the knee as it drapes over her other leg.

I crawl up on to the bed and run my hand up her smooth thigh until I'm cupping her butt. "If you told me this is what you slept in, I would have been over sooner."

"You're here now. Whatever you had planned can wait." She flashes me a salacious smile.

Fuck me. I consider her offer. Who would turn down a drop-dead gorgeous woman who's offering herself up on a silver platter? Me, apparently. I shake my head.

"No. No. I see what you're trying to do. Your temptations won't work on me. We have plans. I'm sticking to the plans." I sit up and yank her hands with me. Then I'm crawling off the bed and forcing her to stand. "Go get ready. I'll wait."

"You're no fun." She juts out her lower lip. I grip her shoulders, twist her around, and give her a gentle push. Before she can get too far away, I playfully swat her ass. She yelps then turns her head and flashes me a sexy smile as she saunters into her en suite bathroom.

Luckily, Hollyn isn't one of those girls who needs two hours to get ready. Twenty minutes later, she's dressed in a slouchy t-shirt and yoga pants. Her hair is up in one of those messy buns plopped on top of her head. She's comfy and casual, and beautiful as ever.

"What's the plan for today that couldn't wait? Are we doing more practice baking?" She stands in front of her dresser putting cupcake shaped earrings in her ears.

"Actually, I think it's time we step outside of the bakery for a day. Do something fun."

She freezes. "We have so much to do before the wedding event. We need to finish prepping."

"If we lose one day, it won't kill us. Remember, you need to let loose." From behind, I grab her wrists, lift, and give them a shake like one of those inflatable tube characters. "Where's the girl I met at the club? She was fun."

"Hey! I'm fun!" She twirls around so she's facing me. Her hands rest on my shoulders. "Plus, that night involved a very hot guy getting naked and lots of champagne. Will today involve either of those?"

"Something could be arranged, but afterward. We have other things to do first." She pouts.

She peers down at her outfit. "This seems like a date. Are you sure I don't need to change before we go?"

"No. You're perfect just the way you are." A smile plays on her lips. "Now, let's go." I tug on her hand, leading her out of her bedroom, down the stairs, and out the front door.

Thirty minutes later, we're standing on the Lakewalk, granted we spent ten of those minutes finding parking, I always forget how busy it gets next to the lake during the summer. The gentle breeze rolling off the lake keeps the temperature cooler. People mill around in the warm sun, most of them tourists, as they take in the iconic views of the lighthouse and the lift bridge that Harbor Highlands is known for. Others bike, jog, and rollerblade up and down the path that spans eight miles along the shore of Lake Superior. Some people have dogs on leashes while others feed the seagulls, even though there are signs stating, "Do Not Feed The Birds."

"Um. I've been down here a million times. What are we doing?"

I point to a corner of the parking lot. "We're riding one of those."

"Wait. We're riding a Surrey bike?"

"Yes, we are." I grab her hand and tug her to the bike stand. I greet the man in charge of rentals and pull out my wallet to pay for ours.

After we sign the waiver, we stroll toward the rows of bikes. She stops next to one at the front of the line. "Are you sure this isn't a date? This is very date-like."

"Consider it a non-date date."

Her eyes crinkle in the corners before she lowers her sunglasses from the top of her head and climbs onto the bench seat of the four wheeled quadricycle. The roof shields us from the sun shining down.

"I've lived here all my life and I've never rented a bike down here."

I hop in next to her. "First time for everything."

Each of us rest our feet on the pedals and push. The wheels propel us down the paved walkway. Other bikers pass us as we leisurely ride along the Lakewalk. A train passes us to the left as steam billows from the chimney. Passengers gaze out the windows and we wave to them as they pass by. We continue down the paved path, weaving in and out of families and couples as they stroll next to us on the wood boardwalk. Once we reach our destination, I steer the bike into a small parking area.

"I can't believe how much fun this is. It's funny the things you take for granted when it's so easily accessible to you." She rests both her hands on the steering wheel and glances at me.

"Life moves pretty fast. If you don't stop and look around once in a while, you could miss it."

Her sweet laugh fills the air. "Is that so?"

"Wise words from a wise man." I flash her a dimpled grin.

With a smile still on her lips, her gaze never leaves

mine. "I can't say much about Ferris Bueller, but you, Van Bailey, surprise me more and more every day."

I lift one shoulder. "I need to keep you on your toes. Life's more interesting that way. Now, on to the next part of our non-date date." I hold out my hand for her, and without hesitation, she takes it. "Let's see, we did an activity and now it's time I feed you."

"Are you sure this isn't a date? It's sounding more and more like a date." She tilts her head and rests her other hand on her hip.

"Non-date date. And I'll be going in for a non-kiss kiss when I drop you off." I'm half tempted to kiss her right now.

Her mouth falls open. "Oh, you already think this non-date date will end with a kiss? Cocky much?"

"Confident." She releases a giggle that sounds as enchanting as the birds singing in the trees.

We climb a set of metal stairs that leads from the Lakewalk up to the main road. Once we reach the top, a small brick building sits to our right. Her eyes light up when she notices where we're going.

"We're getting malts?"

I nod my head, her excitement contagious.

"I've passed this malt shoppe so many times, but never stopped. It's like you know all the things I've never done." She tugs on my hand like an eager five-year old and drags me to where a small line is already formed.

When it's our turn, Hollyn orders a strawberry cheesecake malt, and I get cookies and cream. A few minutes later, they call my name and I collect our order and we find a picnic table in the shade to sit at. Both of us dive in, and the cool, sweet ice cream melts on my tongue.

She takes a big bite and moans around her spoon.

"This is so delicious." She picks up her vanilla wafer and takes a bite. "You know what's an underappreciated treat?"

"What's that?" I ask around a mouth full of ice cream.

"These wafers. They are so good. I should find a way to use them in a cupcake." She inspects the wafer more closely before taking another bite.

We finish our malts, toss our garbage in the trash, and descend the stairs back to our bike. Our ride back to the bike rental is more leisurely than when we left. We take our time soaking up the sun and fresh air. There are more people enjoying the Lakewalk now than when we first got here. Everyone watches sailboats cruise through the waves and wait for the Lakers, freight ships that stay within the Great Lakes, and Salties, salt water ocean freight ships, to come into the harbor.

She breaks the silence. "It's crazy how many people are down here. Could you imagine if we could put a bakery down here to cater to all the tourists? Summers would be non-stop customers."

"There isn't anything like that down here. I bet it would make a killing." I steal a glance her way. She stares wistfully off into the distance as if she's dreaming of things she wishes she could have. There's an ache in my chest wanting to be the man who gives it to her.

After we return the rental bike, we hop into my car, and I drive her back to her house. I pull into her driveway and shift into park. She opens her door and steps out, and I do the same. We meet at the hood of my car and I hold out my hand for her.

"Always with the hand holding." She claps her fingers around mine.

"Any way I can touch you." I've never been one for holding hands but with Hollyn it's different. Any chance I get, I want to hold her close. Maybe so I don't lose her again.

We stroll hand in hand up the sidewalk until we reach her front door. She presses the code into the keypad, opens the door, and turns around, waiting for me to enter.

"Are you coming in?"

I step up to her and wrap a hand around the back of her neck. My fingers thread through her hair as I bend down to kiss her. One of her arms wrap around my waist and pulls me closer while she deepens the kiss. Her tongue peeks out and presses at the seam of my lips. I open up, caressing my tongue against hers. Her other hand reaches up, fingers gripping the fabric of my shirt, and tugs me into the open doorway. Reluctantly, I pull away and she whimpers.

Her eyes flutter open. "You don't want to come in? Finish this non-date date the way it started, in my bed." She winks.

I tilt my head back and look at the ceiling of the covered doorway and blow out a breath. "I wanted a non-date date. I got that. I wanted a kiss. And I got one hell of a kiss. I'm going to keep it at that. For tonight."

She rests a hand on her waist and pops a hip. "I recall you promised me either nakedness or champagne and I got neither. What kind of date is this?"

"A non-date date and one where I'm going to be a gentleman. I wanted to spend the day with you, no sex, and if I step through that door, all bets are off." I never wanted today to be about sex. All I wanted was a day with Hollyn outside of the bakery. A day for us to get to know each other more.

"But you're so close. Just one more little step."

I glance down and the toe of my shoe rests against the footplate of the door. Then I meet her lust filled eyes. "Nnope." I shake my head. "I won't let you tempt me with your temptress ways. Have a good night, Hollyn. I'll see you tomorrow at the bakery." I'm sure I'll regret this later while I'm lying in my cold bed, just me and my blue balls, but for now, I'm holding my ground.

"I don't think I would have to tempt you too hard." She trails a finger from her mouth, down her neck, across her chest, and between the valley of her tits.

A guttural groan erupts from my throat. "You're right. When it comes to you, I have no will power." My foot twitches. It would be so easy to step through the door and have her panting and moaning my name. "Fuck," I mutter to myself. "Tomorrow. All bets are off tomorrow. See you tomorrow." With my feet planted outside the doorway, I lean in and place a kiss to her lips.

I turn around and without a single glance back I stride to my car. Hold your ground. Don't give in to temptation. Once I reach my car, I open the door and flop into the seat. She watches me as I turn on the ignition, her smile never faltering. She's trying to call my bluff, but I can be strong. I need to be strong. I shift into reverse and back out of her driveway. As I'm pulling away, I glance to the door at the same time as she closes it. I blow out a breath, pleased I defeated Goliath, or in this case a beautiful and sexy Goliath.

When I pull up to my apartment, my phone vibrates with a message. I pull it out of my pocket and see Hollyn sent me a picture. She's laying in her bed wearing a tank top and panties similar to the ones she was wearing this morning except this one is white and definitely see-through.

The message that follows the photo reads, "Wish you were here."

Just as I predicted, a night of blue balls.

YOU'RE JEALOUS

Van

After our non-date date, we made plans to open the bakery for customers to have a cupcake on Della. Since we were already making cakes for a wedding, Hollyn said it made sense to make extra base batter and make the cupcakes at the same time. For the three hours we were open the bakery was jam-packed with customers wanting to pay their respects and get a cupcake. Everyone who stopped in had a story to share about my mom. I didn't realize how many people loved my mom and her bakery.

Now, it's the weekend and the day of the Wilson/Carter wedding. After the Celebration of Life gathering, we immediately got to work baking cakes and making decorations. When I say we, I mean Hollyn. She made the important cakes while I jabbed sticks into the cake pops and rolled them in chocolate. Who knew little balls of cake on a stick would be so popular?

"Why do brides go all bridezilla on their wedding day? It's only a day. It's not like this day is the one that defines you for the rest of your life." I stack the boxes holding the individual nine inch decorated cakes for each guest table into the delivery van.

"But for some it is." She lifts a shoulder and lets it drop. "There's nothing wrong with a girl wanting a special day. Where all eyes are on the bride while she wears her beautiful white ball gown. One that she's spent years saving up for because when she laid eyes on the v-neck cathedral train with lace and tulle, it was the perfect dress."

"All that for a dress you'll wear for like twelve hours, get ripped off your body at the end of the night, and then sit in the back of your closet, taking up space for way too many years." I place the last box on top of the stack.

"Well, aren't you the romantic? What's your dream wedding?" She rests her hand on her hip.

"First, I would axe all this extra cake bullshit. A cake for the bride and groom, individual cakes for each table, and a variety of cake pops. Come on? A little overkill, don't you think?" I raise an eyebrow.

"Well, this extra cake bullshit keeps this bakery in business, so I'll take it." I wave my hand over all the cake boxes in the back of the van.

"Fine, but I don't want it. I would want only me and my bride. Destination wedding. Somewhere tropical and on the beach at sunset. Then afterward we wouldn't need to worry about entertaining everyone and we could get right to consummating our marriage." I wiggle my eyebrows.

She snickers. "You've put a lot of thought into this."

"A wedding should be for the couple, not for entertaining everyone else."

"It's hard to argue with that. But I would still want the white dress." She cracks a small smile.

I rest my butt on the back edge of the van and cross my arms over my chest. "What about you? What's the dream wedding? It sounds like you already have the dress."

She drops the stack of table linens in the van and her shoulders deflate. "I already had that wedding. The ending wasn't part of the dream."

"Whoa. So, you've been married? I hope you're not still married?" I raise a questioning eyebrow.

She opens her mouth, then closes it. She wrings her fingers together. "No and no. There was a wedding, but the groom took off before I could walk down the aisle."

"Shit. I'm sorry." I reach for her wrist and tug her between my legs, and she comes willingly. My fingertips drag up and down her arms as she casts her gaze to the ground. "What happened?"

"He decided he no longer wanted the life we'd spent the last five years building together. Which also included starting a bakery. But he did leave me with one thing, all the debt from the startup." She swipes at the moisture in her eyes.

"He's a dumbass. You deserve so much better than him. You deserve someone who'll wipe away your tears, not create them." I use the pad of my thumbs to swipe at the wetness under her eyes. "You deserve someone who'll spend all his time making you smile and laugh, and not bring you sadness." I grip her chin and force her to meet my gaze. When our eyes meet, I flash her a giant grin, and she gives me a small one in return. "I think you can do better than that." The corner of my lips turn up to one side. I wrap both my arms around her waist and pull her closer and tickle her sides. She squeals and wiggles in my arms. I keep going until she's full-on giggling.

"Okay! Okay! Stop!" she says between breaths.

I stop tickling her and rest my hands on her hips. "You deserve the best. Never think otherwise."

She nods.

"What do you say we finish packing up and we can laugh at the drunk bridal party while they embarrass themselves as they dance to the 'YMCA' or 'The Cha Cha Slide' or whatever people dance to at weddings."

"That sounds oddly refreshing. But you'll need to refrain from jumping up on a table and taking your clothes off. It's not that kind of party." She gives me a flirty wink.

I hold up my hands in surrender. "If NSYNC comes on, I can't make any promises."

Tulle and twinkle lights drape across the ceiling from the perimeter and meet in the middle of the room. The head table sits in front of a wall of windows that overlooks Lake Superior. Purples and blues paint the sky as the sun sets. Dinner has been served and toasts have been given. People dig into their nine-inch table cakes while others stop and pick up one of my amazingly delicious cake pops.

An older woman in a tight blue dress saunters up to the table. Her cherry red lips call out like a siren even in the low light. She comes to a halt in front of me. Her striking blue eyes meet mine for a brief second before she glances down and reaches for a cake pop.

"That one is a champa—" Before I can finish, she's reaching for a stick and bringing it up to her mouth. Her tongue peeks out, wetting her lips before she opens and places the cake ball in her mouth. Her lips wrap around the thin stick as she pulls out. She chews and then swallows.

"Not the balls I'm used to, but not bad." Her voice is soft and seductive.

I choke from her words and cover it up with a cough. An unladylike snort sounds from behind me. Trying to maintain my composure, I wave my hand over the table and say, "We have a wide variety of other balls if you'd like."

She rests one hand on the table, and waves her finger, silently asking me to move closer. I lean in, hesitantly.

Once I'm close enough, she trails a finger down my chest. "Which one is your favorite? Because I think I already know which one I like."

"You can't go wrong with the red velvet." Without breaking eye contact, I reach for one of the red velvet cake pops and hold it between the both of us. Her soft manicured fingers graze mine, and she plucks the stick from me. Before she can put it in her mouth, a younger man around my age runs up to the table.

"Mom, there's an emergency. Ben needs you." The woman scoffs, appearing irritated at the interruption. Both of them scamper off into the crowd.

I stand to my full height and shake my head, unsure of what exactly happened right then. Hollyn comes to stand next to me, and I glance down.

"Could she have been any more obvious?" She crosses her arms over her chest.

"About what?" A coy smile plays on my lips since I know exactly what she's talking about, but I want to hear it from her.

"She was so flirting with you. Not like discreet flirting, but like 'oops, my boob popped out' flirting. Which I'm really surprised it didn't with how low cut her dress is. Who wears that to a wedding?"

I tilt my head to the side. "That must be some new kind of flirting. Maybe you can demonstrate how it works?"

She side eyes me. "She's what, twice your age? I bet she's old enough to be your mom."

"Apparently, I like my women older." I shrug.

"She had no shame walking up to you at her son's wedding to hit on the baker. Who does that?" Her hands move in front of her animatedly.

"That went over your head," I say, but she continues to ignore me.

"Running her fingers down your chest. I'm surprised she didn't start purring and rubbing against you."

"You didn't hear me, did you?" I laugh.

"No, she would probably pounce on you and try to groom you into being one of her fuck boys or something."

I grip her shoulders and turn her to me, my voice low. "It's kind of hot when you get all jealous."

"Jealous?" She scoffs.

"You're totally jealous." I smirk.

"No, I'm not." She busies herself with rearranging the cake pops.

I bend down and whisper against the shell of her ear. "So, if I went over to her right now, wrapped an arm around her waist and pulled her to me. Her body flush against mine."

Her breath hitches.

"And bend down and press my lips to hers. You're telling me you wouldn't be jealous?"

Her nostrils flare, and she straightens her shoulders before peering up to meet my eyes. "No, I wouldn't."

I bark out a laugh. "Okay. If you say so. I'll just go over there…"

"Go for it." She stands to her full height and crosses her arms over her chest.

I take a step, then another as I get closer to the corner of the table. "Here I go. I'm going to do it."

She shifts her weight from foot to foot and her teeth sink into her bottom lip.

"Last chance to stop me." I round the corner of the table and her gaze shifts from me to the older woman in question on the other side of the room and then back to me. I guess I'm doing this, not because I want the other woman, but to prove a point. I propel my legs forward, but only make it a few steps.

"Stop." She throws her arms to her sides.

A face splitting grin covers my face. I've won. She's going to admit she was jealous. Hollyn stalks toward me. Once we're toe to toe, she brings her hands up to my shoulders. Her delicate hands brush down my chest. She lifts her head, her eyes staring into mine. Her tongue peeks out and she licks her lips, slow and sensual. Her fingers brush over the top button of my white-collar shirt.

"You're a little stiff, this will make you look more relaxed." She pops the top button and opens the collar slightly. "There, that's better."

I release a boisterous laugh that draws the attention of a few wedding guests. "Are you joking me?"

I grab her hand and drag her out of the reception hall and down a long hallway. When I find a quiet spot, I twist her around and press her back against the sheetrock. With my hands on the wall next to her head, I cage her in. My cheek resting against hers.

"You like to test my limits. Now it's time I test yours." I trail a finger across her collarbone, over her heaving chest, down her stomach until I reach the button at her waistband. I push the button through the hole and slide my hand down the front of the now loose fabric.

Her breath hitches. "Van." She pants. "We can't do this. We shouldn't do this here." She lifts her knee and bucks her hips as I run a finger over the front of her panties.

"Are you sure you want me to stop? Because your body says otherwise." I push the material to the side and run my finger through her folds. Sure enough, she's already soaked for me. "If this is your body's reaction to getting jealous when another girl talks to me, maybe I should make sure that happens more often."

"You wouldn't dare." Her breathing increases with every dip and swipe of my fingers. She bites on her lip to hold back her moans. I know she's struggling to keep quiet when her eyes pinch shut. "Van. You're fingers… fuck. Keep going."

"Tell me what I want to hear," I whisper against her heated skin as I continue to rub my finger over her clit.

Between pants she replies, "Tell. You. What?"

"That you were jealous," I mumble into her neck.

She huffs. "You've got to be kidding."

I pull my hand from her panties. I wrap my lips around my digits and suck her arousal off. "Now, if you tell me what I want to hear, I'll get on my knees right here, bury my head between your legs, and lick your pussy dry. What do you say?"

She drops her leg, pushes off the wall, and buttons her pants. "I say, not going to happen."

She gently pats my cheek with her hand. Then she turns and saunters away, adding an extra sway to her hips. It shouldn't be this fun to rile her up, but it is, and it's my mission tonight to get her to admit she's jealous. I can see it in her eyes, I can see it in her posture. Now I need to get her to admit her feelings.

A few minutes later, I'm entering the reception hall again. Hollyn is shoving German chocolate, champagne, and red velvet cake pop sticks into their holder.

She stomps her foot. "Ugh. I hate you. Fine, I was jealous. I hated her touching you. Hell, I hated her looking at you. Like she was undressing you with her eyes. Are you happy? Is that what you wanted to hear?" Her shoulders deflate.

I step into her space and cup her cheeks with both hands, forcing her gaze to meet mine. "Yes. Now I know the feeling is mutual. You're the only one I want. When we get back to the bakery, I'll show you."

SURPRISE RUN IN

Hollyn

The pavement pounds beneath my feet as "Blinding Lights" by The Weeknd pumps through my ear buds. Each step matches the beat of the song. Bright blues cover the sky as the blazing sun shines above me. The nice weekday afternoon draws a crowd to the lake as I weave in and out of walkers on the boardwalk that snakes along the shoreline.

The past weekend with Van was one of the best I've had in a long time. After we left the wedding, we went back to the bakery where he finished what he started at the reception and then again when we arrived at my place. Waking up with his arms wrapped around me Sunday morning was bliss. Why is the sex so much more intense after we've gotten under each other's skin? After the birthday party when Lucas was flirting with me and now with the older woman flirting with Van. It was never like this with my ex-fiancé, even early in the relationship. Maybe those feelings were only superficial, and everything with Van runs deeper.

I round the final curve before I reach the long stretch before the boardwalk ends. I glance down at my watch to check my time. On my last mile, I push my legs forward to shave off a few extra seconds. As I approach the end of the boardwalk that stops before the lift bridge and the canal, I slow my pace to a brisk walk. My chest heaves as I catch my breath. The aroma of sugar rolled deep fried dough from Donut Dan's food truck swirls through the air as a warm breeze circles around me. My belly rumbles from the sweet smell. Needing a distraction from my stomach wanting to eat itself, I tilt my head toward the sun. I close my eyes and soak up the warmth. Thoughts of the other night with Van flit through my mind.

A hand grips my bicep. I whirl around and throw my hands up as if I'm about to karate chop whoever's in front of me.

"Whoa there, Kung Fu Panda." Krystin holds up her hands in defense. "I've been yelling your name for the past five minutes. Didn't you hear me?

I yank out my ear buds and hold them up. "Sorry. I didn't hear you." *Or I was purposely ignoring you.*

"I never took you for a runner." She eyes me up and down. "It's done well for you." Most people would take her words as a compliment, but from her, it's anything but.

"How are you, Krystin?" I wipe the sweat from my brow.

She scrunches her nose in disgust before talking about her favorite subject, herself. "I've been great. Enjoying the married life." She flashes me her two-carat princess cut diamond ring as if I didn't already see it when she shoved it in my face when she asked me to bake her wedding cake. "Also, I'm sorry to hear about Della passing. That must be really hard for you. Being out of a job and all now that she's gone. What are you going to do?" She rests her hand on my forearm and leans into my space. "You know, if you need anything like a job, I'll talk to my dad. I'm sure he can find something for you. It would only be entry level—"

"Thanks, but I still have a job," I interrupt, mostly so I don't have to listen to her talk anymore.

She claps her hands in front of her excitedly. "Oh great! So you can make some cupcakes for a gender reveal party."

My face falls and I glance down to her flat stomach. The action doesn't go unnoticed.

"It's not for me. Josie is expecting again. I don't know how she does it."

Josie's expecting child number two. Krystin is married. And what do I have? A guy who I occasionally sleep with. At least it's good sex.

She stares at me, waiting for an answer. Her impatience increases with each passing second that I don't answer. I shake the thought from my head.

"Uh. Yeah. Sure. Message me with what you want and how many."

"You're the best. Josie's going to be so excited." She rests her hands on my shoulders and leans in for a fake hug before sauntering away.

I scrub my hands down my face. What did I agree to? And what am I going to tell Van?

After a trip home and a shower, I arrive at the bakery by late afternoon. I send a message to Van asking him to meet me here. I run scenarios through my head on how I'm going to tell him I booked us another job, even though we've never discussed taking on more than the two parties that were already booked.

Van, don't be mad, but we have to make cupcakes for a gender reveal party. Something I want for myself but will never get. No.

So, Van, here are my naked breasts. Also, we have to bake cupcakes for a gender reveal party. No.

So, Van, I booked us another party. Cupcakes for a gender reveal party. Here, let me give you a blow job so you forget all about it. No.

I pace back and forth, so stuck in my own head that I don't hear anyone come in. A pair of hands grip my waist and I twist around with a scream.

"Did I startle you?"

I clutch my chest. "Yes. I didn't hear you come in."

"What has you so jumpy?" He wraps his hands around mine, intertwining our fingers.

"I did a thing today. Don't be mad." I wrap my other hand around our hands and clutch them to my chest.

"It can't be that bad. What did you do?" He bends down and places a kiss on my knuckles.

"I booked us to make cupcakes for a gender reveal party. The good thing is we only need to bake the cupcakes and deliver them to the party. We don't have to stick around." I hold my breath, waiting for his reply.

"We can do that. Why'd you think I would be mad?" His eyebrows draw together.

I twist away from Van, our hands still linked. "I don't know. We haven't talked about what you wanted to do after we completed the two jobs. And then I booked us for another one." I pause. "This woman drives me crazy. I've known her all my life, but she likes to rub it in my face how much better her life is. And ugh! The pity in her tone when she assumed I was jobless. I couldn't let her win."

"Hey. Hey. It's okay. Take a deep breath." Van smooshes my cheeks between his big, firm hands, his gaze on mine. He inhales deeply through his nose and exhales through his mouth, and I mimic his actions. "We'll give her the best damn gender reveal cupcakes any gender reveal party has ever seen. By the way, what's a gender reveal party?"

I bark out a laugh. Only Van would know how to make me laugh at a time like this.

"No, I'm serious. I've never heard of this."

"It's when a couple has a party to reveal the gender of their unborn child to all their friends and family."

He blinks once. Twice. "And people have a party for this?"

"Some people do." I shrug a shoulder.

"Would you want a party like that?"

"I don't know. I'll need to get to that point first before I decide."

Van nods his head in understanding. "Okay. So, what are we making?"

"We'll be making a lemon cake filled with blue sprinkles and a duo of pink and blue frosting." I pull out my tablet from my bag and pull up a picture and pass it to Van.

He studies the picture for a moment. "So, I take it the blue sprinkles means it's a boy?"

"You got it. Also, we only have three days to make one hundred cupcakes." I raise my eyebrows and flash him a tight smile.

He stares down at the picture and back at me. "Uh… is that even possible?"

"If we get started right now."

Van glances back at the tablet. "But the most important question is, who invites a hundred people to a baby party?"

"Gender reveal party. And if you knew this girl, you wouldn't be surprised." I pull up the recipe to write down all the ingredients we'll need.

"I don't even know a hundred people. Let alone know them well enough to invite them to a party. Now that I think about it, I know a girl who would do exactly that." Van rubs his chin.

I jot down the list and toss the tablet back into my bag. "We better get shopping. We've got a lot of work ahead of us."

An hour later, we arrive back at the bakery with arms full of ingredients. We set bags on the table and organize everything.

"This should be easy. We make all the cupcakes, frost them, put them into boxes, and wait until the day of the party to deliver them." Van rubs his hands together like he has everything figured out.

"Well, not really. Of course, the host wants cream cheese frosting, which is a pain when it comes to baking ahead of time because the frosting needs to be refrigerated." I pull out the bricks of cream cheese from the bag and hold them up. "The cream cheese frosting should only be at room temperature for about two hours for food safety reasons. With these, timing is everything. We can start with baking the cakes and we can make the frosting ahead of time to keep in the fridge. The morning of the party, we'll have to come in early, let the frosting come to room temperature for an hour, frost them, and deliver them to the party."

Van stares at me, jaw open and wide eyed, as if I spoke to him in a foreign language. "I trust you know what you're doing because all of that just went over my head."

"Don't worry, I'm good at telling you what to do." I flash him a wink.

"In the bakery. I got it covered everywhere else."

We spend the next several hours baking cupcakes and mixing frosting. Baking with Van is so easy, and he makes it fun. I don't remember the last time I've smiled and laughed so much. It was never like this with my ex-fiancé, even after years of working side by side in culinary school and even afterward when we had plans to start our own bakery.

I steal a glance over at Van as he scoops frosting into a bowl. He has a smear of frosting on his cheek. I take a few steps toward him and bring my hand up to brush off the frosting with my thumb. The contact startles him and his eyes meet mine.

"You had frosting on your cheek." My voice is low.

"Thanks." His voice is deep and throaty.

Desire pools behind his dark chocolate irises as if he doesn't kiss me this instant, he might die. Butterflies swarm in my belly. Instantly, my nipples pebble beneath my shirt and I nibble on my bottom lip. His gaze darts down and watches the movement. He drops the spatula and prowls toward me. His hand comes up to rest on my hip.

From behind us, my phone buzzes, interrupting our moment. "I better check that."

Reluctantly, I break away from Van and check my phone. I quickly scan the message and type out a reply.

I turn back around to face Van. "Parisa's having a crisis. She's trying to hang something up in the nursery but

Seth is at The Lilith House so she needs my help." I glance around the messy kitchen. "I hate to leave all this for you to clean up…"

"Don't worry about it. Nothing needs to get baked, so I can handle it."

"You're the best. I promise to make it up to you later." I pull my apron over my head and toss it on to a table.

"You know, I'm going to hold you to that."

I give him a flirty smile. "I know." I rise to my tippy toes and press a kiss to his cheek. I grab my bag and walk out the backdoor.

VAN

I peer around the kitchen. Dirty dishes fill the sink, flour dusts the worktable, and I still have bowls of frosting to fill. I continue scraping the cream cheese frosting into the bowl when my phone vibrates in my pocket. I wonder if Hollyn forgot to tell me something. Setting the spatula down, I fish my phone and unlock the screen. Except it isn't a message from Hollyn. Instead, it's a message from Trey.

TREY

Beers at Porter's. Get your ass down here.

A small smile pulls at my lips. I haven't been back to Harbor Highlands in five years and I've either lost touch with all my old friends or they've moved away, so I'm ecstatic to have some new friends to hang out with. I type out a reply.

VAN

I need to clean up at the bakery and I'll be down.

TREY

Hurry because when you get here, you're playing catch up. The longer you take, the more beers you're drinking.

Shit. I've seen these guys drink. They can definitely toss them back. I hustle around the kitchen, first starting with scraping the last of the frosting, wash the dishes, and wipe down all the surfaces. Once everything is done, I take one last glance around the kitchen when I notice a covered bowl still on the counter. I grab it, open the fridge door, move a few things around to make room, and toss it in. I release the door handle. Without a glance back, I flick off the lights and lock up.

BARTENDER THERAPY

Van

I pull open the back door to the bakery, a smile on my face, excited to spend the day with Hollyn again. When I enter the kitchen, all the excitement drains from my body. She's standing in front of the worktable, shoulders deflated. That's when I notice the fridge door open and all of its contents sitting on the steel table, including the containers of frosting we made yesterday.

Something's not right. I approach her as if she's a scared animal. Unsure what type of reaction I might get. That's when a lone tear rolls down her cheek.

"Hey, is everything alright?" My voice is soft, still unsure what the issue is.

Her chest rises as she inhales a slow, deep breath. "No Van, it's not."

"What's wrong?"

"What's wrong? You want to know what's wrong?" She rises to her full height.

"Yeah. That's why I asked."

She turns to face me. "Well, it turns out when you left last night, you didn't close the fridge. So all night it ran and eventually the motor burned out, causing everything inside to spoil. Including the frosting we need for the cupcakes. That's what's wrong." She whirls around, grabs boxes and containers off the table, and hurls them into the trash.

"I closed the fridge last night. I put the last container of frosting in and closed the door."

"Well, it wasn't closed when I came in. There was a box pressed against the door, so it didn't seal. Did you not double check?"

"No, I didn't think I had to double check. I shut the door and left to meet up with the guys at Porter's."

"Oh, I see." She grabs a carton of eggs and flings it into the trash. The crunch of eggs breaking fills the room. "Beers with the guys was more important. Glad to see where your priorities lie."

"What's the issue? We'll make more frosting."

She inhales a deep breath before meeting my gaze. "It's not only the frosting, Van. We have to spend money for more ingredients, but most of all we need a new fridge."

"Calm down. Everything will be fine." I rest my hands on her shoulder. Her head snaps my way. Her eyes narrow, giving me the death glare. Slowly, I pull my hands away and retreat.

"I'm fooling myself. You're young, know nothing about baking, and know even less about responsibility." She throws her hands in the air.

I scoff. "You'd be surprised how much I know about responsibility."

With a hand on her hip, she snarls. "Oh yeah, like what? How to do a keg stand without spilling a drop?"

My gaze bores into hers. "More like dropping everything to be with my pregnant girlfriend, busting my ass off to provide a future for her, only to find out eight months later that it may not be mine. Spoiler alert, it wasn't. She'd been cheating on me with my best friend. So yeah, I know a thing or two about responsibility."

She slinks back. "Sorry. I didn't know."

"Because you didn't care to ask!" Heat floods my entire body as my pulse pounds.

"I didn't know we were at the 'tell me your life story' stage of whatever this is." She shakes a finger between us.

"Clearly, you don't know a lot of things about me and didn't bother to ask because you were too focused on yourself. Maybe this was a mistake." She flinches and inches backward. I snatch my keys off the counter and stomp past her. "I gotta get out of here."

My knuckles crash into the door, forcing it open, and I don't wait around for it to slam behind me. I throw open my car door and jump inside. Adrenaline courses through my body as I fumble to shove the key into the ignition but don't turn it over. Hurt and anger bubble through my pores. Who's she to make snap judgments about me? She knows nothing about me or my life. What am I even doing here? Running a bakery... this isn't my life. This was never supposed to be my life. I turn the key and the engine roars. The tires squeal on the blacktop as I stomp on the gas and exit the parking lot. Unsure of where I'm going, I just drive. Newly built unfamiliar buildings pass by, along with new businesses that sprouted up since I left. I lived here for most my life, but everything seems foreign, like I don't belong here anymore. Maybe I don't, until the sign for Porter's Ale

House comes into view. At least it's a place I'm semi-familiar with. I pull my car into the parking lot and proceed inside.

There're a few people scattered amongst the high-top tables and a couple sitting at the bar. I decide to take a seat at the bar, a beer and the baseball game playing on the tv hanging behind it might distract me from Hollyn and the bakery. I find an empty seat at the end and plop down. Before I can decide what I want, a brunette greets me from the opposite side.

"What can I get you?"

"Whatever you got on tap." Her gaze drifts to the row of ten different tap levers, then slowly comes back to me with a raised eyebrow. "Oh. Um. Castle Danger." She grabs a pint glass and rests it below the spout and pulls the lever. The dark brown liquid fills the glass as the tan foam forms at the top. Once it's full, she sets a coaster in front of me and places the beer on top. "Thank you." But she doesn't move. She studies me as if she's trying to see into my soul, and I think it's working.

"You look familiar." She tilts her head and squints.

"I'm not from around here. Well, not anymore anyway."

"You've been in here before."

"A couple of times. I've met Jake. I'm friends with Trey, Seth, and Bennett."

She snaps her fingers. "That's it. You're the new guy. Van. I'm Rylee." She pauses. "So, what brings you in here without your posse?"

"It's a long story." I reach for my beer and take a gulp.

"They always are."

Over the next twenty minutes, I spill the entire last twenty hours of my life to this stranger. And it feels refreshing. She listens, pours me a new beer as soon as mine is empty, and all this without judgment. Or so I thought.

"So let me get this straight. You got into a fight with your girl—"

"She's not my girl," I correct.

"Oh, she's definitely your girl, otherwise you wouldn't be at the bar in the middle of the afternoon pouring your heart out to a bartender you don't know."

Well, shit, maybe she's on to something.

"As I was saying, you got into a fight. You told her to calm down. That pissed her off more, and then you called her selfish. Did I get all that?"

"You missed the part where she called me young and irresponsible."

"At this point, it's irrelevant. I'm going to give you some free advice." She narrows her eyes at me. "If a girl is visibly upset, the last thing you want to do is tell her to calm down. Anything that happens afterward is on you."

I curl my lip. "That's kind of shitty advice. She needed to calm down. Everything that happened was fixable."

She slams a cutting board down on the railing. "Do we need to add not listening to your list of strikes?"

"I listen. Maybe *you* should calm down." For the second time today, a woman shoots daggers in my direction, and I hold up my hands in surrender. "Okay, okay. Fine. I get it. But what's done is done. What do I do next?"

She leans back and crosses her arms over her chest. "Do you like the girl?" I nod. "Good. Because Hollyn's a good person and doesn't deserve some asshole playing with her heart."

"How'd you know I'm talking about Hollyn?"

"I'm a bartender. I know shit. Plus, the entire gang comes in here. It's like their second home or something and they talk. A lot. Anyway, here's what you gotta do."

She raises a finger in tandem with each statement she makes. "Apologize for being an asshole. Fix her fridge. Then make it up to her in a more behind closed doors kind of way."

"Her fridge? I'm the owner of the bakery. If anything, it's my fridge."

"But she's been there for the past seven years. You've been there for what, a month?"

"A month and a half."

She narrows her eyes at me.

"Good point. But I can't just buy a new fridge…"

She pulls out her phone from her back pocket and types away on the screen. A moment later she's setting it down, screen side up, and sliding it toward me. "Call this guy. Tell him about your broken fridge and mention Rylee told you to call him. He'll get you situated."

"This guy's legit? He won't murder me and bury me in his backyard."

"If you keep asking all these damn questions, *I'm* going to murder you and bury you in my backyard."

"Noted. Thank you, Rylee." I add the name and number into the contacts on my phone. Rylee goes back to cutting up lime wedges. "One more question." Rylee holds up her knife and tilts her head to the side. Oddly enough, I think she could gut someone like a fish with the paring knife, but I cross my fingers and take my chances anyway. "How much does the bakery mean to Hollyn?"

Rylee drops the knife to the cutting board and leans toward me. "After her ex-fiancé left her, it was the bakery that brought her back to life. She lives and breathes that bakery. I wouldn't be surprised if she had frosting running through her veins."

"It's probably more along the lines of icing. It's thinner and runnier. Would flow better than frosting." I smile to myself, knowing that little tidbit of information Hollyn told me stuck.

"Whatever. Not the point. The bakery means a lot to her, and she prides herself in the work she does there. And whoever you want to blame it on, that work is in jeopardy. So, make it right." She goes back to the lime wedges. "Ugh. It wasn't this hard with Bennett," she mumbles under her breath.

"Thanks for all your help." I rise to my feet.

Rylee stops what she's doing. "One more thing since I'm doling out free advice like candy at a parade. If a girl says it's fine. It's not fine. It's far from fine." She points her paring knife at me, and I nod in understanding.

While she slightly terrifies me, gut instinct tells me she knows what she's talking about. I toss some bills onto the bar top to pay for my drinks and I'm out the door, loaded with some new information and the need to make everything right with my girl. My girl? I like the sound of that.

A short while later, I'm back at the bakery. When I step into the kitchen, Hollyn's rearranging the other smaller fridge to make room for the new frosting we'll have to make. I clear my throat and she glances up at me.

"I'm sorry. I was a little bit of an asshole earlier."

She quirks an eyebrow at me.

"Okay. A lot of an asshole. I'm sorry. I have a call into a repair shop, and he'll be out to look at the fridge tomorrow and figure out what we need to fix it."

"Thank you. I'm sorry for calling you irresponsible. You've gone through a lot in your life to prove otherwise. My emotions got the best of me. I'm at a loss on what to do, with everything, and I took it out on you." Her gaze casts downward.

Cautiously, I inch closer to her. When she doesn't move

away, I take another step until I'm standing in front of her. "Did we have our first fight?"

She peers up and nods. "We did."

I hold out my open arms. When she doesn't move, I give her a head nod to coax her into my arms. She breaks eye contact and nibbles on her bottom lip. A second later, her arms wrap around my waist and her cheek rests against the cotton of my shirt.

"Huh. And we've managed to come out the other end stronger." I rest my chin on top of her head and rub my hands up and down her back.

"That's what they call being in a relationship. You make mistakes and you work through them."

"Is that what this is? A relationship?" I squeeze her tighter.

"I don't know. But whatever it is, I like it."

"Me too." I bend down and place a chaste kiss to her lips.

Still in my arms, she peers up at me. "There's one thing I'm wondering about. After your girlfriend told you the baby wasn't yours, why didn't you move back to Harbor Highlands?"

Exhaling a sigh, I glance up at the ceiling, unsure how I want to answer. This is the first time I've really talked about it. "Pride, I guess. No one knew me down there. If I came back to Harbor Highlands, I would have to deal with all the hushed whispers and pity glances. Plus, she and my best friend moved back here. Less of a chance of seeing them if I wasn't around."

"You're not afraid you'll run into her now?"

"I've been here for almost two months, and I haven't yet. So, either she moved, or I've been lucky."

"I'm surprised she didn't show up at the bakery to show her respects to Della, at least."

I stifle a laugh. "They weren't exactly each other's favorite people."

"Huh. For what it's worth, I'm sorry you had to go through all that." Her fingertips brush over my stubble covered cheek until she's cupping my jaw.

I lean into the warmth of her hand. "If I didn't go through all that, I would have never met you. Or stripped for you. Or your friends."

She giggles. God, I love making her laugh. I pull away, but she grips the front of my shirt with her other hand and tugs me back to her. She rises to her tippy toes and presses her lips to mine. What starts off innocent, heats up as I deepen the kiss. With my arms wrapped around her waist, I twist us around and push her against the fridge.

Twenty minutes later, we're both catching our breath. I'm tucking myself back into my jeans, and Hollyn is straightening her dress.

"Do we get to do that every time we fight? If so, I think we should fight more often." I secure the button on my jeans.

"Only if you're sweet with your apology." She flashes me a sultry smile.

"Done. Also, give me a list of all the ingredients we need. I'll go shopping while you finish the fridge and get everything set up for the frosting."

She jots everything down on a piece of scrap paper and hands it to me. I place a kiss to her forehead and once again I'm out the door, but this time to do some shopping.

EXES AND OHS

Van

We were at the bakery well into the night making frosting and piping all one hundred cupcakes, so we'd be prepared to deliver them by early afternoon. Luckily, we were able to fit all the boxes in the fridge. Unfortunately, we had to sacrifice other refrigerated items to make room. After we load the van, Hollyn hops into the driver's seat, since she said she knows where we're going.

We head north, winding through neighborhoods of familiar houses. Not much has changed since the last time I was in this area. I glance at every passing green street sign. Birch Street. Fern Street. Oak Street. Then the van turns onto Maple Street. My heart rate spikes when I remember who lives down this road. I turn to Hollyn.

"Where did you say we are going?"

"This girl I know, Krystin."

I glance into the back of the van to read the name on the boxes. "Jenkins." I rack my brain to think if I know any Jenkins.

"That's her new, shiny, married name," Hollyn says, not hiding the sarcasm in her voice. "She was Murray."

My heart drops to the floor. Ding. Ding. Ding. We have a winner. That's a name I know. Fuck me.

Hollyn spares a glance my way. "Is something wrong?"

"You know the ex I told you about? That's her sister."

"Oh. Oh! Shit. The party is actually for Josie." My stomach curdles at hearing her name out loud. "Do you want to wait in the van, and I'll drop off all the cupcakes?"

As much as I want to say yes, I can't make Hollyn do that. We only had boxes that would fit twelve cupcakes. She'd have to make five trips, at least. If I help, we'll get it done twice as fast, and then we can get the hell out of there.

"No, the faster we get this done, the sooner we can leave."

Between the seats rests a baseball cap with an embroidered The Sweet Spot logo on the front. I pick it up and dust it off before shoving it on my head.

"I'll just wear this, keep my head down, and hopefully no one recognizes me."

"Oh, the good old baseball cap disguise trick. No one will know it's you." She laughs.

"It's better than nothing." I tug the hat tighter on my head.

As soon as we pull into the driveway, my chest tightens while my foot bounces on the floorboard. My gaze darts from one side of the property to the other, expecting to see a familiar face, but there isn't a person in sight. I can do this. In and out. Real quick. James Bond did this all the time. Granted, he wasn't trying to dodge an ex-girlfriend while delivering cupcakes.

Hollyn stops the van in front of the garage and turns off the ignition. "I'll see where they want the cupcakes, then I'll come back and get you."

All I can do is nod. When she's out of the van, I slink down into the seat in case someone walks by.

A few minutes later, Hollyn returns and stands next to the passenger side door, and I roll down the window.

"They said to bring the cupcakes around back and set them on the table. They'll take care of the rest."

"Okay."

I exhale a deep breath and exit the van. We meet at the rear and I open the doors. She reaches in for two boxes of cupcakes and I do the same and we make our way to the backyard.

After I set my last stack of cupcakes on the table, I turn on my heel, but then I hear my name. I quicken my pace, ignoring the voice, but it's too late. I hear my name again, only louder this time.

"Van? Is that you?"

I freeze. I haven't heard that voice in over four years. To this day it still haunts my dreams. I close my eyes and slowly turn around. When I catch sight of her, it's like I'm ripping the knives out of my back all over again.

"Oh my God, it is you! What are you doing at my gender reveal party?"

My heart pounds in my throat, still at a loss for words. This is the girl who broke my heart all those years ago. I was hoping I would never have to see her again and now I'm here delivering fucking cupcakes to her gender whatever party.

"I'm sorry to hear about your mom."

I stare at her unblinking. I know she's asked me a

question, but I can't seem to form any words. It's as if I'm having an out of body experience. The entire situation plays out while I watch from the side.

She tilts her head and furrows her brow. "Van? Are you okay?"

Finally, with a shake of my head, I come to. I find my voice as I choke out a reply, "Um. Thanks."

"But also, why are you here? If you've come to win me back, I'm afraid you're way too late." A smile plays on her lips as she rubs her growing baby bump. "I should find Joshua. You two haven't talked in what, four years? It would be so fun to see his expression when he sees you." Josie glances to the left and then to the right.

Fun for who? Josie? Or the ex-best friend who slept with my girlfriend and got her pregnant. Not a single moment of this situation is fun for me.

Luckily, Hollyn passes us on her way back from dropping off the last box of cupcakes and halts in her tracks. Her gaze bounces to Josie and then back to me. It takes her two point two seconds to notice my current state of distress. Without a second thought, Hollyn hooks her arm with mine, brushing her chest against my bicep.

"Van's not here to win you back." Her voice is sugary sweet. Hollyn continues to rub against me as Josie watches her every movement. "I can't believe you let this one go."

"Oh. Oh!" Josie leans in, her voice a whisper. "Are you two together?"

Hollyn beams up at me. Then turns back toward Josie. "He's the best lover. Did he do that thing with his tongue with you? Like, oh my God. I might have an orgasm right here thinking about it." She tilts her head back, closes her eyes, and forms a perfect O with her plump pink lips. She jerks her body somewhere in between a shiver and a convulsion, and I can't hold back the rumble in my chest.

Not a day goes by that Hollyn doesn't surprise me. And each day, I find myself falling even more for her.

"Well, uh, we better get going before this one starts foaming at the mouth. It was good to see you."

Bile rises in my throat as I choke out those last words because it was not good to see her. In fact, my day would have been a hell of a lot better if I didn't see her. I grip her shoulders and turn her toward the direction of the van, then give her a slight push to move her feet.

While still in earshot, she yells over her shoulder, "What's that Van? You want to lick my frost—"

I wrap my arm around her shoulder and cover her mouth with my hand to keep her from finishing that sentence. She giggles into my palm, and I drop my hand but keep my arm wrapped around her.

"Thanks for that."

Her gaze drifts up to mine. "You looked like you saw a ghost."

"I think I did. Ghost of girlfriends past comes back to haunt my life." We walk in silence for a moment before I shake it off. Josie doesn't need to occupy any more of my thoughts than she already has. "I think we should talk about that show you put on back there."

"I can't stand her or her sister. They think they are so much better than everyone. Also, I can't believe she's your ex. I can see why your mom didn't like her."

"Young and dumb, I guess." I exhale a humorless laugh.

"What are you talking about? You're still young."

"But I'm much wiser now. More mature. I think I even saw a gray hair this morning." I pull off the cap and run my fingers through my locks.

"You're so full of it." She playfully smacks my chest.

"But also, lover? And what's this thing I do with my tongue that you love so much?"

"It's like a triple threat. A lick, a nip, and a suck. It's a move you should get patented. You could call it the Van Pussy Pulsator." She flashes me a snarky smile.

I throw my head back in laughter. "Oh. Now you have jokes. I think you've been hanging out with me too long."

"I enjoy hanging out with you."

"Your company isn't so bad."

"Hey——" She tries to push away from me, but I grip her tighter and pull her close. She gives in, realizing it's going to be a losing battle, and wraps her other arm around my waist. We amble in unison back to the van.

Once we reach the van, I hop into the driver's seat as Hollyn crawls into the passenger side. Both of us buckle our seatbelts and I turn the key. The engine roars to life. I shift the lever into drive, and step on the gas with hopes of never coming back here again. Since I'm familiar with the area, I take a different route back to the bakery. Every attempt to think of anything but Josie falls flat. Everything I sacrificed. I worked my ass off to give her, give us, give our family a better life, and it was all for nothing. My pulse speeds up and my grip on the steering wheel tightens.

"Van? Van?" Her voice pulls me from my daze, and I glance toward her. "I've been saying your name for the past thirty seconds. What has you so distracted? And the poor steering wheel. If you squeeze it any harder, I think you'll crack it in half."

I loosen my grip and the color comes back to my knuckles. "Sorry. Just Josie."

"Do—Do you still love her?"

"Hell no. What she did… hurt. I thought I was going to marry her. Start a family. Live the white picket fence dream. But then it was gone. She got to go live that life with my best friend, while I became a shell of myself."

"I'm sorry, Van. I know all about having a dream and then having it ripped away from you."

"I have a shitty ex. You have a shitty ex. Welcome to the shitty ex club. The price of admission… your heart." I hold my hand out toward her and squeeze my fingers as if a beating heart rest in my hands.

She scrunches her face. "That's so morbid."

I drop my hand and it falls into the empty space between the two front seats. "Love is morbid. Feelings are scary. Taking chances are even scarier. That's why I'd rather keep it fun. Then I don't have to worry about all the messy stuff and no one gets hurt."

"Fun is better anyway." She pauses for a moment. "How about no more talk about exes or how they've wronged us? We should move on to other things, much happier things."

Movement causes me to glance over to the passenger seat. She unbuckles her seat belt and twists to face me. The air in the cab suddenly shifts. No longer is it filled with hatred for our exes, but instead buzzes with heated electricity

She leans over, rests a hand on my jean covered thigh, her tongue runs along the shell of my ear before she whispers, "I want you in my mouth, licking you, sucking you, tasting you."

Jesus Christ. Her words catch me by surprise, and I jerk the van to the right. Instantly, my cock goes stiff, straining against my zipper. The denim fabric doing nothing to hide my growing hard on. I'm sure there's a zig zag imprint on my dick from pressing against the metal teeth.

Her hand dances up my thigh until she's cupping me

over the fabric. With her lips still near my ear, her teeth nip on my earlobe. Her warm breath feathers against my skin.

"My pussy is aching for you, needing to be stuffed with your big. Fat. Cock." She continues to rub and stroke me over my jeans. "If I touch myself right now, I'd be so wet for you. Should I find out?"

She leans back in her seat, one foot resting on the seat and the other on the floorboard. She lifts the hem of her dress and slides her hand under her panties.

"Fuck. Are you trying to kill us?" My head flits between the passenger seat, where Hollyn is currently touching herself, and the boring view outside the windshield.

"There's a park a few blocks up. Just off the main road. If you stop, you can find out for yourself how wet I am." She exhales a throaty moan and throws her head back. "Because I'm so wet for you."

I slam down on the gas pedal, needing to get to this park like five minutes ago. When the entrance sign comes into view, I flip on the blinker. The tires squeal on the pavement as I make the turn. Immediately, the parking lot she was talking about comes into view. I find an empty spot on the far end of the lot where there are no other cars. The view overlooks the city and Lake Superior, but I'm not focusing on that. Instead, my attention travels to the gorgeous redhead sitting next to me. I press the button on my seat belt and pounce on her before it can retract back into place. My palm rests on the edge of the seat, so I don't put all my weight on her.

I slam my mouth to hers, capturing her moans. Her hand continues to pleasure her pussy until I push it away, replacing it with mine. I want to be the one who gives her an orgasm. I want it to be my hand, my mouth, or my dick. Whichever way it is, I want it to come from me. She breaks our kiss and brings her fingers that were just in her pussy up to my mouth. She paints her wetness over my lips until I suck her digits into my mouth. I swirl my tongue around each finger, wanting to lick every last drop off them.

I release her fingers. "Fuck. You taste so fucking good, but I need more."

I pull my hand from between her legs and sit up. The hem of her dress is still bunched at her waist exposing her panties. A wet spot darkens the cotton fabric. I bend down and run my nose along her covered slit, inhaling her sweet scent. My cock grows increasingly harder and I'm surprised it hasn't busted through the zipper yet. I cover the white cotton with my mouth, sucking on her clit through the fabric. Her hand flies to the back of my head, her fingers threading through my locks. She thrusts her hips up as her fingers tug on my strands. I'm driving her as wild as she drives me, and I'm loving every second of it.

With my free hand, I tug her panties to the side, exposing her bare, glistening pussy to me. I bend down and run the tip of my tongue between her lips, lapping at her arousal. And I've tasted nothing better. I continue my assault on her pretty pussy with my tongue like a thirsty man in need of water. My stubble rubs against her sensitive skin causing her to shiver beneath me. I wrap my lips around her bud and suck. Her hips buck upward, and she lets out a cry of ecstasy. I continue my triple threat, as she calls it, of licking, nipping, and sucking. Every second that passes, I bring her closer and closer to exploding.

"Oh, Van. Right there. Van. I'm coming." Her labored breaths increase, and her whimpers and cries fill the interior of the van. I continue licking. Nipping. Sucking.

With one last suck on her clit, her body writhes under me. Her fingers in my hair hold my head still as she thrusts her hips up, and her pussy pulsates on my tongue. She chants my name as I continue to lick every last drop of her orgasm until her body stops quivering. I can't get enough of her.

Once her orgasm subsides, I sit up and wipe my mouth with the back of my hand. "We should move this party to the back of the van so I can watch your pretty pussy take my dick."

I don't have to say anymore. Her eyes light up and she sits up eagerly as if the doors just opened to her favorite kitchen store that's having a half off sale. I move back to the driver's seat so Hollyn has enough room to maneuver in the small cab to crawl into the back of the van. My gaze fixes on the hem of her dress that barely covers her ass cheeks as she bends over. When she's in the back and turned around, I follow her through the small opening. Being a delivery van, there isn't much room back here. Shelves line the two sides with an open strip down the middle. The two back windows are tinted so you can see out, but no one can see in. I lie down on the floor, undo my pants and push them to my ankles. My dick bobs up and down, thankful to finally be free from the confines of my pants.

"As much as I want you to sit on my face right now, I want your tight, warm pussy wrapped around my dick."

"How about this?"

She moves to straddle my chest, but then turns around. My heart rate spikes with excitement. This woman is full of surprises. My hands reach up and skate up her smooth thighs until my palms rest on the globes of her ass. I knead the soft flesh with my fingertips. With her ass in the air, she bends down and places a soft kiss on the tip of my dick. Then like a flip of a switch she goes from sweet to dirty simply by wrapping her lips around me and sliding down, swallowing me whole. A guttural groan escapes my chest.

Her tongue runs along the topside of my shaft and when she reaches the top, she sucks the tip into her mouth. I grip her hips and pull her down to my face. I just had her on my tongue, but damn, I want more. She continues sucking and licking my dick and I fight the urge to thrust up into her mouth and feel her swallow my head. So, instead, I distract myself with her perfect pussy in my face. I pull her panties to the side. Her pussy once again glistening with her arousal.

"I had no idea how much sucking on my dick turns you on."

All she can do is mumble since she has a mouth full of cock. The vibrations send a jolt of electricity straight to my balls. If she keeps doing that, I'm not going to last much longer. With my thumbs, I open her up and run the flat of my tongue up the length of her. Her body shivers above me and she releases a moan. Fuck. I'm definitely not going to last much longer. Before I pull away, I run my tongue up her core a few more times.

"I'm about to blow my load and when I do that, I want to be inside you. Turn around and sit on my dick." She does what I say and sits up and turns around. "Good girl. Now lift your dress so I can watch my dick disappear inside you."

Her fingers grip the hem of her dress and bunches it at her waist, giving me the perfect view. With her other hand, she reaches between us and wraps her fingers around my dick. Slowly, she rubs the head up and down her slit. Once at her entrance, she slides down my length, inch by glorious inch. Her warm heat wrapping around my cock. Sucking me in. She throws her head back, her mouth falling open as I stretch her open and she adjusts to my size. When she's fully seated, she stops, and takes in the pleasure of being full of my cock.

"You feel so fucking good. Like your pussy was made for my dick. It fits so fucking perfect." I buck my hips up. "Now ride me."

With no hesitation, she slides up and back down, taking everything that she wants. Everything that she needs. I may be the one giving orders, but she's the one in control. She bounces on my dick like she's riding a pogo stick. But I can guarantee this is much more fun. Her strides become faster and longer. Her moans mix with my grunts as the van rocks back and forth. Both of us are only a moment away from climaxing.

Tink. Tink. Tink.

We both freeze. My heart jumps to my throat as both of us hold our breaths.

The tapping sounds again, followed by a deep voice. "Hello? Anyone in there?"

She glances down at me, the whites of her eyes are the only thing visible. She scurries off of me, and I fumble to tug my pants back up. Once they're buttoned, I turn to Hollyn with my finger over my lips, signaling for her to be quiet. She nods her head. I peek out the front and through the driver's side window. On the other side is a police officer in a blue uniform. I turn the key to accessory so I can press the button to roll down the window.

"Hi, officer. What can I help you with?" My mouth goes dry as I try to keep my voice as neutral as possible.

"I was driving through and saw some commotion coming from your van and wanted to stop and see what was going on. You got your driver's license and insurance on you?"

"Yeah."

My fingers tremble as I reach for my wallet in my back pocket. I flip open the flap and pull out my driver's license and pass it to the officer. I spare a quick glance at the back of the van and Hollyn is sitting on her knees. Turning back around, I pop open the glove box and pull out the insurance card.

"I took a turn too sharp earlier and some stuff tumbled to the floor. I was working on picking that up. That must have been all the commotion."

From the corner of my eye, I peer back at Hollyn, this time she's covering her mouth to hide her giggle.

"Anyone else in the van with you?"

My head snaps back to the officer. "N-no, sir." A bead of sweat forms on my brow.

"Are you sure?" He bobs and weaves to sneak a glance into the back of the van, but I shift my weight to block his view.

"Yes. Sir. It's just me."

"Alright. I'll be right back with these." The officer holds up my cards and retreats to his squad car.

I twist to see Hollyn in a full-on belly laugh now. "Oh, you think this is funny? I'm lying to an officer, so he doesn't know that I was fucking my girlfriend in a public place. And doing it while my dick is trying to bust out of my pants like the Hulk." This causes her to laugh harder.

The officer returns to the window, startling me. "Everything checks out. But next time, make sure everything is secure in the back."

I glance at her one more time, expecting to find her laughing at me again, but she's not. Instead, she is sitting back on her haunches, knees spread, and running a finger up and down her slit. My gaze drifts up and her eyes are hooded as she nibbles on her bottom lip. Fuck me. Is she trying to get caught? Then I remember getting caught turns her on.

"Here are your cards." The officer draws my attention

back from Hollyn. He passes my cards back to me. "Are you sure everything's okay?"

He peers into the cab again, then his gaze lifts to the rearview mirror. Shit. I don't know if he'll be able to see her, but I don't want to take any chances. I lift my arm to roll my shoulder, purposely bumping my hand on the mirror so it tilts the opposite direction.

"Yeah. Everything is fine. I must have done something to my shoulder moving things. I'll finish up and be on my way." I avoid eye contact with the officer.

"Alright then." He turns to walk away, but then stops and turns back toward me. "Also, sorry to hear about your mom. She was a good woman. She made the best damn cinnamon rolls."

"Thank you." I glance down to read the name on his shirt. "Officer Reynolds. Stop by the bakery and we'll get you one of those cinnamon rolls."

"Will do." With a wave he's strolling back to his car, only this time when he's inside he pops his car into drive. I hold my breath as red taillights exit the park. Once he's out of sight, I roll the window back up and turn to Hollyn, whose legs are still spread open.

"You dirty cupcake vixen." Then I pounce on her.

THE ELEPHANT IN THE VAN

Hollyn

Thirty minutes later and we're finished "reorganizing the back of the van." I lay my head on Van's chest, listening to the thumping of his heart. One of his arms wraps around my waist while his other hand plays with the ends of my hair. With each passing day, Van gets closer to melting the hard candy shell surrounding my heart. He challenges me to try new things, have fun, and be adventurous. That's exactly what has been missing from my life for the past seven years. Who am I kidding? It's been longer than that, I just never realized it.

"You really know how to bring a man to the brink of insanity, don't you? With that little stunt you pulled earlier." His chest rumbles beneath my cheek.

I raise my head and rest my chin on his chest. "I

learned from the best. I recall a certain someone teasing me and not letting me come." I raise an eyebrow.

"The student has become the master. Just so you know, there's a chance Officer Reynolds might have seen you playing with your pussy."

I bury my face in his chest, inhaling his clean, masculine scent. "If he did, I hope he enjoyed the show."

There's a quiet pause. "I don't think I like the idea of some other man seeing you touch yourself."

"So, you think you can put a claim on me?"

"For now, yes." He presses his lips to my forehead.

I contemplate if this is a good time to mention this or if he actually meant it, but I'm dying to know, so I blurt it out. "Since we're on the topic of claiming, earlier you called me your girlfriend. Is that what we are? Boyfriend and girlfriend?"

His hand freezes and I'm worried I've scared him. Maybe he didn't mean it and it slipped out. "I thought it sounded better than 'woman I enjoy giving multiple orgasms to'."

"That's kind of a mouthful, isn't it?" I give him a half-hearted chuckle.

"A little bit. But is that what you want?"

"I don't know. Maybe." I sit up and move to sit alongside him.

Van sits up, so he's facing me. "I don't know how long I'm going to be here. My life is down in the Cities. I have an apartment there."

"And the bakery?" And I point the spotlight on the giant elephant in the room, or van, once again.

"I don't know. Baking's not really my thing." Van shrugs a shoulder.

Our once blissful bubble we were in bursts into a million pieces. Van still doesn't know what he wants to do.

It's like he's stringing me along until he figures it out. My heart sinks into the pit of my stomach. "We better get back to the bakery."

I scurry to find my panties. As I stand hunched over I shove my legs through the holes and pull them up. When they're in place, the dress fabric falls over my thighs and I glide my hands down the skirt of my dress to straighten it.

Van gets up and gets dressed himself. He shimmies his way through the opening and into the driver's seat. I do the same and plop down into the passenger seat. Both of us buckle our seat belts. The twenty-minute drive back to The Sweet Spot is quiet. Nothing but my noisy thoughts running through my head.

When we arrive back, neither of us want to talk about the conversation we just had. I'm guessing because neither of us knows how to navigate this. I need him to keep the bakery, at least until I have enough money to buy it from him, but for him it's a distraction keeping him from his real life. Van's phone buzzes in his pocket. He checks the screen, types out a quick message, and shoves it back in his pocket.

"I'm going to get going. But we'll talk tomorrow, okay?" Van presses a kiss to my cheek and before I can respond, he's out the back door.

I glance around the bakery. Everything is already neat and tidy so, no need to clean. And I don't want to go home and be alone with my thoughts so, I pull out my earbuds, open my phone, and find my baking playlist. The best distraction from myself… baking. Plus, I'll get an early start for tomorrow. I hit play and "American Pie" by Don McLean blasts through the earbuds. Van mentioned his mom's cinnamon rolls earlier. I bet I have everything to make those. I pull out bowls, rifle through the baker's rack to find all the dry ingredients, and then dig in the fridge for the rest.

With everything laid out on the table, I rest my hands on my hips, and a smile tugs at my lips because this is a recipe that I've had memorized since I started here. I get to work on making batch after batch of cinnamon roll dough.

Two hours and four batches of dough later, my head is a little more clear. There is something soothing and relaxing about baking. You stop worrying about everything else because your concentration must be on the baked goods, otherwise you'll miss a step or forget an ingredient. Both of those can be very costly to the final product. But now that I'm done, and everything is cleaned up, all my thoughts flit back to Van. Instead of wondering if he's selling the bakery, I ponder all the possible scenarios for his sudden departure earlier. None of them are looking good.

I WISH I WAS THERE

Van

While I was at the bakery yesterday with Hollyn, I got an email from a construction company that wants to set up an interview. But the kicker is, it's back home in the Cities, not in Harbor Highlands. Now, I need to tell her I'll be gone for a few days for a job interview, which I'm sure won't ease her fears of me selling the bakery. I don't know what else to do.

I pace the kitchen of the bakery, sweat collecting in the palms of my hands. Scenario after scenario of her possible reaction flash through my mind. I would like to think she'd be happy for me, but I might be too optimistic.

The back door opening and closing draws my attention. When I turn around, Hollyn's gorgeous smile lights up the room. Like two opposite sides of a magnet,

I'm instantly pulled toward her. In a few quick strides, I'm in front of her, wrapping my arms around her shoulders and tugging her to my chest.

"Did I tell you how much I hate arguing with you?" I bury my nose into her hair, inhaling her sweet vanilla scent.

"I hate it too." Her grip around me tightens.

"I'm hoping what I'm about to tell you doesn't lead to another argument…" Her body goes stiff in my arms, as if she's bracing for impact. "I got a phone call about a job interview—"

"That's great!" She beams up at me.

"Well, it's not here. It's in the Cities, so I'll be gone for a couple of days."

"Oh." Her face falls. I know she's been hoping, at the very least, if I didn't continue working at the bakery, I could at least find a job around here so I could be around as the owner.

"I'll only be gone for a couple of days." I press my finger under her chin and force her to meet my eyes. "I promise I'll make it up to you."

"It's not that." She pulls away from my grasp.

"You're still worried about if I'm going to sell or not?"

She shrugs her shoulders like it's the only question worth asking.

"Look, I need to figure out what I'm doing. Currently, I'm paying rent for my mom's apartment, and I still have to pay rent at my apartment until I can find a sublet. Something's got to give and soon because I can't keep paying both. There's no reason to get upset when we don't even know what's going to happen yet. Alright?" All I can see is the disappointment swimming in her hazel eyes.

"Yeah. You're right. But I can't keep waiting like this. What am I supposed to do?"

"What am *I* supposed to do?"

There's another question that's been eating away at me that I haven't asked yet, mostly because I'm afraid of her answer. But now is the perfect time.

"Are you sleeping with me so I don't sell the bakery?" As soon as the words come out and I see the expression on her face, I instantly wish I could take it back.

Her stride falters as she takes a step away from me as if my words smacked her across the cheek.

"Wow. Is that how you really feel? I could ask you the same. Are you stringing me along until you leave town with your fat stack of cash?"

"That's absurd. I don't have time for this. I have to go."

"Just leave when things get tough. I've seen that before." She crosses her arms over her chest, but her feet stay firmly planted on the ground.

Needing to get out of here, I stomp past her. I can't give up my entire life for a girl, again. It didn't work the first time so I can't imagine it will be any different the second. But the thing that hurts the most is she didn't deny it.

The entire two hour drive I spent thinking about Hollyn. Maybe I wasn't being fair to her. Everything exploded around us and now we're trying to sort out the pieces. When I arrive in the city, instead of going to my apartment, I send a message to my friend Jason to meet me at a local bar.

There are a dozen or so people gathered at the bar when I arrive, but it's nothing like Porter's. I've been here many times before, yet it lacks comforting familiarity. Within a few seconds, I spot Jason by his unruly blond hair sitting at the bar. I stroll past the tables and pull out the barstool next to him.

"Dude, where have you been? I was ready to call the cops and file a missing person's report." He passes me a pint of beer.

"Generally, you do that within forty-eight hours, not forty-eight days." I take a drink of my beer.

"Shit. Has it been that long?"

"Probably closer to sixty." I shrug.

"Damn. Where did the time go?"

"You got me. Things got a little complicated up in Harbor Highlands."

"Oh shit. Josie again?" He peers over to me.

I bark out a laugh. "No. But I did run into her. So that was great. This is a little more complicated than that."

"Unless it's another girl, I don't think it could get more complicated than Josie." His jaw drops when I don't answer him. "Shit. You always find yourself surrounded by girl drama. Speaking of which, your ex-girlfriend's been looking for you. She said she sent you some messages that went unanswered."

My eyebrows knit together, unsure who he's referring to.

He senses my confusion and says, "Jami."

"Oh. She's not an ex." I shake my head.

"She was only your foreman's daughter who you fucked on his desk?"

"Yeah. Pretty much." My stomach twists into knots. After my time with Hollyn, the way he says that makes me feel like a scumbag. I couldn't imagine doing that to her, yet that's exactly what she's accusing me of. I bring the pint glass of beer to my mouth and take a big gulp.

"Good. So, I hope you don't mind, I offered her my services as a distraction since you weren't around."

His comment catches me off guard, and I choke on my beer. "She's all yours, man."

Jami isn't my cupcake vixen. Hell, she doesn't even compare. Hollyn's grounded and knows what she wants. She knows when to take the reins in any situation and when she wants me to take over. In and out of the bedroom. Every day she surprises me, especially with the dirty talk.

"What's up with your face? You're glowing."

Jason pulls me from my thoughts of Hollyn. "Glowing? What are you talking about?"

"You have that wistful, looking off into the distance look because you're thinking of someone. It's like when chicks get those cartoon hearts in their eyes when they're in love… wait…" Jason leans in and whispers, "Are you in love? Is that the complication?" A few seconds pass and I don't give him a reply. "Holy shit. You're in love.

Is this love? Do I love her? Dammit. I think I love the girl.

"Stop holding out on me. Who is she?"

"Her name is Hollyn. She worked with my mom at the bakery. I met her when I went up there after my mom passed." I decide to keep the stripper part of the story to myself.

"Is she hot?" Jason wiggles his eyebrows.

"She's not hot. She's absolutely breathtakingly beautiful. The type of beauty that lights up any room she enters. For the first time in a long time, a woman has made me feel again. She makes me want to be a better man. Not just for myself, but for her."

"That sounds depressing. Keep that shit away from me."

"But it's not. She sparks new life in me. And every day it gets better and better."

"Hard pass. You keep all that lovey dovey shit to yourself. Why are you in town then if your girl isn't here?"

"I have two job interviews set up for tomorrow."

"Why here? Shouldn't you be doing those in Harbor Highlands? Where your girl is."

"Yeah." Why am I here? I've only been in town for four hours and I've spent every minute thinking about Hollyn. I don't want to be here, yet here I am. Not being near her is a sad and lonely place. "Thanks for meeting up and having a beer. I think I'm going to get home and prepare for those interviews."

"It was good seeing you. Don't be a stranger. Also, for what it's worth, I never saw you look like this when you were with Josie." Jason stands at the same time I do and stretches his hand out. I grip his with mine and give it a shake. We say our goodbyes and then I'm out the door.

Luckily, traffic is light and within twenty minutes, I'm pulling into the parking lot of my apartment complex. When I reach my apartment, I unlock the door and push inside. As soon as the door shuts behind me, I take in the living room. Everything is the way I left it, yet something feels off. All my belongings are here, but I'm the one that doesn't belong anymore.

I toe off my shoes and leave them by the door, ambling into the living room and flopping down on the couch. I pull out my phone and see I have no new messages. I press the button for contacts and scroll to Hollyn's name. My finger hovers over her name for a few beats until I exit out and shove the phone back in my pocket. Even when I was dealing with everything with Josie, I never felt this conflicted. Granted, that situation was more betrayal. And maybe that's why I'm at a crossroads.

Once again, do I give up everything to be with the girl and pray I don't get burned again or sell the bakery and continue living my regular life? I sit in silence. All my thoughts and feelings bull rush me all at once, but there is only one thing that stands out. My head falls to the back of the couch and I close my eyes. The only future I see, the only future that holds any meaning, has Hollyn in it. When I think about it, my regular life is pretty fucking boring. And I don't want boring anymore. I want something thrilling and exciting. Unpredictable.

In the short time I've been with her she's been all that and more. Fuck. I'm falling for her. And it's not just sex, even though that's phenomenal, but I enjoy being around her. Her presence alone, jolts me back to life. She makes me want to be a better man, any way possible. I dig my phone out of my pocket again and pull up Hollyn's number, only this time, I send a message.

VAN

I miss you.

Not waiting for a reply, I rise to my feet and make my way to my bedroom, stripping off my shirt along the way. When I'm inside the room, I tug off my jeans and crawl under the covers. As I lie on my back, staring up at the pitch-black ceiling, my phone buzzes. I jump out of bed and pull it out of my pants pocket and see it's a message from Hollyn.

HOLLYN

I miss you too.

A wide grin takes over my face. With a simple text message, she can light up my day. I've never felt as much happiness as I feel when I'm with her. Instead of continuing with the text conversation, I want to see her face. This time when I pick up the phone, I FaceTime her.

After a few rings, she picks up. Her head rests against the pillow, she isn't smiling but she's still beautiful.

"I'm sorry. I didn't mean what I said. There's a lot going on." My chest tightens as I wait for her response.

She sits up and sags against the pillow. "I'm sorry, too. We're both under a lot of stress and accusations came out. To answer your question. No, I'm not sleeping with you so you keep the bakery."

My shoulders sag in relief. "I don't know why I asked that. It just came out."

"No. It's a completely valid question. Things are complicated. But I like you. I enjoy spending time with you. That's why I'm sleeping with you." Her warm smile lights up the screen.

"I like you too. More than the fat stack of cash."

She softly giggles. "Good to know."

"I wish I could wrap you up and fall asleep with you in my arms right now."

Her eyes soften as she tilts her head. "I love falling asleep in your arms. But it's getting late, and you have your job interviews tomorrow. We'll talk later."

I steal a glance at the clock and she's right. Seven in the morning will come soon enough and I should get some sleep, even though I would much rather stay on FaceTime with her. "Sweet dreams, cupcake."

"Good night."

I set my phone down on the bed next to me and roll to my back. I spend the entire night tossing and turning until eventually falling into a restless sleep.

The next morning, I get ready and head to both interviews. Both had potential, but neither offered what I really wanted. And that was to be in Harbor Highlands. To be with Hollyn. Once I get home, I check the time. It's still early, but maybe she's done at the bakery. I pull out my phone and instead of calling her, I decide to FaceTime again. The phone rings a few times before her face lights up the screen.

"Hey. I wasn't expecting a video call. I'm sure I look like a train wreck." She attempts to finger comb her hair, but the wind continues to blow strands into her face.

"You're as beautiful as ever. Did you leave the bakery?"

"Yeah, I'm walking into my house. How did the job interviews go?"

"They went alright."

Who am I kidding? They went terribly. Perhaps it was my subconscious sabotaging me because the entire time, all I could do was think about Hollyn and how I don't want to lose her. She's the first girl since Josie who's held my attention for more than a night. The first girl I've wanted to move mountains for. Every question they asked me, I gave them some muddled version of skills and work ethic. At the end of the day, I couldn't do it. I wouldn't be happy. So, instead, I made a new plan, but telling her will have to wait until we're in person.

"How was your day?"

"It was good. Oh, I met Officer Reynolds this morning. He popped into the bakery to get that cinnamon roll you promised him. I had to come up with some excuse that you wrote him an IOU or something since you weren't here." She chuckles.

My heart rate spikes. "Were his eyes on you? Like maybe he saw something?"

"No. Not that I could tell."

"Well, you aren't very good at noticing things like that, especially when a guy flirts with you."

"I know when you're flirting with me."

"With you, I make it pretty damn obvious that I'm flirting. Because I know flirting leads to kissing, kissing turns to touching, touching leads to fucking. And I really enjoy doing that last one with you." A tint of pink paints her cheeks and I love that color on her. "God, I wish I was there with you right now."

"Me too. When are you coming back?"

"I need to do a couple of things tonight, so I'll be back tomorrow afternoon."

"I have to spend another night without you?" She pouts.

"I promise I'll make it up to you."

"Hold on a second. I need to change."

"Why don't you prop the phone up? Give me a little strip show."

Her cheeks turn rosy pink again, and fuck, I want to see what else is pink. "You want me to strip? On FaceTime?"

"I do. Thinking about it has my dick hard." I shift the camera down to my crotch to show her the visible outline underneath my slacks. "See how much I want you. Just seeing your smile has me on the cusp of coming."

She nibbles on her bottom lip for a moment, deciding if she wants to go through with it, before propping her phone up on her dresser. She stands in front of her bed, giving me the perfect view from her knees up. Her dainty fingers undo the top button of her chef's coat and slowly she moves down, releasing each button until the sides fall open, exposing her white tank top underneath. She shrugs out of her coat, and it floats to the floor. Her hard nipples poke through the thin fabric.

"If I was there right now, I would run my hands up your stomach, taking your tank top with me—"

"Like this?" She moves her hand up her stomach, exactly like I described.

"That's perfect. I would stop as soon as I got to the top of your tits. I would put a finger into each cup and pull your bra down, exposing your hard perky nipples to the cool air."

Her hands continue to do everything I say. She pulls down her bra and her nipples spring free. She cups each breast, squeezing and massaging them. I reach down and adjust my growing dick in my pants.

"Van, I wish you were here, and these were your hands." With her thumb and forefinger, she pinches her nipples and exhales a moan.

"I wish I was there too, cupcake. But keep going. Pretend your hands are my hands. How much do you ache for me? Is your pussy wet for me? Slide your pants off and tell me how wet you are."

She drags her hand down her torso until she reaches the waistband of her pants. She flicks the button open, and they fall to the floor. Slowly, she slides her hand under the elastic band of her panties. Her hand moves up and down under the fabric.

"Van. I'm so wet for you. My finger is coated."

"Move your panties to the side. Let me see you."

She follows my instructions. Her fingers glide up and down her slick folds glistening with her wetness. I unbutton my pants and pull down the band of my boxer briefs and my cock springs free. A bead of pre-cum sits on the tip. I use it for lubrication as I slowly stroke myself tip to root and back up again.

"Cupcake, you got me so fucking hard."

I point the camera down so she can watch while I stroke myself. Her gaze fixates on the way I pump myself up and down, her own strokes on her pussy increase. I fight the urge to meet her stroke for stroke because I'm not ready for this to end so quickly.

"If I was there, I would get on my knees and hike your leg over my shoulder and bury my face in your pussy. I would open you up and run my tongue up your slit, savoring the taste of your arousal. Suck on your clit and make you moan."

"Oh God, Van. I want that. So bad."

"I would eat you up until your legs tremble and you detonate on my tongue. I would taste your sweet arousal, sucking until I got every last drop."

Her moans and whimpers float through the phone speaker.

"Bring your finger up to your lips, taste yourself."

Again, she does what I say, except she takes it a step further. She brings her finger up to her mouth and instead of sucking on the digit; she paints her wetness across her bottom lip with the pad of her finger. Moisture glistens on her pretty plump lip. When she's finished, her tongue peeks out and licks at the wetness, then she sucks her bottom lip into her mouth.

I groan. Jesus Christ. I'm trying to execute some self control, but with each passing second, it's getting harder and harder. And something else is getting harder and harder. My grip around my cock tightens as I leisurely stroke myself. Her cheeks hollow as she sucks her finger into her mouth. I pinch my eyes shut. Fuuuck. This girl might be the death of me, but I'm not playing around anymore. My lids slowly lift, and I stare into the camera.

"Take your shirt and bra off, then grab the phone and get on the bed."

FACETIME SEXY TIMES

Hollyn

I pull my finger from my mouth with a pop. His demanding voice, deep and gruff, turns me on even more. I know I'm affecting him as much as he's affecting me. Wanting to please him, I do what he says. I grip the hem of my shirt and slowly drag it over my head. After I drop it to the floor, I thrust out my chest as I reach behind, unhooking my bra. One white strap falls down my arm, followed by the other, until my bra flutters next to my coat on the floor. Once I'm naked, I stalk toward the camera. With each footfall as I get closer, I glide my hands up, making sure Van has a good view as I cup each breast. The pads of my fingertips dig into the soft flesh. When I reach my erect nipples, I give them a pinch.

"I wish it were your hands on me right now. Touching,

squeezing, and caressing. I want you licking and sucking each hard nipple into your mouth."

"Fuck, cupcake. I want that too. I'm tempted to get in my car right now, so I can be with you. Just looking at you and how goddamn sexy you are has me rock-hard. Look at what you do to me." He pans the camera down. His hand grips his thick cock as he slowly strokes up and down.

Lifting my phone, I bring the screen closer so I can get a better view. I backstep until my legs hit the side of my bed. While holding my phone with one hand, I use my other to grab a couple of pillows and prop them against the headboard before I crawl on top of the comforter. I never thought watching another person pleasure themselves would be so hot. Everyday, he's teaching me something new about myself, about life. Plain and simple, he's been everything I've been missing. My feelings have never been this intense with anyone else. Sure, we fight but our passion for each other always wins.

"I wish it was your hand wrapped around me. Even better, your pretty, plump lips sucking me down." He thrusts his hips up in motion with his hand. His voice draws my attention and I go back to watching Van while he masturbates. "The tip of my cock hitting the back of your throat, swallowing me whole." His voice is low and hoarse like he's hanging on by a thread.

A bead of pre-cum sits on the tip of his deep red, almost purple tip. Instinctively, I lick my bottom lip, wanting it to be the head of Van's cock. The pad of his thumb brushes over the tip and he smears the moisture down his shaft.

I glide my hand over my collarbone and over my right breast. "Van, I need you so much right now." I arch my back as I cup my breast and pinch my nipple between my thumb and forefinger.

"How bad do you want me?"

"I don't just want you, Van. I need you. I ache for you." I continue to trail my hand down between my breast and over my stomach until I reach the apex of my thighs. Goosebumps pebble all over my heated skin. I pinch my eyes closed, imagining Van's hand roaming my body.

"Let me see how much you need me. How wet is your pussy? Is it dripping for me?"

With hooded eyes, I watch through the small screen as Van continues to pump his cock. His strong fingers grasp the hard flesh as he strokes his fist up and down, growing faster with each stroke. When he comes, I want us to come together.

Once my hand reaches my pelvic bone, I spread my knees, opening up myself to Van. With a finger, I circle my clit before sliding down my slit. My arousal coats my finger as I spread the moisture around.

"Fuck, cupcake. Your pretty, pink pussy is primed for me. Imagine me running my tongue up your pussy, devouring you, savoring your taste. My hand wraps around my fat, throbbing cock. I line up to your hole and thrust inside. With each pump of my hips, I'd kiss you and swallow your moans as I sink deep inside you."

I exhale a moan as I push a finger inside. It's nowhere near the size of Van, but it'll have to do. When I pull out, I add a second finger, stretching me a little more.

"Van." I pant. "I feel you inside me. My fingers are drenched with my arousal for you."

I pull my fingers out, rub my clit, and plunge back in. I repeat this over and over again. My back arches as my orgasm builds. Stars dance behind my eyelids, and I know at any moment I'm going to burst with pleasure. It builds and builds until I've reached the point of no return.

"Oh God, Van. I'm going to come."

"Me too, cupcake. You're gripping my cock so tight right now. I'm thrusting harder. Faster. I'm ready to explode."

My motions mimic his words, thrusting harder and faster.

"I can't hold on any longer. Fuck. I'm coming."

Both of us release at the same time. My entire body ruptures like a volcano. I pinch my eyes shut and call out Van's name as my body rockets to the stars. Each of my extremities tingle with bliss. Slowly, I fall back down to Earth. Sated and satisfied. When I open my eyes and stare at the screen, Van's grip on his cock slows. A splatter of cum covers his stomach.

My chest heaves as I roll over and lie on my side. I prop the phone on the pillow next to me and hold it steady with my hand. "I have to admit that was a first for me."

"I'm inclined to go away more often, so we can do more of that."

"Maybe we can just go to separate rooms. I don't like when you're not here."

"I'll be back tomorrow. What do you have planned for the rest of the day?"

"After that, I might need a nap. Then the girls want to meet for dinner later. What are your plans?"

"I have a few things to take care of around here. I'll let you get to your nap, and I'll see you tomorrow."

"See you tomorrow." I blow a kiss to the camera. We say goodbye one more time before ending the call. I set the phone down next to me, deciding I do need that nap. I reach down and grab the corner of the blanket, tug it over me, and drift off to a relaxing sleep.

Several hours later my eyelids flutter open, the setting sun casting a warm glow in my bedroom. I was having the best dream where I got to watch Van's fingers wrapped around himself, up and down, as he stroked himself to orgasm. I shut my eyes, hoping to continue where I left off, but all I can picture is a black screen. Wait? Was that a dream? I lift the end of the blanket and peek under. Well, shit. Maybe it wasn't.

My phone buzzes next to me on the bed. Butterflies swarm in my belly, hoping it's a message from Van. When I flip the phone over, the butterflies turn to wasps when I see the name.

Josie: I have a huge favor. I need a cake for a birthday party. I'm thinking about three tiers. A coffee layer cake with vanilla espresso buttercream. Oh, and I need it by next weekend. You can do that right?

I slam the phone down. I don't have the energy to answer her right now. Plus, a three-tier cake in a week? Does she think I have nothing else to do except wait for her cake orders? Ugh! I climb out of bed, grab my robe dangling off the back of a chair, shove my arms into the holes, and tie the belt around my waist. I slide my phone into the pocket and descend the stairs. My hand flies to my chest and I cup a breast with my hand. Normally, I'm used to wandering around my house without a bra, but today my boobs are sore and tender to the touch. I lighten my steps in order to prevent any bouncing as I pass through the living room and into the kitchen. When I cross the threshold, my stomach growls on cue as if it knows where I am and demands food. I check the time on the digital clock on the stove. Four-thirty. I'm meeting with the girls in a couple of hours, so a quick snack will tide me over.

After I have some of my favorite BellaVitano black pepper cheese cut into chunks, I toss a handful of crackers on a plate and place the cheese in the middle. I pull out a jar of Kalamata olives, spoon out several, and place them next to the cheese. My mini charcuterie board might be a little more than a snack, but I'm sure I'll enjoy every bite and I might even lick the plate when I'm done.

I plop down on my couch and rest my snack board on my lap. I prop my feet up on the coffee table and turn on the Food Network. I need something to occupy my time for a bit. Because I'm a glutton for punishment I text Josie back letting her know I'll do the cake. It's hard to turn down the money.

I cover my mouth to stifle a yawn. We've been at Porter's for over an hour. I pick a french fry from the basket and dip it in my half mayo and half ketchup mixture and pop it into my mouth. We've talked about everyone else's lives, so it was only a matter of time before I became the topic of conversation.

"What's happening with the bakery?" Charlie asks.

"Nothing new. Everything is still up in the air. He did agree to opening a few days a week to serve our usual customers and I was able to hire back our two part-time employees. One moment it's like we're moving in the right direction, and then we're standing still the next. But right now, he's in the Cities for a couple of job interviews, so, it's not looking good." I lazily swirl a french fry in the dip before tossing it in my mouth.

"He's moving away?" Olivia asks.

"I'm not sure what his plan is. I'm always left with more questions than answers. I hate being in limbo. With my life. With the bakery. Everything. I want to move forward." I sigh.

"Can't he move back to the Cities and you run the place since you practically know how to do everything, anyway? It'll be like he's a silent partner," Parisa says.

"I've mentioned that, but he hates the idea of being two hours away if something were to happen. He doesn't feel comfortable doing it. I can't blame him. I don't think I could do it either."

Another yawn creeps out, and I cover my mouth. I don't know why I'm so tired today. All week it's been like this. I've even gone to bed early and I still can't manage to stay up past 10 p.m.

"Is the weather changing? Or the barometric pressure dropping. All day, my boobs have been so tender." I shimmy in my seat to discreetly adjust myself, but secretly want the fabric to brush against my nipples to release some of the ache.

"Your boobs can sense the weather?" Charlie asks.

"That would be a pretty cool party trick." Olivia cups her breasts and moves them in sync as she talks. "Tomorrow will be mostly cloudy with a chance of rain in the evening."

I lean over the table toward Olivia. "People can see you." A table of twenty somethings next to us quickly turns around, hiding their snickers.

"Wait a second. That's the third time you've yawned and now you're complaining of tender breasts. The last time that happened to me…" Parisa's eyes go wide. She leans in and whispers, "Are you pregnant?"

"Me? What? No. I'm not pregnant." I shake my head because I can't be pregnant.

"When was your last period?" Parisa asks.

"I've had my period." Shit. When was my last period? I glance up at the ceiling as I think back. "I know I got it right after our trip to the Cities. And… I'm sure I've had it since."

"That trip was over two months ago, so there's still a month that's unaccounted for," Olivia says.

"And with all the sex you and Van have been having, I'm surprised you're not double pregnant," Charlie says. Everyone laughs but me. Double pregnant? Is that a thing?

"Have you been using protection?" Olivia swirls her drink with her straw.

"We did our first time together. But after that, no. I'm on birth control. And I know it's not one hundred percent effective, blah blah blah, but I think I have a better chance of getting struck by lightning."

"Well, I think Zeus hit his target." Charlie chuckles.

"You're totally pregnant. I can sense it. It's the twin thing." Parisa points between the two of us.

"No. What you're feeling are *your* pregnancy hormones."

"I didn't want to tell you, but I had a dream you were pregnant. We were pregnant together," Parisa says.

If I am pregnant, it would be a major inconvenience. Not the baby, but the timing. I rack my brain, trying to think when this could have happened, but I'm drawing a blank.

"We need to get to the store!" Parisa hops up as fast as she can with her growing baby bump.

"We have to do this now?" My gaze shifts between my three friends.

In unison, they all reply, "Yes!"

"Oh. Okay." I climb out of my seat. Olivia catches a passing waiter and gives him some cash for our bill, and then we're out the door. All of us pile into Olivia's SUV. Once everyone's inside, she peels out of the parking lot and drives to the nearest drugstore.

As soon as Olivia shifts into park, the three of them throw open their doors and are halfway in the store before I've even got out. A minute later, I'm meeting up with them in aisle D3, each with a box of pregnancy tests in their hands.

"Are all those necessary?"

Parisa glances up from the back of a box she's reading. "Yes. You need more options in case one is faulty."

"I don't think I have enough pee in me for all those." I eye all the boxes they have.

"Well, you better get a bottle of water, too," Charlie says.

We scurry to the front of the store, and everyone unloads their boxes onto the conveyor belt. Charlie finds a standing cooler and grabs a bottle of water and tosses it with the rest of the things.

"Where's your restroom?" Olivia asks the cashier as she shoves her card into the card reader.

"It's located toward the back of the store." She points to a giant restroom sign hanging on the wall.

"Thanks. We don't need a bag." Olivia grabs the boxes and hands them out to everyone as though she were Oprah. You get a pregnancy test and you get a pregnancy test. I wish it were cash because if I am pregnant, I'll need some of that instead.

Before I realize it, the girls are strolling to the back of the store. I pick up my pace to catch up with them. "Wait. What are you guys doing?"

"You have some sticks to pee on." Parisa holds up a box and shakes it.

"Here? Why here?"

"The sooner we find out, the sooner we can celebrate." Olivia holds open the bathroom door and everyone enters, single file, with me following at the end.

"The bathroom at the drugstore?" My nose scrunches. I run my finger down the white painted metal of the stall and inspect the tip. At least, it's fairly clean in here.

"What do you want? Candles and a bubble bath?" Parisa asks.

"That would be nice." I nod.

Parisa tears into the boxes one at a time, pulling out a test from each one.

"Drink this." Charlie shoves the bottle at my chest.

"Then pee on these." She holds out several sticks of various shapes to me.

"If I'm pregnant, I'll have to tell my child I found out about him or her while in a drugstore bathroom."

"There are worse places. Plus, it's not about the place, but that it happened. Now go." Olivia rests her hands on my shoulders, twists me around, and pushes me toward an open stall.

I take a few steps until I'm inside the cramped stall. I rotate to close the door and move the lever to the left, locking it. With my hands full with a bottle of water and several pregnancy tests, I whirl around and wonder how I'm going to do this. I set the bottle of water on the toilet paper dispenser and with my free hand I undo the button of my jeans and shimmy them down my legs. I sit down, the cold seat sending a chill through my body. Or maybe it's because I'm about to find out if I'm pregnant. I shove a stick between my legs, hold it there, and wait.

"What are you doing in there? Why don't I hear pee yet?" Parisa calls out, her words echoing off the tiled walls.

"There's not much room in here and I have a handful of pee sticks and now you're all listening, so it's a lot of pressure."

Someone turns on the sink, who I'm assuming is Olivia, since she asks, "Does that help?"

"No. Not really."

She shuts off the water. A few seconds of silence pass, and then it happens. After I've peed on one stick, I do a juggling act to hold a different one under the stream and by the third I only get a few lingering drops. Somehow, I've managed to hold the sticks in one hand while wiping and pulling up my pants with the other. With these multitasking skills, maybe I can handle having kids.

I step out of the stall and the three girls part like the Red Sea. I set the pregnancy tests on the sink and wash my hands. When I glance up into the mirror, everyone is staring at me, waiting for me to say something. Needing to fill the silence, I ask, "How long do we have to wait?"

Each of them flips a box over and reads the directions. "The one with the blue tip takes two minutes, and a plus sign means you're pregnant," Charlie says.

"The all-white one takes one minute. Two lines for pregnant," Olivia says.

"The pink test takes three minutes, and it will tell you yes or no," Parisa says.

I push off the sink and turn around. My feet carry me to the back wall of the small bathroom and I lean against the cool tile. The tests are still in view, but I'm too far away to read them. I can't watch. My heart pounds so hard, I'm surprised it hasn't busted through my rib cage. I want to know, yet I don't. I slide the palms of my hands on my jeans, needing to do something, but mostly to dry the clamminess. As time passes, seconds feel like minutes and minutes are like hours.

What if I am pregnant? How will I tell Van? Will he be happy? What if after what happened with Josie he doesn't want kids? What if he decides to sell the bakery and leave? I'll be left with no job and a single mother. My pulse races as all these questions flit through my mind. I rest a hand on my belly. Whatever happens, happens for a reason.

"We're here for you. No matter what it says." Parisa wraps her arms around my shoulders.

"For anything." Olivia hugs me on the other side.

Parisa rests her head on my shoulder. "I know this isn't what you had in mind when you said you wanted to move forward."

I drop my head to hers. "Not really. But oddly enough, it beats standing still."

Charlie glances down at the tests and then peers back to meet my eyes. "You have your answer."

My hands fly up to cover my face. "I can't look. Tell me what they say."

Parisa and Olivia move to stand next to Charlie and one by one they each give an answer.

"Plus sign."

"Two lines."

"Yes."

My hands fall to my sides. I'm pregnant. I'm having a baby. I swallow hard. Then the corner of my mouth tips up and I inhale a deep breath. "I'm pregnant."

IS IT MINE?

Van

When I arrive back to Harbor Highlands, my first stop is the bakery because I know that's where Hollyn will be and I need to see her. I pull up to the curb at the building's front. I unlock the door and jog into the kitchen.

All night I thought about her. The two-hour drive back, she was the only thing on my mind. We've both said things we didn't mean, and I know we'll work past everything because deep down I know she's the one I'm supposed to be with.

She's standing at the center worktable, rolling out dough. When my footfalls hit the linoleum floor, she glances up. A sparkle lights up her hazel eyes and her mouth tips up into a smile. I stalk toward her, and she turns to face me. As soon as we're toe to toe, my hands grasp her cheeks and I crash my lips to hers, not wanting to spend another second not touching her. Her hands reach up to my chest and her fingers clench the fabric of my shirt, holding on as if I'm her lifeline. And I want to be that for her. I want to be her everything.

Her eyes are still closed when I pull away. Slowly, they flutter open.

"Hi." Her voice is almost a whisper.

"Hi."

"I won't complain if you greet me like that every day." She brushes the flour handprints from my shirt.

"Done." I wrap one arm around her waist and pull her so she's flush against me. Bending down, I press my lips to hers once more, except this time it's a quick peck. "I have some news for you."

"I have some news for you too, but you go first."

I reach for her hand and intertwine our fingers. "I have a car full of boxes."

Her eyebrows squish together in confusion.

"I packed up my apartment, or most of it. I'm staying in Harbor Highlands. A friend's sister is actually looking for a place, so he sent her a message about subletting my apartment."

"You're staying? You're really staying?" Her face lights up with excitement. She releases my hand and wraps hers around my neck, drawing me in for a hug.

"I am. I don't want to be without you."

"But what about the interviews? What if they call you?" Her eyes search mine as if she's unsure I'm telling her the truth.

"I'm pretty sure they won't be calling me. My heart wasn't in it because all I could think about was you and I couldn't bear being away from you."

A wide smile covers her face. "I'm really glad to hear

that because my news is big. Life changing. And having the extra money from not paying for your old apartment is going to help. A lot."

"What is it?" I can't help but share in her excitement with a smile of my own. Whatever has her this happy will make me happy as well.

"I'm pregnant."

Those two words have haunted me for a long time. Not because of what it entails but because the last time I heard them it was a lie. My mind flashes to when Josie told me she was pregnant. I was ready to take on the responsibility of being a parent and taking care of my family. But then she dropped the bomb that it may not be mine. Without thinking, I word vomit the only thing that comes to mind. "Is it mine?"

Her face falls and her eyes widen. She takes a step back, then another, her arms drop to her sides. "Excuse me?"

I'm pulled back to the present. The shock and hurt on her face is evident. "Fuck. No. I didn't mean that." I reach for her, but she pushes my hand away.

She furrows her brow. "This was supposed to be an exciting moment for us, and you ask if it's yours. Who do you think I am?"

"Based on my past, can you blame me for asking?" I shrug.

"I'm not your past. I'm your present. I'm not your ex. In fact, I'm far from it."

"I'm sorry. You're right." My voice is soft, and I reach for her hand. Reluctantly she allows me to take it and tug her to me. "You're nothing like my ex. And I love you for that." I rest a finger under her chin and force her to meet my eyes. "I love you. You've given me new life, and I never want to let that go. I never want to let *you* go."

For the first time in forever, I say those words. But with her, they were so easy to say. No hesitation. No second guessing. It felt natural, like I've said them a million times to her. Never in my wildest dream did I expect to meet an amazing woman, have the best night of my life with her only for her to pop into my life again. Fate does wonderful and mysterious things.

She stares at the center of my chest before her gaze wanders up, meeting my pleading eyes. "I'll let it slide this time because of your past. But if you value your life, don't ever say that again." A ghost of a smile plays on her lips.

"Being with you, I know I'll never have to." I press my lips to hers. Soft and full of promise.

She pulls away. "I love you. You've helped me experience life again. Experience love again. Even if it's been one crazy rollercoaster ride."

It's been so long since I've heard those three words. I never expected eight letters to hold so much weight, but when they come from Hollyn, they mean everything.

"I'll always be here. So, we have a little cupcake baking in here." I place a hand on her stomach.

"We do. And it's yours." She gives me a wink. "At least, according to the three pregnancy tests I took. I'll go to the doctor to confirm."

"I want to go with you. I want to be involved every step of the way." She nods her head. I rise to my full height and cup her warm cheek. "We're having a baby."

Before she can respond, I kiss her again. After everything that's happened in the past five years, this is a moment I'll never forget. It gives me everything I need to let go of the past and move forward toward the future.

Over the next few hours, I work side by side with Hollyn as we make cookies, cake pops, and cupcakes for the display case. As we pop the lid on the last container holding the cake pops, she exhales a yawn.

"I'm beat." She rests her hips against the table.

I glance around the kitchen. We didn't make too much of a mess. "You go home. I'll finish up here."

"Are you sure? I can stay. Give me a second. I'll get my second wind."

"You go home. Get comfy. Get some rest because I'll be over later to start my groveling." I waggle my eyebrows.

"Don't take too long. I might actually fall asleep."

I press a kiss to her forehead and send her out the door. Working quickly, I wash all the dishes and wipe down all the surfaces. For once, I can see what my future holds, and I couldn't be more excited. But then my excitement bursts as fast as a popped balloon. What's going to happen when Hollyn needs to take time off from the bakery? With a baby on the way, we'll need the money and I can't do this without her.

I shut off all the lights and stroll to the front door. I click off the glowing The Sweet Spot neon sign and exit out onto the sidewalk. After I pull the door shut behind me, an unfamiliar voice catches my attention.

"Excuse me? Are you the owner?" I finish twisting the key, securing the lock, and whirl around. An older gentleman in his mid-fifties, wearing a tie and suit jacket, stands in front of me.

"Yes," I reply.

He holds out his hand. "I'm glad I caught you. I'm Elliot Jasper."

I grip his hand with mine. "Van Bailey."

"Yes, I know who you are. Sorry to hear about your mom passing."

"Thank you."

"But that's not why I stopped by. I overheard Keith

Goldberg mention that you were looking for a buyer for the bakery and I'm very interested." His gaze wanders over the building's façade.

"Oh. I've thought about potentially selling, but I'm not committed to anything yet."

"I assure you, I'm willing to offer you a lot of money." He reaches into his inside jacket pocket and pulls out a business card and a pen. He scribbles on the card and passes it to me.

I glance down and my eyes widen. "That's a lot of zeros."

"My offer won't last long, so don't hesitate. My number is on the other side. Call me when you want to sit down and make it official." Elliot turns on his heel and continues down the sidewalk until he rounds the corner at the end of the block.

I glance down as I flip the card back and forth in my hand. This deal would set us up. Not only would it pay off our debts, but also leave us with plenty left over for the baby.

I leave the bakery and drive the twenty minutes to Hollyn's townhouse. When I arrive, I let myself in using the door code. Quietly, I turn the door handle and creep in, not wanting to disturb her. Sure enough, she's curled up into a ball, softly snoring on the couch. I reach for the blanket folded across the top, drape it over her, and take a seat on the opposite end. I grab the remote and flip through the channels until I find a movie worth watching. An hour into the movie, Hollyn's movements next to me draw my attention.

She stretches her legs, her toes brushing against my thigh. Her head shoots up and she rubs the sleep from her eyes. "When did you get here?"

"About an hour ago." I grab her ankle and place it in my lap as I massage the bottom of her foot.

"Mmm. God, that feels so good. Don't stop."

"Usually when I hear those words, my face is buried between your legs." I press the pad of my thumbs into the ball of her foot.

She exhales another moan. "I fully expect that once you're finished with the foot massage."

"So, after you left the bakery, I did some thinking. What are we going to do when you go on maternity leave, and I'm stuck running the bakery myself?"

"That's like seven months away. We have plenty of time to think of a plan."

"I know. I like to be prepared, so I can take care of you and our little cupcake." I move her feet and set them on the couch. Then I lift the blanket and crawl up her body in the dark. When I reach her belly, I lift the hem of her shirt and place a kiss on her warm skin right below her belly button.

"I know you're probably the size of a pea, but I'm your daddy. I promise I will love you and make sure you want for nothing. And I'll feed you all the cupcakes your mommy makes."

She lifts her end of the blanket and peers under. "That was really sweet. Well, until the cupcake part."

I move up the rest of her body until my head peeks out at the end of the blanket, meeting my gaze with hers. "I thought that was the best part."

She rolls her eyes. "Of course you di—"

Before she can finish, I cut her off with a kiss. My hand roams across her cheek, down to her collarbone, until I reach the swell of her breast. I press kisses along her jawline, and down to the crook of her neck.

"I think it's time to satisfy my sweet tooth."

NOT PART OF THE PLAN

Hollyn

Music blast through my earbuds as I shake my hips to Shakira. Pretty soon I won't be able to so I better enjoy it while I can. I continue to stir the lemon custard I'm making for some lemon vanilla cupcakes. Out of nowhere, Van comes barreling into the bakery. Fear takes over and I do the first thing that comes to mind. I throw my lemon custard spatula at him. Custard flies through the air as the spatula cartwheels toward his head. Luckily, Van has quick reflexes and ducks. The spatula hits a stainless steel refrigerator instead of his face.

Van rises to his full height, his eyes wide as he stares at me and then behind him at the splatter of custard on the door and then back at me.

I pull out my earbuds. "I'm so sorry. You startled me. And it was a natural reaction."

"Perhaps you should stop listening to your earbuds while you work." Van bends down, picks up the spatula, and passes it to me. I grab it and toss it into the sink.

"Or you could maybe knock to announce your presence instead of barreling in here like a teenager at a Taylor Swift concert."

"I'll have you know, it's not only teenagers. Adults can get crazy too."

"How many Taylor Swift concerts have you gone to?" I raise an eyebrow.

"Not the point. But I have some news that will benefit us both and our little cupcake." He clasps my hands in his.

My gaze meets his with curiosity.

"I've found a buyer for the bakery. We can pay off your debt from your ex and still have plenty left over for living expenses and the baby."

"You sold the bakery?" My heart drops and I tug my hands from his. This was the last thing I was expecting him to tell me.

"I did. But it's for us and our new family. I did this for us." There's a pleading tone to his voice.

"But you don't understand. This bakery is all I've ever known. This was a dream. I was to take over the bakery from your mom after she retired and now all of that is gone. My dream is gone. I don't know what I'm supposed to do now!" Speckles of light dance behind my eyelids. I frantically glance around, needing something to focus on.

"Shit. I didn't know. I'm sorry. I didn't know." His voice soft now.

After a long pause, I respond, "Of course you didn't. You were never supposed to be part of the plan." I rest a hand on my stomach. "This baby was never supposed to be part of the plan. Della's passing away was never part of the plan. Every time I'm so close to my dreams, I get thrown back ten feet. Each time, it gets harder and harder to crawl my way to the start again." I fight back the tears, but I've reached my breaking point, and everything collapses. My hands fly to cover my face as a sob shudders through my body.

Van wraps his arms around me and pulls me into the crook of his arm. As much as I'm sad about losing the bakery, I need Van more. I need him like I've ever needed anyone. I press my cheek to his chest.

"I wish I could rewind the past twenty-four hours. I would have never taken the deal. Are you mad at me?"

I sniffle and run my fingers along the underside of my eyes to wipe away the moisture. I exhale a long huff. "No, Van. It's fine. It's your bakery and you have every right to sell it. I just wish… you didn't." He continues to hold me tight, and I let him. Not only for him, but for me.

"This was the best option to make sure you were taken care of."

"Look Van, I admire your incessant need to take care of me, but you don't have to. I'm not some damsel in distress that needs saving."

"You're right. You don't need saving, but that doesn't mean I don't want to take care of you. Take care of our family." Van turns and rests his hands on the worktable and bows his head. "My dad left when I was a kid. Left my mom with nothing. Growing up, I watched my mom struggle. She wanted to give me the world but couldn't afford it. When I found out Josie was pregnant, I needed do everything to make sure they didn't go through what my mom did."

I inch closer. His muscles tense beneath my palm that

rests between his shoulder blades. He tilts his head. "You wanted to give them everything."

He nods but doesn't fully lift his head. "I worked my ass off to make that happen, and then it was all for nothing. Then you told me you're pregnant and all those same emotions smacked me like a tidal wave. Except, this time with a lot more uncertainty, so I did what I thought was right for you and the baby."

"Van, look at me." I grip his shoulders and twist him, forcing him toward me. "You're a good man, Van Bailey. Don't think otherwise. Your mom would be proud of the man you've become. I'm sorry. Everything between us has happened so fast. We haven't had much time to fully get to know each other. But moving forward we need to talk to each other more. Work things out together. As a team. As a family."

Moisture collects in the corner of his eyes, and he nods. I wrap my arms around him, crushing him to my chest. He wraps his arms around my shoulders and holds tight. We stand there for several seconds, wrapped in each other's arms, neither of us saying anything. Letting our touch be the glue that holds us together. I don't know what I've done to deserve such a kind, caring, compassionate man, but I'm never letting him go.

Van pulls away and glances around the kitchen. "We've had some good times in this bakery."

I move to stand next to him and rest my head on his arm. "Some of the best I've ever had. Our little cupcake was conceived right here on this worktable."

I run my hand along the smooth surface. After I had some time to think about it, it hit me. The most probable chance of it happening was after I got sick. I must have thrown up my pill and that disrupted my entire cycle. Since we weren't using any other form of protection, the night after the wedding was the next time we had sex.

"We could reenact that moment. You know, for old time's sake." He winks.

I slap my hand against his chest and release a laugh. "Of course you would say that. Why doesn't that surprise me?"

"Damn. You're on to me. I might have to switch up my tactics to keep you on your toes."

"Oh, believe me, you're still full of surprises." I step away, stop, and whirl around. "By the way, who made you an offer on the bakery?"

"Jasper. Elliot Jasper."

As soon as I hear his name, my heart stops. Once the shock dissipates, all I see is red. "That son of a bitch."

"Who is he? What did he do?" Van's eyebrows knit together.

"He owns a bakery in town. Cake and Crumbs Bakery. He's been after your mom's bakery for as long as I've worked here, probably longer." Van stares at me dumbfounded. "Every time he gave her an offer, Della told him over her dead body. Well, I guess he finally got what he wanted."

Van blows out a breath. "Wow. I got played."

"You could have never known. He's a slime ball. He preys on innocent people and strikes when he sees an opportunity that fits his agenda."

"If I had been around more, maybe I would have known and none of this would have happened."

"It's not your fault. Don't blame yourself." I sigh. "Everything is fine. We'll figure it out." Maybe if I keep repeating it, I'll believe it myself. "I'm exhausted. Can we go home?"

"Sure. Anything you want." Van clasps his hand in mine.

IT'S NEVER FINE

Van

The early morning sun shines through the window, stirring me awake. I roll to my side. Auburn strands of hair contrast against the white pillowcase. It's been two days of wracking my brain, trying to figure out how to make this right. Not for me, but for Hollyn. She says everything is fine, but I know that's far from the truth. Her hazel eyes have lost their sparkle, and it hasn't been there since I told her I sold the bakery. She deserves everything and I want to be the one to give it to her, not take it away. Sitting up, I bend over and brush a strand of hair off her cheek. I press a kiss to her temple. She stirs but doesn't wake.

Slowly, I slide out of bed and grab my jeans. I tug them on and fasten the button. Bending over, I pluck my shirt off the floor and pull it over my head. With one last glance back, I exit her bedroom and head downstairs and out the front door. I need to figure out a way to get the bakery back. On the drive to my apartment, the roads are quiet, but my mind isn't. Once I'm almost to my place, I get an idea. It's crazy and I don't know if it will work, but there's only one way to find out. I step on the gas and get home as soon as possible.

Two hours later, I'm showered and dressed in slacks and a dress shirt. I pull the door open to Cake and Crumbs and sugar and caramel waft into my nose. The dining area is light and airy with white walls and splashes of color splatter the walls, as if someone took a bucket of paint and threw it. The left side is full of bakery cases that wrap around to an L shape with a check out at the end. Small, two person tables fill the rest of the area and right now, most of them are occupied. People mill around as they collect their muffins, pastries, and scones for the morning. I can see why he wants a second location. I move to the end of the line that's ten people deep and wait until I reach the front counter. When it's my turn, I ask to see Mr. Jasper. Another employee sticks their head into the kitchen. A few moments later, Elliot exits.

"Hello Mr. Bailey. What can I do for you?" He brushes his hand on his chef's coat before extending it out.

I grip his and give it a shake. "I was hoping I could have a few minutes to talk to you."

"As you can see, we're a little busy." He turns his attention to the girl behind the counter. "Sara, I told you to fold the corners in first when you wrap the pastries." Sara's cheeks redden with embarrassment from the scolding.

"It will only take a minute, sir. Please."

Annoyed, he glances around before turning back to me with a huff. "Give me a minute." He storms off into the kitchen.

I stand off to the side as I wait. A few seconds later, he steps out of the kitchen and directs me to follow him down a hallway and into an office. He steps to the side to allow me to enter, then shuts the door.

"Have a seat. How are you doing? Enjoying your new found fortune?" He takes a seat and leans back in his leather office chair.

"I wish I could say I was, but unfortunately, I can't. See, Mr. Jasper, I made a big mistake. When I sold the bakery to you, I wasn't in the right headspace. I made the decision while I was in distress. My girlfriend told me she's pregnant and the only solution I could come up with to provide for my family was to sell the bakery." He leans forward, resting his elbows on his desk, and I keep going. "Then I found out the bakery means more to her than either of us could ever know. Unfortunately, I didn't realize it until it was too late. I beg you, please allow me to cancel the sale or buy it back. Whatever I gotta do. I need the bakery. I'll do anything." Silence fills the room, except for the thumping of my heartbeat in my ears.

Elliot leans back in his chair and crosses his arms over his chest. "I admire your determination Mr. Bailey, and your dedication to supporting your family is very admirable. But the deal is done. You've signed on the dotted line."

"There has to be something I can do. This can't be the end all be all."

Leaning forward he rests his elbow on his desk. "I assure you Mr. Bailey, if you attempt to back out of the deal, you'll be hearing from my lawyer and going to court will cost you more money than it's worth. You should consider yourself very lucky. I've paid you twenty percent over market value. Now, take the money and provide for your family." He rises to his feet. His large frame towers over me from the other side of the desk.

I stand, a giant pit sits in the bottom of my gut as I realize this is it. One moment in time can change everything. One wrong move and the carefully crafted foundation you've built comes crashing down. That moment is right now. The bakery and possibly Hollyn are gone.

I tip back the pint glass of beer, taking a giant gulp. When it's empty, I set the glass on the bar top and push it away. The beer does nothing to ease my conscience. My stomach turns each time I picture her expression. The hurt in her eyes. The sadness. And I caused it. All of it.

A moment later, Trey, Bennett, and Seth stroll into Porter's and find my sorry ass sitting at the bar. Bennett and Seth take the empty seats on my right, and Trey takes the seat on the left. As soon as I realized my mistake, I made some phone calls. These guys have become my friends and they've known Hollyn longer than I have, so hopefully they'll know how I can fix this.

The bartender takes their order and sets a new beer in front of me. No one says anything for a few moments until I break the silence. "I fucked up with Hollyn. Like really fucked up. And I don't know how to fix it."

Seth clasps my shoulder. "We've all been there. Bennett unknowingly catfished Charlie on a dating app, but once he found out who she was, he continued with the ruse. I pushed Parisa away and kept her away after accusing her

of making me her dirty little secret. And Trey is just…
Trey."

"Moral of the story. Don't get yourself emotionally involved," Trey deadpans.

Bennett leans in. "Don't listen to him. We're waiting for the day a woman makes him forget his own name. But first we need to know what you did before we can determine if this fuck up will require flowers, chocolate, or jewelry."

"I don't think any of that will fix what I did." I twirl the base of my beer glass on the bar top.

"Oh shit. What did you do? Burn down the bakery?" Trey elbows me, humor in his voice.

I stifle a laugh. "I wish I burned it down. That would have been a lot easier to explain instead of telling Hollyn I sold it."

"Wait? You sold the bakery?" Seth asks.

"I did, and apparently it was to someone who's been after the bakery for several years."

"What did Hollyn say?" Bennett asks.

"Her expression said it all." I take a long drink of my beer, wanting to wash away the disappointment on her face that's imprinted in my mind. If she said she hated me, it would have been easier to process. How do you fix disappointment?

Seth leans in. "But she didn't say anything?"

"She said it was fine. We would figure something out."

"There you go. She said it was fine. What's the big deal?" Trey says.

Bennett and Seth lean against their chairs and glance everywhere but at me. I tip my head to Trey. "What's the big deal? A very scary woman once told me when a girl says 'it's fine' it is, in fact, not fine. It's the opposite of fine. I've now witnessed this firsthand, and it's not fine."

Trey glances past me to Bennett and Seth. Both of them nod their heads vigorously. "This is why I'm never settling down. Shit's way too confusing." He takes a drink of his beer.

"Could you ask for the bakery back? Maybe explain it was a big mistake," Seth asks.

"I tried that. Then he said he would take me to court if I tried to withdraw from the deal."

"Oh shit. This guy means business." Bennett takes a drink of his beer.

"Yeah, so that's out. And I have no plan B." I stare at my half empty glass.

"You know, a property came across my desk today." Trey pulls out his phone and taps a few times on the screen. He slides his phone to me. "It's a small building but in a prime location by the lake. They used it as a seasonal pop-up restaurant for the tourists. With a little remodeling, it could make a great location for cupcakes, especially with the foot traffic."

"I hate to admit this, but Trey might be on to something. You could start anew," Seth says.

Bennett points to Seth. "It could be something you own together."

"The Sweet Spot two point oh," Trey says, excitement in his tone.

I scroll through the photos on Trey's phone. He's right. This place has a lot of potential. And I could see the foot traffic being crazy during the summer. Most of all, there isn't any type of bakery in that area. Gourmet treats on the go. Finally, after days of misery, I'm finally excited about something. And it's an idea that's crazy enough to work.

"Trey, get me an appointment to see that building." I glance between the three guys. "And don't tell Hollyn. I want this to be a surprise. And tell Charlie, Parisa, and Olivia I'll need their help too."

THE SWEET SPOT 2.0

Van

Trey got in touch with the realtor of the small building he showed me and set up a meeting for the following day. The sun peeks over the building rooftops as I stroll down the sidewalk. I glance down at the address, then up to the numbers above the door. My feet come to a halt, 532 Lake Shore Avenue. The building is a sliver of bricks sandwiched between two much larger ones. If someone blinks, they'll miss it. The curb appeal is severely lacking with the overgrown hedges and cracked patio bricks, but looking past that, this place has potential.

"Hi. You must be Van?" A woman in her mid-forties exits the door. She maneuvers her way over the split and missing bricks and holds out her hand for me to shake.

"Yes. And you're Denise?"

"I am. Let me show you inside." Denise strolls to the front door and holds it open as I walk through. She waves her hand in front of her. "I would give you a tour, but this is about it." She lets out a small laugh.

When Trey mentioned it was small, he was talking *small*. The size is shy of one thousand square feet, and it appears to be exactly that small. I glance around the space. It's a little dark with the small windows in the front. There's only about twelve feet between the front door and an old, rickety, wood counter that runs the width of the building. I run my fingers over the rough wood top. Dust covers my fingertips and I wipe it on my jeans. The wood needs a good sanding and a fresh coat of stain and finish. I peer to my left and then the right. The walls could use a fresh coat of paint. I kick my toe at a chip in the black and white checkered tile floor. Denise leads me behind the counter and into the kitchen, if you could call it that. There is a prep table along one wall, an open space for a fridge, but definitely not enough room for a commercial fridge. A flat top grill sits along the far wall with a double oven next to it. The kitchen would need a complete remodel. It would need to be more bakery than restaurant. I take one last glance around. This building needs a lot of work in order to get it into properly working conditions.

Then everything comes to life when I imagine Hollyn in the kitchen, dancing around without a care in the world as she bakes. She'd softly sing as she twirls from one side of the room to the other all while whisking something in a bowl or shaking her hips as she pipes frosting. I know this would be the perfect place for us to start new. Start together.

"So, Van, what do you think?" Denise asks from the doorway.

With one last glance around the old and dilapidated building, I turn toward her. "It's perfect. I'll take it."

When I took on this project, I had no idea what I was actually getting myself into. While I know my way around a tool bench, all of this is over my head. Once I signed the closing documents, I immediately went to work on fixing this place up. I want to get the new bakery running as soon as possible. The hardest part is keeping all of this a secret from Hollyn. Selling the bakery was the worst decision I've ever made, but also the best because now we get to do this together. She's always wanted to have her own bakery. It's been her dream and I want to make her dreams come true.

I dial Bennett's phone number. After a few rings, he picks up. "I need help. All the help. So much help." Desperation laces my tone, and I'm not afraid to admit it.

Shortly after, Bennett strolls into the bakery with Trey and Seth in tow. "I brought reinforcements." Bennett hikes his thumb behind him.

"I had no idea you guys knew anything about construction," I say.

"I'm good with a paint brush." Seth holds up a bag of various paint brushes and rollers.

"I've brought beer and my superior supervisory skills." Trey sets a twelve pack on the counter.

"Honestly, I'll take whatever I can get."

The four of us start with gutting the kitchen. With Bennett's knowledge in woodworking, he's tackled the project of refinishing the wood countertop. With the kitchen cleaned out, Seth started applying a fresh coat of paint in there to avoid the sawdust in the front. Trey is excellent at telling all of us what we should do but also, he has connections and is very good at making phone calls. New appliances will arrive in a week. A contractor will install new flooring later this week. I'll finish the outdoor patio within the next couple of days.

My phone vibrates and I pull it out of my pocket. Hollyn's name flashes on the screen and I press talk.

"Hey cupcake. What's up? Is everything okay?"

"Hi Van. Everything is fine."

A car horn blares in the background.

"What are you doing? Where are you?" Concern laces her voice.

"I'm downtown… wanted to get a bite to eat." I pinch my eyes shut, hoping she takes the lie. All week, I've been avoiding her so I could finish things up at the bakery. I can't keep this up much longer, otherwise she's going to suspect something, if she hasn't already. Plus, I hate being away from her.

"Oh. Okay. I miss you. Maybe we can hang out tonight. Have dinner together?"

My heart sinks. I hate that I'm doing this, but I know she'll love it when she sees it. "I miss you too, cupcake, but I promised Trey I would help him with something tonight. How about tomorrow?" I hate that I'm involving all of Hollyn's friends in this, but I need this to be perfect.

"Okay." I can hear the disappointment in her voice. "Tomorrow. Come over and I'll make us dinner."

"It's a date. I love you."

"I love you too."

The call disconnects and I shove my phone into my

front pocket. I charge toward the bakery and fling open the door. "Trey, if anyone asks, I'm hanging out with you tonight!"

WORSE CASE SCENARIOS

Hollyn

All week, something's been off with Van, but I haven't had too much time to dwell on it, which I'm grateful for. On Monday, Charlie called me and said she needed me to help her with baking cookies. When I asked her what they were for, she said it was National Sugar Cookie Day and wanted to celebrate. I missed being in the kitchen, so I wasn't about to say no to any opportunity to bake. We spent the entire day making enough sugar cookies to feed the entire city. By the time we were done, it was late. I called Van, and he told me to get some rest and he'd talk to me tomorrow.

On Tuesday, Parisa called me for a lunch date and then, when she was done with work, she wanted me to go to her house and help organize the nursery. But mostly we daydreamed about how amazing it's going to be having our kids around the same age and growing up together. Van called to tell me he was pretty tired from packing up The Sweet Spot and he would talk to me tomorrow.

Olivia called me on Wednesday and wanted a girls' night. She invited me over for dinner and we had a Gerard Butler marathon. This time I called Van to tell him I was too tired, and I would talk to him later.

The next day, I spent the morning finishing packing up the bakery with Van. But the tension in the air was thicker than a buttercream frosting. Normally, he's playful and full of banter, but this time, he was all work. The bags under his eyes tell me he's been running on empty. But he hasn't been with me. When I asked him if he wanted to come over that night, he said he was helping Seth pick out patio bricks for The Lilith House. I called Parisa to confirm that's what he was doing.

On Friday, Charlie unexpectedly showed up at my townhouse, wanting me to help her redecorate her home office. She said she wanted my eye for decorating. I told her I was better at decorating cakes than rooms, but she wasn't having it. Several hours of shopping later, I arrived home and crashed. I sent a text message to Van.

Come Saturday, something was off. I called Van, wanting to spend a night with him, and he brushed me off and said we could get together tomorrow. It took everything in me to not break down. Then, I called Parisa and told her to meet me at Porter's. Ten minutes later she strolls in with Charlie and Olivia on her heels. A girl's night is exactly what I need.

"I'm so happy you guys are here." I stand and give them each a hug.

Parisa takes the seat next to me as Charlie and Olivia sit across from us.

"So, what's going on? What's with the emergency meeting?" Parisa asks.

"It's Van. He's been acting weird all week." I take a sip of my virgin margarita. I choke back a gag as I swallow the overly sweet yet tart yellow drink. "And this is disgusting. Virgin margaritas shouldn't be a thing."

"You need to try a pineapple and ginger punch. It's so good and refreshing." Parisa waves down a waitress and orders us a round of non-alcoholic drinks while the other two lucky bitches get alcohol.

"So, what's going on with Van?" Olivia asks.

"I don't know. Something's wrong. He hasn't been himself lately. No playful banter. No trying to lick my frosting."

Charlie leans forward and whispers, "The last part… do we want to know?"

"Use your imagination."

"Nevermind, I'd rather not." Charlie laughs.

Olivia glances between Charlie and Parisa and shifts in her seat. "What do you think is going on?"

"I have no idea." I throw my hands in the air. "Things have been different ever since he sold the bakery. We've talked about it, and everything will be fine. We'll figure something out. I can find a new job. I've already talked to a few places in town, including a restaurant about doing their dessert menu."

"Is that what you really want to do?" Olivia asks.

"I don't know what else to do. I need a job. I can't depend on Van. He's already paid off the debt from my ex, even though I told him he didn't have to. But he insisted." I shrug. "But there's something else that's been eating away at me."

"What's that?" Charlie asks.

"I hate to even put this out in the universe, but how

much do I really know about Van?" All three of them stare at me, waiting for an answer. I exhale a deep breath. "What if he's seeing someone else?"

"He wouldn't do that. Would he?" Olivia asks.

Parisa leans toward me and rests a hand on mine. "That's not possible. He adores you."

"Thanks. I hate even thinking it, but every time I try to make plans with him, he's either too busy or too tired. I don't know anymore. Every time I think my life is moving in the right direction, I get smacked in the face. As if the universe is telling me I can't be happy." I play with the cocktail napkin in front of me, tearing off little pieces and scattering them on the table.

"Well, if he's doing anything of the such, he'll have to answer to us." Olivia slams her palms on the table.

"All of us," Parisa adds.

"He said he'll come over tomorrow for dinner, so I'll talk to him then. It's probably pregnancy brain getting to me, making me delusional." I redirect the conversation to anything but myself. I'm emotionally and physically exhausted from thinking about it. While everyone shares what they've been up to, I can't help that all my thoughts continue to revert to Van.

Opening the oven door, I pull the chicken out and set the dish on the stovetop. I finished mashing the potatoes while stirring the honey glazed carrots. I don't know why, but I imagine this is my last meal before my execution. Maybe not my execution since that's harsh, but at the very least, my last meal before my life changes forever.

As I finish scooping the potatoes into a serving dish, a creak from the front door catches my attention. I peer around the corner and Van trudges through the door. His hair is disheveled, and his clothes are worn and wrinkled like he's been wearing the same outfit for the past week. He toes off his shoes. When he enters the living room, our eyes meet. The corner of his lips tip up into a smile. I can't help but give him one of my own. He stalks my way and wraps his arms around me, hugging me to his chest. I glance up and he bends down. I think he's about to kiss me. A kiss I've craved all week. Then his lips press to my forehead. My heart falls to the floor. Now, I'm waiting for him to stomp on it and walk out. Instead, he leans over to the stove.

"It smells delicious. I'm starving."

"It'll be finished in a couple more minutes. Why don't you sit on the couch, and I'll let you know when it's done." He kisses my forehead again and strolls into the living room.

Ten minutes later, I've finished setting the table. I call out to Van, but I don't get a response. So, I call out again. Silence. I round the corner from the kitchen to the living room and Van is sitting on the couch, his head bowed, as he softly snores. I lean against the door jamb, rest my head on the wood, and sigh. So much for spending time together.

THE EDMOND FIZZGERALD

Van

A pain shoots up my neck as I stir awake. I lift my hand and rub the sore spot at the back of my neck and cringe. My heavy eyelids lift open. It takes a moment for my sight to adjust to the darkness, but when everything comes into focus, I remember I'm at Hollyn's. Her living room, to be exact. I toss the buffalo plaid blanket off me and rise to my feet. Dammit. We were supposed to have dinner last night and instead I fell asleep on her couch. I'm surprised she didn't throw me out onto the sidewalk. If I were her, I would have. I pray all of this is not for nothing.

I climb the stairs to the second floor two at a time. When I reach her bedroom door, I stop shy of entering. She's curled up on her side, sleeping peacefully. Her hair is a wild mess, and she's never looked more beautiful. With soft footsteps, I walk to the side of the bed. I bend down and kiss her cheek. She stirs awake and her eyes flutter open.

"Hey. Sorry about dinner last night. I have to get going, but I'll call you later. Okay?"

She purses her lips and nods. I brush a strand of hair from her face and press my lips to her forehead. I rise to my full height and exit the bedroom, but what I really want to do is crawl into bed with Hollyn, wrap my arms around her, bury my nose in her hair, and never let her go.

Once I'm at the new bakery, I race around the room, wiping down the already clean surfaces. I straighten already straight pictures hanging on the walls. Using a rag, I wipe down the glass to remove any smudges.

"If you keep rubbing, you're going to rub a hole right through the glass." Bennett rounds the corner from the kitchen.

I drop my hand. "I want this to be perfect. She deserves perfect."

Bennett clasps my shoulder. "Trust me, she's going to love it. If not, you'll look adorable in that pink apron baking cupcakes."

I give him a half smile. Lifting my wrist, I check the time. Parisa, Charlie, and Olivia should arrive at the end of the block with Hollyn in ten minutes. "Alright. Remember the plan? Shut the lights off and when I come in with Hollyn, we'll surprise her."

"Got it. We've gone over it a hundred times. I have Charlie on standby to text in case something goes awry. You have nothing to worry about," Bennett says.

"Worry about what?" Trey exits the kitchen with a

cupcake in hand. He removes the bottom half of the cake and plops it on top of the frosting like a sandwich and shoves half of it into his mouth.

Bennett slaps his hand away and Trey does a juggling act, catching half the cupcake with both hands before it hits the floor. "Hey, that was uncalled for. Now I have frosting all over my hands."

"Those aren't for you," Bennett scolds.

"We've been here all day, and I'm famished," Trey whines, shoving the other half of his cupcake in his mouth before finding a napkin to clean his hands.

"We've been here an hour, and you took down a hamburger two hours ago," Bennett says.

"That's not the point. Besides, I'm a growing boy." Trey rubs his stomach.

Bennett shakes his head. His phone chimes from his pocket and he pulls it out to read the message. His gaze meets mine with a smile on his face. "It's showtime."

I stop pacing. This is the moment I've been waiting for. All the late nights sneaking around while Hollyn was at home. If this entire plan is an epic fail, then this baker goes down with his bakery. My stomach quivers. What if she hates it? What if she decides she can't do this anymore because I sold her dream? What if she leaves me?

"Van. You gotta go." Bennett gives me a shake.

Breaking me from the doubt currently running through my head, I nod and bolt out the door. My legs propel me down the sidewalk as I pass groups of tourists window shopping. Ahead of me I spot all of them and then my girl. Once I get closer, I slow my stride. My chest heaves as I try to catch my breath. Parisa spots me first. A huge smile covers her face. One by one, all the girls turn toward me.

Hollyn is the last to turn, her brows furrowed. "Van, what are you doing here?"

I step in front of her so my toes are touching hers. "Waiting for you."

"We'll let you two talk," Parisa says as she rounds up the other girls and they all stroll down the sidewalk toward the alley.

"What's going on?" Hollyn's eyebrows knit together.

"Walk with me." I hold out my hand. She peers down at my open palm before placing her much smaller hand in mine. Walking hand in hand, we move down the sidewalk toward the bakery. I blow out a breath, needing a moment to find the right words. But I realize there will never be the perfect words. All I can do is give her my best and pray it's enough for her.

"I'm sorry."

"For what?" She glances up at me. The green and gold in her irises swirl in the sunlight.

"Everything. Throwing your life into a tailspin. Derailing all your plans. Selling the bakery and essentially killing your dream." I peer down at my feet and kick a lone pebble on the sidewalk.

"Van." Hollyn stops and tugs me into a small, empty patio between buildings. "You've done none of that. Yes, things went a little unexpected, but that's life. You don't walk away when it gets tough, you work through it. Together. I'll admit I was upset when you sold the bakery, especially not talking with me beforehand, but I understand why you did it. The thing about dreams is they can come true, they might not, or sometimes those dreams change." She pauses for a moment to collect her thoughts. "I thought my happily ever after was the bakery, but now, it's you. You're my happily ever after."

I bring her hand up to my chest, holding her close. "I want nothing more than to be that and everything. In my head, it was the right thing to do. After the fact, I realized how big of a mistake it was. I met with Elliot to try and cancel the deal or buy it back…"

She looks up to me, eyes wide as her body goes still in anticipation.

"But he didn't budge."

Her face falls.

"That brings me to my next thing. I hope you still have dreams to own a bakery because I did a thing." I step to the side and wave my hand over the empty patio with freshly laid bricks and a single red door framed by two bay windows.

Hollyn eyes the patio, then cuts back to me. "What is this?"

"This is your new bakery." I bite back the smile that fights to take over my face. Unease settles in my stomach, and I'm not sure what her reaction will be. Everything was done without her knowing, and this could be something she doesn't want anymore.

"You bought me a bakery?" Her tone is flat and her face void of any expression.

Maybe after all her talk of dreams and happily ever afters, she's given up on the idea. The pit in my stomach turns into a black hole. "I did."

"I don't know what to say." She does a three-sixty, taking in everything around her.

"Please say you like it, and I didn't make a huge mistake. Again." My heart pounds in my chest, waiting for her to answer.

Hollyn takes a few steps and meets my gaze, her eyes shine bright as she rests a hand on her breastbone. "I love it. You bought me a bakery…" Her voice is so soft I barely hear the words tumble from her mouth.

I close the distance between us and grip her hands in mine. "I know it's small. It still needs some work and I know it's not in the best location to run a full-size bakery—"

"Van, it's perfect." Moisture wells in her eyes.

With my thumbs, I brush away the wetness. "I take it those are happy tears."

"The happiest. You bought me a bakery!" Her face lights up.

Her hand trembles as I clasp mine around hers. "Let me show you around." I take a few steps forward and Hollyn follows. "This is the patio. There isn't much room for seating inside so I figured during the spring through fall we could set up some tables. There's enough room for two four person tables and four two person ones." I point out potential spots. "This is a prime location for tourists during the summer. We could even set up dog stations and cater to those who travel with their pets."

"We could make dog friendly cupcakes." She claps her hands. The excitement in her voice prominent. Hollyn glances around, visualizing everything I'm explaining. Her foot smooths over the freshly laid cobblestone. "Is this new? It's gorgeous. I love the vintage look it creates."

"It is. One of the many things I was working on all week."

"You did this yourself? Is that why you've either been tired or gone all week?"

I nod. "I was in a rush to finish so I could show you."

"This is just… wow. I'm speechless."

"Let's continue with the tour. I have lots to show you." A full grin covers her face. "Then I was thinking we could have an awning over the door with the bakery name over the top." I wave my hand in front of us. "I wanted to wait for you before giving her a name."

"I don't know what to say, Van. This is all so unexpected. I love it. All of it."

"Wait. Now there's the inside." When we're at the front door, I twist the handle and hold it open as she walks through. The lights flicker to life, and everyone jumps up from behind the front counter with a collective "SURPRISE!"

Hollyn's hands fly up to cover her mouth, her eyes go as wide as cake pans. Tears roll down her cheeks this time.

"You guys were in on this?" Everyone steps out from behind the counter and all the girls surround Hollyn in a group hug.

"I'm surprised you didn't catch on after we hounded you all week, trying to keep you occupied," Olivia says with a laugh.

"It never even crossed my mind. I must have been thinking about so many other things I didn't make the connection." Hollyn wipes away the wetness under her eyes. Then she turns to me. "I still can't believe you did all this."

"Well, let me finish giving you the tour. There will be display cases over here." I point to an empty spot to the left of the counter. "Parisa gave me a bunch of framed photos of Harbor Highlands to hang on the walls. Above us hangs a chalkboard to post pastries and prices."

She glances up. The Sweet Spot logo is drawn in chalk at the top of the board. She then reads what I've already written below. "Sea Smoke and Caramel Cupcake. The Edmond FIZZgerald Cupcake, North S'more Cupcake, Wafers of Lake Superior, and Ganasheen Cupcake." She turns to me. "Did you come up with these?"

"I did. And let me tell you, it's a lot harder than it looks."

Trey leans forward and interrupts. "I tried to help, but they shot down every single one of my ideas."

"No one would want to eat something named Split

Cock Lighthouse. Plus, children would see these, and it sounds like the name of a porn," I deadpan.

"That's why there would be a super-secret adult menu. Like those menus at fast food restaurants that you only find out exist because of the internet." Everyone stares at Trey with blank expressions on their faces. "Fine, that's the last time I offer any suggestions." He throws his hands in the air and sulks off to the other side of the room.

"Anyway. The Sea Smoke and Caramel is a smoked sea salt and caramel frosting on a chocolate cake. My favorite, The Edmond FIZZgerald is a vanilla cake with a vanilla frosting sprinkled with pop rocks. The North S'more, that one is self-explanatory, Wafers of Lake Superior is a lemon and blueberry cake with blue frosting and a wafer on top, and then the Ganasheen has a layer chocolate ganache with a peanut butter frosting on a chocolate cake."

Tears well in Hollyn's eyes. "You remembered my wafer cupcake idea." Her gaze darts from the board and then to me. "I'm at a loss for words. I'm so impressed that you went through all this work. And the cupcake names... they are absolutely amazing, and the tourists will love them."

"We can always change The Sweet Spot name too, if you want."

"No. I would love to keep it for your mom. Maybe we can hang her neon sign in the window?" She clasps her hands together.

"Of course, she would love that. But wait, there's more." I jog into the kitchen and return with a tray overflowing with cupcakes. "It took me a couple of tries, but I believe these turned out pretty good. Edible at least."

Hollyn plucks an Edmond FIZZgerald cupcake off the tray. She lifts it up to eye level to inspect it closer. Her fingers squeeze the cake to check its density. "It's nice and springy."

Next, she takes a big whiff of the frosting. All eyes are on Hollyn in anticipation. She peels down the paper liner and takes a giant bite. Her eyes close and her head falls back as she chews. I shift my weight from foot to foot, waiting for her response. She didn't immediately spit it out, so that must be a good sign. Once she's done chewing and swallows, her eyes flutter open and meet mine.

A wide grin takes over her face. "That was one of the best cupcakes I've ever tasted. The popping candy adds a fun surprise when you bite into it."

I mentally give myself a fist pump.

"You made these all by yourself?" She picks at the left-over crumbs in the wrapper and pops them in her mouth.

I nod vigorously.

"Van, I'm so proud of you. These are so amazing. I don't think I could have done any better." Hollyn grabs the tray of cupcakes and passes them out to everyone.

Trey waves his hand, passing on a cupcake. "I ate two earlier."

The room fills with "mmm" and "this is so good" as everyone dives into their cupcakes.

Hollyn moves to stand next to me, wraps an arm around my waist, and rests her head on my chest. "I don't know what to say. All of this is so incredible."

"This isn't everything. I have one more surprise for you." I grab her hand and lead her through the kitchen, where I give her a brief tour before I stop at the backdoor. "Close your eyes."

Her eyes meet mine before her lashes flutter to her cheeks. I step behind her and open the door with one hand and guide her through the doorway until we're standing in a small parking lot next to the alleyway.

Once I get her positioned exactly how I want her, I bend down and whisper in her ear. "Open your eyes."

A small gasp escapes her mouth. One of her hands fly to her parted lips. She takes a second to take in everything in front of her before turning toward me, her eyes bright with excitement. "Is this what I think it is?"

With a wide grin, I nod my head. "The Sweet Spot is hitting the road."

She releases a tiny squeal before racing toward the truck. Her hand runs along the chipped, white metal.

"We'll need to give her a paint job, and add The Sweet Spot logo to the side, but I had a mechanic check the engine, and everything is in perfect working order."

Hollyn whirls around and jumps into my arms. Luckily, with my quick reflexes, I'm able to wrap my arms under her so she doesn't hit the ground. Her gentle hands cup my cheeks as she presses her lips to mine. Soft and warm. I've been craving this all week, and the sacrifice has finally paid off.

She pulls away slightly but keeps her hands on my face. "I love it. Everything. But mostly, I love you. You've changed my life in more ways than one. You've made me live again."

"I love you too. More than anything. And we're starting a family together."

"Our own little cupcake." She kisses me again. "You've done so much for me, the bakery, the food truck… I don't know how I can ever repay you."

"All I want is to make you happy."

Her hands cup my cheeks. "You're my happily ever after. Not a job, not a ring on my finger. You and only you."

"You're my everything." I press my lips to hers. "One more thing. I think it's only fitting this ends how it began."

She pulls back, eyeing me suspiciously. I pull out my phone and press a few buttons, then the opening notes of "It's Gonna Be Me" play through the speakers. A sweet laugh tumbles from her lips as the song continues to play.

I drop a foot back and then another until I have a little room between us. In sync with the song, I roll my hips and lift the hem of my shirt exposing my abs.

A smile as bright as the sun covers her face. "You are not stripping to NSYNC. In the alley. Where other people can see you."

"Oh. But I am. And I'm going to look good doing it." On the last note of the chorus, I thrust my hips.

"Okay! Okay! Stop." Her laughter is uncontrollable. She reaches forward and tugs on my wrists, pulling me to her so she can wrap her arms around my waist. "How about you finish the dance at home where only I can watch."

"You don't want anyone to see this sexy body and my hot dance moves."

"Something like that."

Before I can say anything, she rises up to her tip toes and kisses me. So sweet and tender. I snake a hand up her spine so I can hold her to me and never let her go.

ONE YEAR LATER

Hollyn

"Oh, how cute. Look. A food truck."

I scrunch my nose and squeeze my eyes shut. Even though it's been over a year since I've seen her last, that voice will always haunt me. I whirl around and plaster on the fakest smile I can muster. "Hi Krystin."

"Oh my God, Hollyn! I did not know you ran a… food truck. Josie, come here." Krystin's nose crinkles as she glances from the front of the truck to the back. Josie saunters up next to Krystin.

I roll my eyes. "I'm surprised The Sweet Spot logo didn't give it away."

"I didn't even notice. But since you're here and seeing that you're not busy. I could use your help. I need cupcakes. About four dozen. I placed an order with Cake and Crumbs and they messed up the order twice and I can't deal with them anymore. You should be able to get them done by next weekend, yes?" Krystin asks.

"Unfortunately, I don't think I'll have time." Busy or not, I don't want to take another order from her.

"The food truck business can't be *that* great. I'll pay you double."

A part of me takes great satisfaction from the desperation in Krystin's voice. Of course, I could get it done and the extra money would be nice, but it's not worth the hassle.

Van strolls up next to her with baby Della strapped to his front and boxes of cupcakes in his hand. As soon as we found out we were having a girl, there wasn't even a discussion. We wanted to name her Della, after Van's mom.

"Actually, the food truck business is amazing. Who knew that Harbor Highlands would need a cupcake truck?" Van sets the boxes on the counter. "I have more in the car."

I turn to Molly, our newest employee, and ask her to grab the rest of the cupcakes. She eyes all four of us, a small smile forming on her lips before she strolls off to get the cupcakes. I know she'll be asking what all of this was about later.

Josie does a double take between Van, baby Della, and me. Then she repeats the process. I step out of the truck and greet Van. He wraps an arm around me. I stretch up on my tippy toes and press my lips to his. I grab Della from Van and pepper kisses all over her face. Her little giggles and coos make me kiss her more.

"I didn't know you two were still together. And you have a baby," Josie says with disdain in her voice.

As I turn to her with Della in my arms, both Josie and

Krystin glance down to see if there's a ring on my left finger. Van sees it too. But their whispered words and judgmental glances no longer bother me. I'm happy exactly where my life is. "We are and we do. And our lives couldn't be any better."

"And I know for a fact this one is mine." Van wraps his arm around my shoulder and tugs me to him. I rest my head on his chest. Josie flinches from his words.

"Also, about those cupcakes, we're really busy here and won't be able to do the order." I tilt my head and give her a fake smile.

Molly returns with the rest of the cupcakes and refills our stock. The earlier rush cleared the truck. I had to call Van to deliver more, so we would be prepared for the second rush.

Olivia and Trey stroll out of The Blue Stone Group building and come up to the truck's window. "We needed to get out here before you guys run out of cupcakes again," Olivia says.

Josie and Krystin step to the side. Olivia side eyes them before turning her attention to the window. "Give me two of those new strawberry lemonade cupcakes. Those are so drool worthy." Molly grabs Olivia's cupcakes and takes Trey's order before bagging up their cupcakes.

Olivia pulls a cupcake from the bag, unable to wait, and takes a bite. "Mmm. This is delicious. It's like an orgasm in my mouth." Trey raises an eyebrow and flashes her his panty dropping, flirtatious smile. "Don't look at me like that. Try this." She shoves the other half of her cupcake into his mouth.

He chews and swallows. "That's pretty good. Probably a close second to the orgasm you were talking about." Olivia playfully slaps his chest.

Van leans toward me and whispers from the corner of his mouth. "What's with those two? Are they together?"

I shrug. "No one knows. They're like one of the world's biggest mysteries. Kinda like does Big Foot exist? Olivia says Trey's like her best friend. But if you ask me, more is brewing there."

"I've never licked the frosting off my best friend's fingers." Van laughs.

Sure enough, Olivia peeks her tongue out, licking the lemonade frosting off Trey's fingers. A couple walking past stops at the cupcake menu and then sidle up to the order window.

"Looks like we got here right on time," Olivia says as she points down the street.

A small group of people exit one of the office buildings and get in line. Slowly, more and more people shuffle out and make their way to the truck. Random people strolling down the sidewalk notice the crowd forming and stop to see what's happening. Eventually they get in line themselves.

"It was great talking to you, but as you can see, we're a little busy here." Van waves to Josie and Krystin before turning his attention to the customers.

Both of them turn on their heels and sashay down the sidewalk. I hold Della as Van and Molly handle all the customers. Once the line dies down, we're left with only a couple dozen cupcakes. Molly takes over helping any new customers as Van steps outside the truck.

I turn to Van, unable to fight my grin. "It was kind of great to tell them no. And you had impeccable timing."

"Everything was impeccable timing, especially the crowd of people. Hopefully, we won't be hearing from them for a long time."

"I'm okay with never." I press my lips to Van's again,

but I pull away, keeping the kiss chaste since we're in public and I'm holding baby Della. "Parisa said she'd watch Della anytime. I could call her, and we could have a night to ourselves."

"I like where your head is at. I believe we've never properly christened the cupcake truck." His lips press to my cheek and slowly, he kisses all the way up my jaw until he's reached the shell of my ear. "I could spread you wide while you're bent over, hands splayed out over the counter. I would lap at your pussy until you explode all over my tongue. Then and only then would I know you'd be primed to be stuffed full of my rock-hard dick."

I exhale a low moan and rub my thighs together.

Twisting my head slightly, my voice low and soft I say, "I'm soaking wet just thinking about it. I'll make the call."

All he does is flash me his wide, dimpled grin and I know he's game.

Thank you for reading Flirting with the Stranger! Want more Van and Hollyn? Claim your copy of their fun and steamy bonus scene when you join my newsletter!

Olivia finds love in the most unexpected place. But how does she navigate the grumpy, tattooed bad boy, especially after she find out he's her best friends brother?

Continue reading for an excerpt of the next standalone book in the Harbor Highlands series, Flirting with the Bad Boy.

"Kiss me."

Did I hear her correctly?

Slowly, I turn my head toward her. I'm greeted with topaz blue eyes. Even in the dim lighting, they sparkle. Her voice is sugary sweet, just as I suspected. I don't do sugary. Or sweet. "Did you just ask me to kiss you?" I tip up an eyebrow at her, wanting confirmation that I heard her correctly.

"Yes. I need to know if I'm broken."

Again, I give her another questioning eyebrow.

She sits up straighter on her stool. "Have you ever kissed someone and there was no spark?"

"Uh. No."

"Of course, you haven't." Her shoulders deflate. "You're a guy. Guys care about one thing..." She glances down at my denim covered crotch, but the way her eyes linger doesn't go unnoticed.

"I could say the same thing about you." I peer down at my crotch, then meet her eyes. She says nothing, just lifts her beer and takes a sip. I wasn't expecting her to give up so fast. I figured it would take a little more than her getting caught red-handed checking me out to get her to keep quiet. Grabbing my beer, I take a celebratory gulp.

She places her beer on the bar, then swivels her stool so she's fully facing me. "I just need you to kiss me."

I choke on my beer as I fight not to spray it all over the bar top. As soon as I finish coughing, I turn to her. She's not going to give up.

She inches closer to the edge of her seat. Her knees almost touching my thigh. "Kiss me. I need to know that whatever I'm feeling is just a rut, and I'm not broken."

"Where I come from, we don't ask. If we want to kiss someone, we just do it."

She gives me an exasperated sigh. "I don't go around just kissing random strangers."

"And this is... what?"

"This is an experiment. So don't worry about that." She waves me off.

I bark out a laugh. For the second time in our brief conversation, she made me laugh. It's a foreign sound as of late. What is she doing to me? I shake it off. "So, now you're just using me?"

Her lips tip up into a smile. "For experimental purposes. You're not really my type."

I scoff. But truth be told, I'm hypnotized by her plump cherry red lips and curious how they would feel pressed against mine. "Wow. An insult on top of using me. How could anyone turn down your offer? I'll let you in on a little secret." I lean toward her so my face is inches from her cheek. She smells sweet and rich, like jasmine. I regain my train of thought and whisper, "You're not really my type either, duchess." I pull away while keeping my eyes trained on hers, wanting to catch her reaction. Her breath hitches. Then she squares her shoulders as she composes herself.

"My name's not duchess. It's Oli—"

"Don't care." I take a drink of my beer.

"Well, there's no reason to be rude about it. All I want is one simple little favor." She pinches her fingers centimeters apart in front of her. "Just a kiss. It's not like I was asking you to father my children. Also, just so we're clear, I wouldn't want that," she glances down at my crotch again, "anywhere near me."

Now it's my turn to scoff. "I guarantee you'll be thinking about this later tonight." I nod toward my lap. "You'll be squirming on top of your expensive as hell silk sheets wishing I was there to take away the ache between your legs."

Her nostrils flare as she narrows her eyes. "How dare you make assumptions about me? You know nothing about me. Hell, you don't even want to know my name. You just think you're some big gruff guy, with a sexy bad boy vibe, and all the women will just flock to you like a seagull to a french fry. Well, guess what? That's all you are. A seagull."

"Did you just compare me to a bird?" I raise an eyebrow.

Without missing a beat, she replies, "I did. Because you're annoying with a cocky attitude."

"You're the one who sat down next to me and rambled on about kissing me."

"Clearly, it was a big mistake. The last thing I would

want is a limp kiss from you. And I'm sure something else would hold the same limpness." Her eyebrows raise as she nods to my crotch again.

"You're on a roll. Now you challenge my manhood?"

She shrugs a shoulder. "I call it like I see it."

I lean in, my voice low. "Well duchess, I guarantee you I'd have you moaning my name in under five seconds. But I'd hate to dirty up your perfect good girl persona."

"Good thing we're not on a first name basis so I can't moan anything. And once again my name isn't duchess. What is it with guys and pet names? Is it so you can call all the girls the same name, so you never have to remember their real—"

Done with this conversation, I'll give her what she wants and grease covered hands be damned. I wrap one hand around the nape of her neck and haul her to me. Her eyebrows shoot to her hairline in surprise, and I slam my lips to hers.

To continue reading, get your copy of Flirting with the Bad Boy!

If you enjoyed *Flirting with the Stranger*, I would love it if you let your friends know so they can also experience Van and Hollyn's cupcake and stripping adventures as they find their happily ever after. Please feel free to leave a review on the retailers, Goodreads, or BookBub. Reviews help other readers discover my books.

You can stay up-to-date on upcoming releases and sales by joining my reader group or following me on social media.
Gia Stevens' Sassy Romance Readers
Facebook
Instagram

First and foremost, I want to thank everyone who picked up this book. I think I will forever be in awe that someone wants to read my stories.

I have to thank my husband. I don't know if I would have ever started writing and publishing journey without his words of encouragement.

A big shout out to Brandi Zelenka. You were there for me every step of the way and I don't think I could have done this without you.

To my creative team, you pushed me to put out the best book possible and I am so thankful to have you on my side. Thank you to my editor, Brandi at My Notes in the Margin. I tend to give you a hot mess and you make it brilliant.

Thank you to Katy Cuthbertson for all your work and support, especially your eye for commas. You've been a huge help.

Thank you to my beta readers Jessie Bailey, Quinn Anderson, and Randi Gauthreaux. You gave me invaluable feedback to help make my manuscript sparkle. Thank you to my proofreaders Teagan Reichuber and Tonya Fender. You helped me out so much.

Thank you Enticing Journey Book Promotions and Xpresso Book Tours for your amazing PR work. You made everything run smoothly. Thank you to my amazing ARC and Bookfluencer teams. Thank you to everyone in my group, Sassy Romance Readers.

Most of all thank you to all the bloggers, bookstagrammers, and booktokers for reading and sharing your excitement for this book. It means the world to me and I can't thank you enough. And of course, thank you to all the readers for reading my words. I hope I've been able to give you a fun escape for a few hours.

See you at the next book! Stay sassy!

Gia Stevens resides in Northern Minnesota with her husband and cat. She lives for the warm, sunny days of summer and dreads the bitter cold of winter. A romantic comedy junkie at heart, she knew she wanted her own stories to encompass those same warm and fuzzy feelings.

When she's not busy writing your next book boyfriend, Gia can be found binge watching TV shows that aired five years ago, taking pictures of her cat, or curled up with a steamy romance novel.

Want to read more sassy heroines, swoony heroes, and fun and flirty romance books?

Visit Gia's website to find a complete list of all her books.